GW00469966

DEATH AT FORT DEVENS

Peter Colt

SEVERN
HOUSE

First world edition published in Great Britain and the USA in 2022
by Severn House, an imprint of Canongate Books Ltd,
14 High Street, Edinburgh EH1 1TE.

Trade paperback edition first published in Great Britain and the USA in 2022
by Severn House, an imprint of Canongate Books Ltd.

severnhouse.com

British Library Cataloguing-in-Publication Data
A CIP catalogue record for this title is available from the British Library.

ISBN-13: 978-1-4483-0766-1 (cased)
ISBN-13: 978-1-4483-0789-0 (trade paper)
ISBN-13: 978-1-4483-0788-3 (e-book)

All Severn House titles are printed on acid-free paper.

MIX
Paper from
responsible sources
FSC® C013056

Typeset by Palimpsest Book Production Ltd.,
Falkirk, Stirlingshire, Scotland.
Printed and bound in Great Britain by
TJ Books, Padstow, Cornwall.

Sergeant Major Christopher L. Callan
28 November 1970 – 18 July 2020
Requiescat in pace.

GLOSSARY

10th Special Forces Group: Also known as 10th Group or 10th SFG, US Army Special Forces (Green Berets) responsible for operating in Europe. They were based out of Fort Devens, Massachusetts in 1985 and had a battalion stationed in Bad Tölz, West Germany.

A-1 Skyraider: Also known as the 'Spad,' a propeller-driven aircraft that held a large amount of ordnance and guns, with a long loiter time on target. Used to provide lifesaving close air support to Recon team.

Blackjack (or slapjack or sap): Impact weapon involving a weight at the end of spring steel encased in stitched leather. There are many improvised and manufactured variants. 'Sap' can also be used as a verb or adjective.

Bright Light: Recon team or Recon teams on standby to assist other Recon teams or downed pilots in trouble.

CAR-15: Compact version of the M16, with collapsible stock and shortened barrel firing the 5.56mm cartridge, capable of semi-automatic and fully automatic fire.

Huey: Bell UH-1 helicopter, the workhorse of the war.

Indig: Indigenous SOG Recon team members.

MP: Military Police.

One-Zero: Designation for SOG Recon team leader.

P5: Walther P5, an updated, compact version of the venerable German 9mm Walther P38 pistol.

POW: Prisoner of war.

PT: How the Army refers to its Physical Training program in which units will work out together. Can also be used to refer to an individual working out.

PT'ing: The act of exercising.

Ring Knocker: Derisive term for a Service Academy or military school graduate due to their tendency to buy and wear large class rings.

S3: Military nomenclature for brigade of lower operations staff section. Can also be used to refer to the Operations Officer.

Slungshot: Impact weapon made up of a weight wrapped in cord or twine, often inside a 'monkey's fist' knot.

Tokarev TT-33: Russian pistol chambered in 7.62mm, also known as the Type 54 if manufactured by China. It was made by numerous Soviet Bloc countries and could best be described as 'crude but effective.'

ONE

Winter in Boston is an ordeal. If it isn't miserably cold with enough snow to make an Eskimo feel at home, then it is all cold rain and slush. Spring is like all poems by Russian poets, a chance to hope and in hope to be mortally, tragically disappointed. Spring is what really breaks spirits in New England. Not the long, cold, snowy winter but the promise, the hope of good weather. Then the inevitable cold spell and late snowstorm.

However, toward the end of spring, a miracle happens. That miracle is called June. In June, New Englanders, but most importantly those of us from Boston, wake up and realize that the rain has stopped, and leaves have appeared on trees. Fenway Park is open for business, and by June, flowers are blooming. In June, we can count on more sun than rain, and the whole region suddenly perks up.

I had a rough spring. In March, I had taken a case that had almost gotten me killed. It had been a murder investigation involving two seemingly unrelated killings. The case led to a girl I kind of liked being killed and my car getting blown up. A friend had been murdered in front of me, and I had lost the closest thing to a family that I had since leaving the Army. Spring had offered me hope, and it almost killed me.

I spent the rest of spring in a funk. There were other reasons too; being a private investigator hadn't provided much in the way of interesting cases in the past few months. It hadn't provided much in the way of money either. I hadn't had a steady job since I left the Boston Police Department six years ago. For me the cops hadn't been a great fit. All the BS and the order taking that the Army had to offer, but none of the sense of purpose. The thing about being a private investigator that was worth the infrequent pay and often dull divorce or insurance fraud cases was the fact that I didn't have a boss.

The Army had been the last job I had loved. I had been in

Army Special Forces in Vietnam, part of a highly secretive elite within an elite known as the Studies and Observation Group. It had been dangerous and exhilarating, and the only thing I had ever really felt I was good at. I had gotten out of the Army before the war ended. I had tried college, tried the cops, finished college in night school, and then realized how much I hated taking orders. Thinking about Vietnam and everything that had happened had left me feeling pretty low.

Then came June, the gateway to summer. The third week in June 1985 I was driving west down Route 2. I had taken Mass Avenue, over the Charles River into Cambridge, and passed by the Massachusetts Institute of Technology where they made smart kids wicked smarter. I passed the NECCO candy factory and other artifacts of dying urban industries. Mass Ave is also known as Massachusetts Route 2A. I made my way through Harvard Square, and traffic was bad enough at two in the afternoon that I had plenty of time to appreciate the Ivy League ladies in their skirts and slacks. Not that I was prejudiced. I appreciate plenty of women who aren't members of the Ivy League too. I try to be open minded.

I followed Mass Ave to the Alewife Brook Parkway and then to Route 2 proper. The city started to shrink, and the buildings seemed to have fewer stories to them the further west I went. Then there were ponds and suburbs and places where nice, civilized people lived and played. I passed through Belmont and Arlington and wound my way toward the place where the first shots of the American Revolution had been fired.

I had the windows rolled down and the air was warm, perfumed by pollen. The radio was playing rock and roll loud, and the Maverick's engine growled every time I pushed the gas pedal down. It was a pure joy to drive that stretch of highway through rolling, green hills on a fine early summer day. I felt like a teenager, except that in my teenage years I didn't have a car. Since March I had felt world-weary, old, and everything seemed gray, but now things were looking up.

Today, I was finally feeling good. Some of that feeling had to do with driving to Fort Devens. It had been a while since I had been there. I had always liked it. It was home to the

Military Intelligence School where scores of GIs in the Army Security Agency had trained during the fifties and sixties. It was also home to the 10th Special Forces Group, Green Berets, whose area of responsibility was Europe. A battalion of the Group was stationed in Bad Tölz, Germany. They trained there and were in place in case the Russians and East Germans tried to invade the West, or the Soviets got up to mischief elsewhere in Europe. Even though I was long out of the Army, it was nice to be around other Special Forces types. SF was a brotherhood. Being near it was a little like homecoming.

This time, my trip to Devens was more than nostalgic – it was business. I had gotten a call from David Billings. I had known him in Vietnam as First Lieutenant Billings when he had come to Recon. He was normally in some hush-hush intelligence gig in Saigon, but sometimes he came up north. We worked together on a few missions, and then several months later, Sergeant Major Billy Justice felt I was getting burned out. He told me I was taking unnecessary risks. He moved me to a position as a Covey Rider, a Special Forces Recon man flying in a plane with an Air Force Forward Air Controller. When Recon men were on the ground in trouble, they could call upon every combat aircraft in the theater. That was a lot of planes, each with a lot of bombs and rockets. It was a lot for one man to fly a plane and coordinate the close air support. The Covey Rider worked the radio, directing air strikes and coordinating with the team on the ground. Being a Recon man, he could direct the team on the ground to likely pick-up points or landing zones. I could attest to this from personal experience: it was nice to hear the calm voice of a Recon man on the other end of the radio.

Covey was a Recon man's savior and avenging angel. Billy Justice had saved my life by moving me to the Covey Rider slot. In turn, it allowed me to save lives by helping the teams on the ground. It was still a dangerous job, and we had some hairy moments, but we made it home. I usually flew with a Covey whose plane had been shot up so many times it had 'Swiss Cheese' painted on the nose. There were too many Coveys who didn't make it back. Too many Recon men too.

Dave Billings was now Lieutenant Colonel Dave Billings.

Last I heard, he had been in Germany, Bad Tölz, as a battalion commander in 10th Group, and then some time in Berlin. I had heard through other SF guys that Dave was on the cusp of being promoted to full bird colonel. Word was that he was going to be given command of 10th Special Forces Group. There was talk that Dave might even have a star in his future, which was rare indeed. There was a lot of resentment of Special Forces by the regular Army types. Not as much as during Vietnam, but there was still plenty left in the mid-1980s. There were not a lot of generals in SF and Big Army didn't consider being a Special Forces officer as being a good career move. Big Army viewed Special Forces officers as either deviants or dilettantes. They weren't far off, but those were shitty reasons not to promote competent officers. If anyone could do it, it was Dave Billings. Dave was more than just competent. He was a superstar. Always had been. I could tell when I first met him back in Vietnam; it was as clear now as it was fifteen years ago.

I had been summoned to the Operations shack to see the Commanding Officer and the Operations Officer, known in Army parlance as the S3 or just 'the Three.' I was between missions, and being summoned meant being offered one. When I walked in, the CO, the S3, and Billy Justice were huddled around a map, like a weird version of the witches in *Macbeth*. I was worried about what trouble they were cooking up in their cauldron.

'Red, good, you're here.' The CO used my nickname which had stuck with me since Basic Training. The CO was standing near the map table wearing a black windbreaker, no shirt, and tan diver's shorts. He had flip-flops on his feet, and he had a pipe in his mouth, all of which looked very unmilitary. He had been dressed the same way when I first met him many months ago, and I wondered then if it was some sort of joke that he played on new guys. It wasn't.

He had been in Korea as a private in the infantry. He had been young, fresh off the farm, when he stepped off the troopship in Korea. When the shooting stopped, he was a buck sergeant. He had seen what things looked like when they were fucked up and decided he could do better, got a commission, and became a paratrooper. From there, he heard that Special Forces was all volunteer, and they got specialized training. He had been there ever since. Now he was a major with few prospects for promotion and more salt than pepper in his hair.

'Red, we're just waiting for one more.' He said it like we were at a cocktail party or waiting for another to play bridge instead of huddled around maps of the Ho Chi Minh Trail.

'Yes sir.' I was trying to see what they were looking at on the map, but there was no point. Another man walked in. Tall and barrel chested, he looked like a college athlete. Not one of the small colleges, but one of the big football schools whose games are on TV at Thanksgiving. His teeth were pearly white, and his light brown hair was cut in a high and tight. With one look at him you got a feeling he had been an all-American team captain type. He was going to grow up to be the president of Ford or GM. He had his Ranger tab sewn on his shoulder and his Airborne wings above his pocket, and I had the feeling that he hadn't felt too challenged by either school. He wasn't a West Point graduate. The boys from Hudson Technical College tended to let you know within the first twenty seconds or so of meeting them that they were a ring knocker. It was a term given to graduates of military schools based on their propensity to compare their class rings. It was not a compliment.

'Dave, good. Dave, this is Andy Roark, the One-Zero I was telling you about.' Dave was a first lieutenant with the crossed rifles of the infantry on his collar. His name tape said 'Billings.' His fatigues were starched once, but the humidity in Vietnam meant that nothing stayed crisp for long. I resisted the urge to look at his boots to see if they were spit shined. He was a sniper magnet and didn't seem to care, or maybe it wasn't an issue at headquarters in Saigon.

'Andy, this is Lieutenant Billings. He is up from Saigon.' We shook hands.

'Call me Dave.' It was common in SF for officers to have their men use their first names. There were a lot of reasons for it, but it spoke to the confidence of the officers and the professionalism of their NCOs. Special Forces NCOs trained and led indigenous soldiers. Your average SF sergeant was doing the job of a lieutenant or captain.

'Andy,' I said. His eyes were bluish green, and I'm sure that they were not a hindrance when chatting up ladies. Later, in the field, I would see them alight with the devil's own mischief as he and I fought the North Vietnamese Army. When he got that look, we were in the shit but bad. The only difference between us being that he was certain we would never be touched, and I was certain we would be killed.

'Gentlemen, we're here because Dave has come up from Saigon with a mission that headquarters has dreamed up. Dave, do you want to tell Andy about it?' The old man was nice enough to phrase his order like it was a question, like the lieutenant had a choice.

'We have a source that indicates there might be some POW sites in Laos, deep in Laos.' Billings stabbed the map with his index finger at three spots that were deep in a sea of green ink further into the map than I had ever traveled into Laos. 'Our source was unsure of the exact location, but this is based on his description of the topography. He said that these aren't POW camps but rather assembly areas and rest points off the Ho Chi Minh Trail where they hold wounded POWs to heal up enough to be moved north. The ones who aren't healthy enough get a bullet.' Nobody had to point out that the NVA only brought up the Geneva Convention when it applied to them. When it came to American soldiers it was a very different story.

'Dave, how sure are you of this source?' POWs were a priority. Every man I knew would risk his life and more to try and rescue one. Conversely, I didn't want to risk my life on the word of a double agent after it had been analyzed by some rear echelon intelligence officer who thought that not having air conditioning or cold beer meant he was living in hardship.

'We think the source is good, but we are worried about the fact that he isn't very precise about the location. He said he saw two Americans, one tall and dark haired and one short with curly hair. Both white guys. We think they may match the description of a Recon man who went missing and a pilot who ejected after he was hit during a close air support mission. The boss thinks it is worth checking out but not worth endangering a Bright Light mission for until we have better intel.' Bright Light was the code name for rescue and recovery missions. It was a task for the Recon team that had Bright Light duty that week. Or it could mean using a large MIKE Force, a platoon or more of indigenous soldiers trained and led by an SF team, if a larger element was needed. It was driven by the situation. It was dangerous work at the best of times . . . then again, all our missions were dangerous.

Billings continued, 'The boss is worried that it could be a trap and doesn't want to commit a Mike Force or large team and the birds to fly them in. It would be a heavy lift.' It would make a juicy target, and the enemy was savvy enough to feed us bullshit intelligence to draw us into an ambush. The NVA liked shooting down helicopters, and they were good at it.

'OK, that makes sense. Let me guess, he wants a Recon team to go deep into Laos to see if they can find these sites and the Americans in them. Is that it?' It was a dangerous and tantalizing mission. I was flattered at being involved.

'Andy, we asked around, and we were told that you are good in the woods.' Being referred to as 'good in the woods' was the highest compliment one Recon man could pay another. 'Sergeant Major Justice and your CO said you were the best One-Zero to lead this mission.' One-Zero was the designation for an SOG Recon team leader. I was surprised, because most of the time Billy Justice acted as though I was a fuck-up and he should fire me, but he needed One-Zeroes.

'OK, I will look at it. It is deep . . . I'm not sure a Recon team has ever gone that far into Laos.' I was looking at the map already calculating weapons, equipment, rations, helicopter capabilities and fuel consumption.

'Oh no, Sergeant Roark,' – suddenly I was Sergeant Roark, not Andy, and that scared me – 'not a Recon team. Just you and me.' I know that these were the words that Dave Billings said with his Ivy League enunciation and his Hollywood whiter-than-pearly-white smile. What I heard was, 'Sergeant Roark, I'm going to do my best to get you killed, and you will love it because we complimented you. We made you feel special, and that is enough. Because, Troop, you are a junkie, and this war is your habit.'

We survived that mission somehow, and a few more really hairy ones. I wasn't wrong – Dave was trying hard to get me killed. It wasn't personal. Dave was the type of guy who had been treated like a god his whole life. Mortality was a completely foreign concept to him, and my mortality even less so. At that point, I was sure that I was going to get my ticket punched permanently anyway. There just wasn't any point in worrying about it. Now it was about acquitting myself well and being welcomed at Valhalla.

I got to know Dave well in those few months he kept showing up from Saigon with wilder and wilder mission schemes. He had married a socialite from Maryland. Her family were railroad people who had literally struck gold, then struck it again by making parts for computers that IBM bought. She and Dave had a daughter who was one or two years old when we had been in Vietnam. The daughter should be a teenager now. Dave hadn't said much when I asked him about his family. I got the feeling that was why he had called after so many years.

I liked Fort Devens because it was small and felt like a community more than an Army base, unlike some bases which felt like they were their own state. Like all small towns, Devens had its own peculiarities. The dependents, wives of current and retired GIs, seemed to have a monopoly on employment in the Army's version of commerce. In the Army, supermarkets were called the Commissary and soldiers bought their uniforms at Clothing Sales, almost always misspoken as 'Clothing and Sales' by generations of GIs. Liquor stores were the Class Six store, because the Army had to give it an Army name. The Army's version of a convenience store was called a Shoppette. There was a movie theater on post, on every post for that matter. They all looked the same from base to base. The movies always started with everyone in the theater standing while a flag flew on-screen, and 'The Star-Spangled Banner' played.

The Army had bowling alleys with snack bars that provided a decent lunch and good clean fun for GIs. The one at Fort Bragg was legendary for its fried chicken, and rumor had it that the barbecue served at the one at Fort Benning was second to none. At Devens you could get Schnitzel and Spätzle or any number of wursts with red cabbage at the bowling alley. They even had a decent selection of German beers. The Army's version of a department store was the Post Exchange, the PX. That was neutral territory where all dependent native languages were spoken freely, and a Frankenstein-mixture English was the lingua franca.

The Army hired wives of soldiers to work in them, so it was possible to hear things like, '*Erma, ein Class A jacket, bitte.*' This had to do with the fact that a lot of 10th Group guys married German *fräuleins* when they were stationed in West Germany. As a bonus, it ensured that the Class Six store had inexpensive German brandy and a constant supply of apple schnapps. I have been known to appreciate both. Going to Devens gave me the chance to practice my ever-increasingly rusty German. It was all that Mother spoke to me until she left for parts unknown when I was six.

There were dependents from other countries and the US working there too, but the Germans were more heavily entrenched at Fort Devens than they had been at the Siegfried Line. For some reason Korean dependents had the monopoly on the tailoring and barbershops. I liked to amuse myself in slower moments imagining something akin to a mafia summit taking place in which the German and Korean ladies had a sit-down to determine who got what turf. The Koreans seemed to be heavily invested in the strip malls on either side of the road outside the main gate. There were Korean restaurants enough to make you wonder if there was that much demand for the food. They left the pawn shops, tattoo parlors, and one depressing strip club to the Ayer natives. The Germans had a small toehold in Ayer, the town right outside the main gate, in the form of two restaurants across the main drag from each other. I imagined that they were there in case they wanted to launch an all-out bid to dislodge the Koreans for dominance of all Army-related commerce in Ayer. Shirley, Massachusetts, where the other gate was located, was wide open territory with no one group more represented than another.

I followed Route 2, letting the Maverick's engine power me over the hills and down the valleys with its throaty engine sounds. The Doobie Brothers were playing, and the sun was shining. It felt good to be alive. Which, given the last few months, almost felt novel.

I took the exit off the highway to the Jackson Road gate. If I turned left and took the bridge over Route 2, I would be going to Range Control, the ammunition supply point where they had bunkers filled with all sorts of ammunition. Also, that would take me to the shooting ranges, the Land Navigation course, and Turner Drop Zone. Special Forces soldiers were on jump status, and that meant they had to jump regularly to stay on status and receive jump pay. My father had been a paratrooper in World War II. He told me he joined up, like a lot of other guys, for the extra jump pay. The extra fifty dollars a month almost doubled his pay. Not bad for a kid from South Boston, coming out of the Depression. Now it was more about the prestige than the money.

Instead of heading left to the ranges, I went to the right and stopped at the small brick gatehouse. Since Fort Devens was home to the 10th Special Forces Group and the Military Intelligence School, and had been home to the Army Security Agency, they took security seriously here. I showed the bored-looking military policeman my driver's license and the DOD ID card that assured him I was a veteran and could buy cheap booze on post. He checked a clipboard, made a tick mark on it, and handed me a laminated placard that just said '10th SFG' in six-inch-high letters. There was some legalese on the back telling me where I could and couldn't go and what laws I would be breaking if I did. It was signed by D. Billings, LTC, SF.

'Colonel Billings called ahead, sir. Put this in your wind-shield, and you will have access to the post, except anything to do with the Intelligence School. Please do not take any photographs while you are on post, as you will be subject to arrest and detention.' He could tell by my longish hair and mustache that I was no longer subject to the Uniform Code of Military Justice, the UCMJ. Soldiers – and anyone in the service – have their own set of laws that are far more restrictive than those the rest of us must follow. I must have looked civilian enough that he had to remind me about the rules. It wasn't his fault. He didn't mean to sound arrogant. The

Army trains their MPs to be that way. They're taught at the MP school to say the phrase, 'Sir, do not confuse your rank with my authority.' It's how they teach nineteen-year-old privates to harass officers and NCOs. They do a good job. I, like most soldiers who were not MPs, harbored a real dislike and distrust of them.

I thanked him with a politeness I didn't feel and eased the Maverick through the gate. I kept the needle just to the left of the twenty-five mile per hour line. MPs saw the world in black and white, and their interpretation of the post ordinances was even less liberal. I passed the golf course on my right with 'Fort Devens' spelled out by a series of privet hedges. I followed the road toward main post and the housing area. It was a little past three when I pulled up in front of the stately red brick building on Walnut Street. It had been built between world wars when Devens was changing from a camp to a fort.

It occurred to me that I hadn't seen Dave in almost sixteen years. I turned off the car and sat listening to the engine ping for a minute. Then he had been an all-American football hero type, with both brains and balls. Now he had a star in his future . . . a general officer. I might not be going places, but one of my friends was.

TWO

Dave's quarters – the Army can't say house or apartment – were a stately brick house with white trim. All the other houses in the area had the same trim, same uniform white paint. As a lieutenant colonel, he rated a single-family home not far from post commandant's house. As lieutenant colonel soon-to-be promoted, he rated a nice one. This was the Army equivalent of Park Avenue. Single enlisted soldiers lived in the barracks, either Vicksburg Square or some of the old wooden ones built as temporary structures in World War II but still used. Enlisted married couples lived in duplexes or some sort of modern ranch house where two were stuck together and shared a kitchen, one family on either side. NCOs and their families might live in duplexes or the newer single-family ranch houses that some architect designed in the 1950s, made of cinder block and looking modern with an abundance of glass brick and a carport. The post commander lived in a stately red brick box not far from Dave's. Many soldiers lived in apartments and rental houses off post too, but not Dave.

Pine pollen was riding around on the breeze, and it was peaceful. It was a little after three in the afternoon, and the post was quiet. Most people would be trying to get their work finished for the day. Now and then, a car drove by at twenty-four miles an hour. I stepped out of the car and shut the door. In the distance, I could hear the hum of engines from the airfield but not much else.

The sidewalks were lined with trees, and the lawns were uniformly cut short. There was a neatness to the housing area that was a bit like a movie set. Here near main post, there were no flags, no exotic paint schemes, no sports team banners. There were no toys left out on the front lawn and no bikes left discarded in the driveway. Dave's driveway had a neat-looking orange two-door BMW in it. A lot of the guys who served in Germany bought German sports cars there. They were much cheaper to buy there, and the Army paid for the shipping when troops rotated home. Not surprisingly, a lot of the officers in 10th Group had BMWs, Mercedes, and even the occasional Porsche.

The hedges on either side of the front steps were neatly, uniformly trimmed. The trim was painted white, and there was a small slot above the doorbell holding a buff calling card with black lettering that read 'LTC David Billings.' Officers were expected to present their calling cards when meeting other officers, diplomats, and foreign military officers. I was thankful that I was never an officer; too much dog and pony show for me. Their life was one of being management, wondering if their subordinates would screw up their careers, sweating out every Officer Evaluation Report and the bullet comments therein. It was a life that forced officers to compete with fellow officers for promotions and plum assignments. Nope, that would never have been for me. As it was, I couldn't hack it in the stateside Army.

I pushed the doorbell and listened to the sound of it somewhere in the house. I waited for a few minutes and then heard footsteps and the sound of the locks turning. The door opened, and through the screen I saw Dave Billings. He opened the screen and stood in front of me and then stuck his hand out. I took it to shake, and he pulled me to him and hugged me briefly.

'Andy, come on in. It's really good to see you.' While it was in vogue for vets to call each other 'bro' or 'brother' these days, it wasn't Dave's style. He had been raised to know instinctively which forks and knives to use at the table when the rest of us had to pause and remind ourselves to work from the outside in.

'What happened to your ear? Looks like it got shot or something.' He was looking at my left ear. Most of the lobe was gone, shot away by a Vietnamese army colonel's last of several attempts to kill me. The bottom was pink scar tissue and had only recently stopped aching or itching.

'I cut myself shaving.' I didn't want to go into it, and I was not sure that Dave would have understood any of it.

'Uh huh. You shave with live ammunition these days?' At least he didn't roll his eyes.

Dave was still tall and looked fit. He had a blue polo shirt with an alligator on the chest, tucked into faded blue jeans. He wore boat shoes and no socks with a pair of aviator sunglasses pushed back on his head. His hair was still brown and on the short side for an SF officer. His sideburns were a little long, neatly clipped, and there was gray nibbling at the bottoms of them. His eyes were still the same color but a little dimmer, like a lightbulb not getting quite enough power. He had wrinkles around his eyes now.

Guys in 10th Group did a lot of skiing, both downhill and cross-country, and mountain climbing. They spent a lot of time jumping out of perfectly functional aircraft too. That was all in addition to hiking and training to fight an enemy deep in their own territory. As a consequence, Dave's face was tanned well enough to rival any beach bum.

I followed him down a hallway which had a stairwell on one side leading upstairs. It struck me that we were walking down a Persian carpet that had been handwoven a hundred or more years before Dave and I walked in the jungle together in Vietnam. We passed by a formal front room on one side, a living room on the other, and a small study. The walls were liberally plastered with pictures of Dave and his wife, then their infant daughter. The daughter got older, and the Billingses stood a little further apart in each photo. I wondered if you were to start at one end and run down the hallway, would they appear to age like they were in the old movie *The Time Machine*? On the opposite side of the hallway was a dining room with a maple dining room set that had let some antique store owner close shop early when the Billingses bought it. The dining room was connected to a kitchen. We went into the study.

The study was good sized but seemed smaller because two walls were taken up by bookshelves. The walls were painted infantry blue, and there was a set of French doors leading out to the backyard. The shelves were crammed with books, mostly military history, histories of the West, Army manuals, and some adventure novels. There was a section with books about

Vietnam that was cheek by jowl with a section of books about German culture and history. On the two opposite walls were pictures of Dave in various wars and conflicts, and framed awards and decorations. There were even a couple of the two of us up on his wall.

A framed certificate for his Distinguished Service Cross, the nation's second highest award for valor, two framed Silver Star certificates, one for his Bronze Star medal, and certificates for his three Purple Hearts and Combat Infantryman Badge all hung on the wall. There was an engraved sabre in a wooden holder with its scabbard below it. There were plaques and mementos from different units he had served with or trained with. Most were from the US Army, but many were from allied nations. Dave had been to see the elephant, had been in the shit, and was a real hero. He had the stuff on the wall to prove it.

A certificate noting that 2LT David Billings had been the honor grad from his class at jump school hung on the wall. It was almost a work of art, with a huge pen and ink of Jump Wings above his name. In the corners were pen and ink drawings of the swing landing trainer, the thirty-four-foot mockup jump tower and the 250-foot tower in which troops floated to the ground on tethered parachutes. It was displayed prominently, speaking to the pride he felt, that most of us felt about being paratroopers. Airborne school was our first taste of something different from Big Army. It was the first taste of being elite, and it was the first step on the way to our being SF. I didn't know a Green Beret who wasn't proud of their Jump Wings. You couldn't be Special Forces without being Airborne. It was as simple as that.

There was a desk with a wooden captain's chair in one corner and a couple of comfortable chairs at right angles to a small, round wooden table. There was small table opposite with an expensive German stereo on it. Next to the stereo were tasteful wooden racks for cassettes and LPs. There were two antique brass spittoons at opposite ends of the room. In some houses they might be decorative, but a lot of tobacco was chewed on Army posts. Dave would have guests who used them. Here and there were non-military mementos: commemorative plates for long-forgotten scotch whiskeys, a Roman centurion's helmet on a wooden stand, and a German beer stein with its pewter lid all competed with the militaria. No matter where you were sitting in Dave's study, there was a view through either windows or French doors. Dave had created for himself a room that was comforting and spoke to his success in the Army.

'Nice to see light colonels live well.' I'm sure that his wife's family fortune didn't hurt, nor his own for that matter.

'This place is a little much for the three of us but living off post wasn't really an option.' Devens was a small post. On bigger posts where they had lots of lieutenant colonels and colonels, even a general or two, Dave probably could have had quarters off post. Here he was one of a handful of senior officers. Also, if he was going to be promoted to command 10th Group, it made sense to keep him close to the Group. 'Can I get you something to drink? Iced tea, coffee?'

'Black coffee, please.' Dave had lived on Army bases in the south long enough that I couldn't trust him not to make sweetened iced tea automatically. This really was a business call, or he would have offered me a beer or something stronger, so coffee it was.

'Sure. I have a pot on.' Dave disappeared and was back in a minute with a thick ceramic mug that said 'Bad Tölz Combined Mess, Snake served daily' across the top. It was a souvenir from the 10th Group mess hall in Germany and referenced the fact that SF troops were also known as 'snake eaters' from their early days of survival training. A lot of the guys liked to take coffee mugs from the various mess halls of the posts they served in. SF prided itself on the fact that it was made up of slightly closeted kleptomaniacs.

He ushered me to one of the two comfortable chairs, and I sat down, the butt of the Smith & Wesson .38 I was carrying in my waist digging into my side a little. It was a new one, a Centennial model with an internal hammer, and replaced my Chief's Special, which was in a safe deposit box in a bank in Providence, Rhode Island. It was there for legal reasons, next to a Colt automatic that I put in there in November of '82 for similar reasons. I probably wasn't supposed to be carrying a gun on an Army post, but my life experience to date had taught me I was much more likely to live to an old age if I had a gun around when I needed one. The problem was that I never knew I needed one until someone was shooting at me.

I took a sip of the coffee, which definitely wasn't from a blue metal can or chock-full of anything, and waited for Dave to tell me why I was there. He sat down next to me in the other comfortable chair. Birds flew by outside, and somewhere in the house an air conditioner was running. It was cool but not uncomfortably so. We spent a couple of minutes catching up, talking about our lives. My portion was short. I was out of the Army, I wasn't a cop anymore, and I wasn't married or a father. I had a job that a career Army officer thought was beneath me. Dave didn't say it, but his lack of questions about my work did.

His career was on the rise, his wife was in Palm Springs for an extended trip, and his daughter, Judy, was seventeen. We skipped the part where we talked about guys we both knew. Too many of the Recon men were names on a black wall in Washington, DC. The ones who were alive would turn into hours of war stories. We skipped the war stories, and Dave said, 'Andy, it's my daughter, Judy. I'm worried about her.'

It was funny that it was always the same with each client. They never come right out and tell you why they need to hire you. It starts with a vague statement and then there is usually a story, often one that paints the client in a better light than is warranted. A lot of them were embarrassed about a cheating spouse, and it took a little longer to get to the point. Missing persons cases weren't much better, for all the same reasons. This business is quirky.

'Judy is getting to an age . . . well, an age where she doesn't want to listen to me, where boys . . . she is sleeping around.' I didn't say anything. There weren't a lot of things to say to an old friend telling you about his teenage daughter's sex life. 'I'm no fool. I know that girls these days . . . that things are different now, but . . . this is different.'

He took a few gulps of air, and I sipped the coffee. Then I asked, 'What is different?'

'She had a boyfriend in Bad Tölz; his dad was a supply

officer. He was a nice boy. I know they fooled around, but . . . you know . . . they were both Army brats. It was . . . what it should be.' I knew what he meant: stolen kisses between bells in school, necking in a theater instead of watching the movie, wrestling around in the back seat of the family station wagon, the sort of thing that all American teenagers are supposed to do.

'We got PC-essed back here.' PCS, Permanent Change of Station, Army-ese for moving, but in typical GI fashion Dave had used the acronym as a past tense verb. It took me a second because it had been over a decade since I had last done it. 'Well, she met some young enlisted soldiers down at the lake.' Mirror Lake was on post, water left over from melting glaciers had formed it, and generations of GIs and their families had swum there. More than one Army family had started on the banks of Mirror Lake.

'She started going with a private pretty regularly. He worked in the motor pool, a black kid. You know I'm not like that, Andy. He wasn't right for her. He was from the inner city. He had a couple of Article 15s.' It was strange to watch a man who I had seen literally run into a hail of gunfire with no regard for his own safety backpedal and justify his casual bigotry. If it was important, he might have mentioned the Article 15s, the Army's form of non-judicial punishment, first. The kid got in trouble, but not jail trouble. 'Barbara and I weren't happy when we had to go to Boston and get them one night. She was high. I could have killed the kid. She said they broke up, and she's started going to Boston more and more, staying out all night; sometimes she doesn't come home for days at a time. Her grades are slipping, and I don't even know if she will graduate, much less go to college with the rest of her peers. The stress has been too much for Barbara, and she is in Palm Springs to rejuvenate.' It must be nice to have that as an option. The best I could do was an occasional weekend on the 'Irish Riviera,' Wollaston Beach, in the summer. If I was really lucky, I could work in a visit to the Clam Box. That and some whiskey was about all the rejuvenation I could afford. 'Andy, I need your help. Judy hasn't been home in a couple of days. She hasn't been to school either.'

'Do you think she ran away?'

'No. I'm sorry to say she does this all too often. She stays out for a couple of days and comes back for a few. She'll go to school and promises that everything will be all right, then does it all again. But she always comes home in the end. Andy, she's a good girl at heart.'

I wrote the name of the private down in my notebook, and his unit on post. The pass Dave gave me would let me go most places, so I could talk to the kid tomorrow. It was now a little past five, they had played the retreat and folded the colors, and there was no one to talk to at the motor pool.

'I want to hire you. What do you charge?'

'Don't be ridiculous . . . you are an old friend and brother. It's on the house. I owe you one.' One of his Purple Hearts and the accompanying medal for valor had both been earned saving my life. You couldn't take a man's money after something like that.

'Andy, please . . . what do you charge?' We argued back and forth for a bit, eventually standing up. Other than the money, we had either too much or not enough to talk about.

'Take out a dollar. Put it on your desk, and when this is all settled if you feel you need to pay me, you can give me that.' It must have appealed to his romantic nature because he took out a dollar bill and put it under an ashtray made from the bottom of a brass artillery shell. We shook hands, and I agreed I would check in with him.

I got in my car and followed Walnut Street out to Sherman Avenue. I crossed over Buena Vista Drive. Almost every Army post had a Buena Vista Drive, whereas a lot of the posts down south seemed to be missing a Sherman Avenue. I passed the post headquarters on my left, and Vicksburg Square with its four giant brick buildings that would look more at home on the campus of Harvard than on an Army post. I passed the Sweetheart Memorial, a stone stairway over a recessed monument. It was said that it was made from stones brought to the post by local sweethearts of Doughboys getting ready to ship out for the war to end all wars.

I drove through the gate and drove down Ayer's Main Street. Saying it had seen better days was generous. I passed the police station, the library, and the southern edge of the post which housed a large maintenance building. Then I was in bucolic countryside which hadn't changed much in the last two hundred years. I followed the country roads until I picked up Route 2 again and retraced my route back to Boston and my lonely apartment.

THREE

When I got home, I parked a couple of blocks away. Three months earlier, some angry Vietnamese guys had blown up my car. They had hoped I would be in it. Unfortunately, someone else was. Now I was leery of parking in front of my building. My neighbors appreciated it, as they seemed to like their cars and windows intact.

I let myself into the apartment. I had shared it with a woman named Leslie whom I had loved, and who left me. I couldn't blame her. I took the 'silent type' part of the cliché too far. She was a graduate student, English Literature; she was writing her thesis, which had to do with comparing fictional private detectives to knights of old. We had met at the Brattle Book Shop when I helped her get a book off a high shelf. That had led to coffee and then a date. It had been surprisingly good for a time, and then it wasn't.

The problem was that most nights my mind was in Vietnam and the war. I was dreaming about my war, my dead friends. I didn't have nightmares every night, but I had them more than enough nights. She would ask me about them. She wanted to help me, but there was no way she could. There wasn't any way for me to explain it to her, the litany of death and gore. I had killed people, friends of mine had been killed. I had, for no discernable reason, survived when better men hadn't. That was the hardest part for me. There was no language to explain things like that to sweet, sensitive Leslie. In the end, I drove her away with my silence.

Sometime after Leslie, there was a woman who came to stay with a cat named Sir Leominster. She left a few months later, but Sir Leominster had stayed. He didn't care if I had nightmares and didn't want to talk about them. He didn't care if I drank too much as long as there was food in his bowl, and I would scratch behind his ears when he wanted me to. He was a very pragmatic cat.

After my car blew up, Special Agent Brenda Watts, with her honey-colored hair drawn back in a ponytail and a .38 on her hip, came looking for me. She found me in the bar across the street, cut up, hard of hearing, and looking like I had survived a slasher film. She came with me to my apartment and made sure there were no bad men waiting to finish what they had started. Later when the case took me out to California and the Suisun Bay, she agreed to watch Sir Leominster. When I got into a gunfight in a Chinese restaurant in Quincy, Massachusetts and then lied to her about it, she was understandably angry with me. She was angry at me because she liked me enough to not tell the FBI I was involved and had compromised her integrity. She was so angry that she had kept my cat.

Sir Leominster is a very practical cat who appreciates that Special Agents in the FBI are making more money than PIs, and consequently have better living conditions. I was pretty sure Sir Leominster was not upset. Watts hadn't returned any of my phone calls or messages offering lunch at any of Boston's more expensive restaurants. I would have offered dinner, but Watts could honestly do better than the likes of me. She wasn't one to forgive me for lying to her anytime soon, so I was getting used to not having the cat around.

When Leslie had moved out, I had an apartment that was half empty. Over the years I had filled in the empty nooks and crannies with books and furniture that the college kids left behind when they fled to their hometowns at the end of the year. There was no one to share it with, but maybe that was better than having a wife in Palm Springs? Dave Billings' nice house with its antiques and family photos seemed just as empty as my apartment. Bigger and nicer but just as empty and somehow a little sadder. I missed the cat, though.

That was one of the reasons I had liked Dave Billings. He seemed to appreciate my skills as a Recon man but was not impressed by my bullshit. By the time Dave had walked into the Operations shack I had been in Recon for a year and a half, and I had been a team leader, called a One-Zero, for a little over six months. I was a little salty and wasn't sure I wanted to deal with a Saigon Commando, but Dave had won me over with his bold plans. No matter how reckless they were, Dave, like all good leaders, convinced me we could pull it off. He imbued me with his confidence and made it seem like we could pull off anything. He always left out the part about 'or die trying.'

I came to learn quickly that Dave was more than a Saigon Commando. He was tough and cool under fire. Frankly, I wish they had made more officers like him. He had no fear of getting us in the shit, but somehow we always managed to get out again. It wasn't that he had a death wish, it just never occurred to him that he could buy it like the rest of us mere mortals. I wish I could say that I had fond memories of our last mission together. It wasn't that I could remember it as if it were yesterday. It was more like I couldn't get it out of my mind.

I was standing on the skid of the bird, a Huey with its distinctive *whup whup whup* rotor sounds. I was scanning the landing zone for signs of danger. It was my call; it was Dave's mission, but I was the One-Zero, and it was my team he was strap-hanging with. If I didn't see anything threatening, I would step off the skid and the team would follow. If I waved us off, then that was that.

My stomach was knotted tight. I had spent the ride in the bird a bundle of nerves as I thought about the mission and all the things we had to do. I would go over it again and again in my head, trying to figure out if I had missed some tiny detail that could mean life or death. The nerves had eased. The only trace was my knotted stomach. I put my feet on the skid and stood up holding on to the door frame of the Huey. It was always like that. I looked over at my One-Two; he nodded. Dave was on the bird behind ours standing on a skid, and across from him was my One-One. Each of us had a Montagnard mercenary standing behind us on our respective skids, every one of us wearing a heavy rucksack and bristling with weapons.

My bird came in fast, flaring its nose. The pilot was good. I didn't see anything and stepped off the skid and jumped the few feet into the LZ. My stomach suddenly wasn't a problem anymore. I hit with a thump that jarred me from ankle to collarbone. The rucksack I was carrying lifted and smashed into my back. Even trying to get my breath back, I moved forward ten yards with my CAR-15 raised to my shoulder. I scanned the area in front of me with the weapon tracking like a third eye, searching for the NVA. I heard the helicopter move off smartly and the next bird flared in. It moved off and we took up positions, listening and waiting.

We waited for ten minutes, watching for the enemy, weapons in hand and radio at the ready so we could call the birds back in. Then we linked up and quickly checked to make sure no one was injured. Jumping out of helicopters, like jumping out of airplanes, can lead to injuries. We started moving toward our target area, the One-One covering up signs of our movement as we went. We were going to plant some new super top secret sensor near the Ho Chi Minh Trail. Dave had hand-carried it up from Saigon. It was so secret he hadn't even shown me.

'Trust me, Andy.' I should have known I was going to get fucked. No good thing has come from being told to trust someone, much less a commissioned officer. 'You will be blown away.' He wasn't wrong. He rarely was. That is probably why they kept promoting him.

We moved away from the LZ. Ger, my best Yard, was on point, and the rest of the team was spaced out as we had trained to. We were moving slowly, silently, through the Laotian jungle, pushing through the steamy air as much as the vegetation. The jungle was alive with noise: insects, birds, monkeys, and other animals adding to their chorus. It was a good sign. When things go silent in the jungle, you are about to be ambushed.

We had been at it for a couple of hours, the LZ far behind us, the sweat stinging our eyes and driving insect repellant into them. Not that the bug juice did much good. Life in Recon was an essay in ignoring discomfort and pain to achieve your mission. We hardly spoke, never above a whisper if we had to. We were eaten alive by bugs, food almost always eaten cold, you couldn't smoke, and sleep was a series of short naps. We had discipline that would have shamed a Roman centurion.

Ger's chest and head exploded when the NVA machine gun

opened up on him. He had been good in the woods and then he was dead. Just like that. Alive one second, then bang . . . dead. The team was good. They were trained and knew their shit. They were doing the things that I was screaming at them to do before I was actually ordering them to do it. Smoke grenades thrown, shooting back at the jungle which had come alive with AK-47 fire. One man would fire a magazine and peel off running back down the trail we had been walking on. The next man would fire a full mag and peel to the opposite side and run back the way we had come. We would peel off this way, firing off full magazines, reloading as we ran. If the man in front of you was shooting, then you were throwing grenades over him. We had practiced it thousands of times.

Rounds were whipping at us, and we were scrambling to get the fuck out of there. Ger was dead before he hit the ground. I wanted to get him, to bring him back to his family, but it would have been suicide. The foliage around his body was exploding in green mist as AK-47 rounds and larger machine gun rounds ripped through it. Grenades went off with their angry blasts and somewhere in all the noise was the bloop of the M79 shooting at the enemy.

We broke contact and withdrew, firing, covering each other as we pulled back. We moved like a well-oiled machine, after having practiced The Peel so much. The fire was intense, and the jungle was being hacked up by bullets. Hundreds of loud cracks whipped by us as the enemy rounds swept past. We kept withdrawing, and two more of my Yards fell. It would have been heartbreaking if I'd had time to be heartbroken.

We ran, shooting, throwing grenades, moving, and reloading as we went. When we stopped at the edge of a series of bomb craters to regroup, I had two Yards left. My One-One was bleeding from his head, and my One-Two had pink foam at his lips, a sucking chest wound. The bullet had pierced his chest, and he would die if we couldn't get evacuated soon. Dave was untouched, smiling as he fired his CAR-15 and threw grenades. My legs were peppered with RPG fragments, red oozed through my pants, and I was not moving well anymore. My legs were rubbery, and my chest was tight. I took magazines from my two wounded teammates and called

Covey. They came up on the radio, and I told them my call sign and said, 'I am declaring a Prairie Fire.' Actually, I just said my call sign and screamed 'Prairie Fire' into the handset three times. I paused to fire off a magazine and then went back to the handset.

'Hey y'all, I got birds inbound, but you all have to wait a bit.' That was not what I wanted to hear, but that was what it was. Dave and I kept shooting and throwing grenades. I was desperate and scared and just working through it. Dave looked like he was watching a ball game. The NVA kept coming and RPGs exploded around us. Eventually air cover arrived, but it was sparse. A couple of Cobras and a couple of A-1 Skyraiders. We had to move back a couple hundred yards to a new LZ. I told Dave I would cover him as he got the guys out.

The NVA knew what was coming, and while Dave pulled the guys back to the new LZ, they picked up their fire. It seemed as though the whole North Vietnamese Army was in front of me, everyone trying to get near to me. They had sensed that our fire had slacked off and were redoubling their efforts. I had used up my last magazine and had one hand grenade left so I wouldn't be captured alive. I had decided I was dead. At first there was just acceptance. The math only worked out one way for this problem. I was sitting and waiting for the NVA to come. The Cobras above moved off. The Skyraiders moved off. I was jerked off the ground and almost dropped my grenade. Dave Billings had come back and thrown me over his shoulder. Then, with machine gun rounds and AK-47 rounds whipping around us like a tempest, he ran for all he was worth to the waiting helicopter. Mr all-American quarterback running into the end zone with me over his shoulder instead of a football cradled in his arm.

There was a Huey waiting, and Dave pitched me in and jumped on. I could hear AK rounds punch through thin aluminum as we pulled away. They were making a slight pinging sound. The pilot was swearing to no one specifically. The co-pilot was praying to no one in particular and everyone all at once. We rose and headed off. Then there was a noise like thunder. The pilot swore louder, and our bird was buffeted by angry winds that smelled like ammonia. We rocked and bounced, and it lessened as we moved away from the LZ.

'Andy, look.' Dave held me up, and the jungle below was erupting in plumes of smoke and dust. Arc Light . . . a B-52 bomber strike. It seemed huge. I had seen the aftereffects during bomb damage assessment missions, but I had never seen one happening from a helicopter. Pulverizing the jungle and all below it. Tons of bomb rained down. 'Andy, it works, the beacon works!'

Later in Nha Trang, Dave came to visit me in the hospital. He told me about the plan, his plan, hatched and executed without any higher authority. Nothing was more dangerous than a lieutenant with an idea. His plan had been called Operation Stalking Horse.

'Andy, we pasted them . . . we pasted them good.' He was gleeful like a kid.

'What are you talking about, Dave?'

'Andy, I saw the beacon and had an idea. What if we could draw an NVA regiment or even a division into a kill zone? A box with no bunkers and less overhead canopy, that Arc Light could pound them to death in. We inserted and moved toward an NVA complex on the trail. It had to be somewhere on the trail. As we moved out toward our extraction point, I turned on the beacon and stuck it in some brush. The B-52s were already orbiting the area, waiting for the word. They just dropped their bombs on the beacon, which was in the middle of the kill box. They sent as many B-52s as they would have bombed a city with. Man, it was brilliant. Instead of flying and releasing in a straight line, we got the Air Force to fly perpendicular sorties using the beacon as the center point of the target.'

'Oh, Dave . . .' My team had fared badly. One dead American, one paralyzed, and almost all my Yards were dead. Not to mention that I was peppered with RPG fragments and had been shot. 'Dave . . .'

'Andy, it was brilliant. It worked like a charm. The only bait that would bring that many NVA into one place was a Recon team . . . I thought about a downed pilot, but that was too hard to do. But I knew you would take the mission, buddy

. . . Jesus, that beacon worked like a charm . . . we blew a whole regiment to kingdom come! I knew that they wouldn't get you! Not you!' He was excited, and I felt sick. Later they gave me a couple of medals and a seat in a Covey plane. Dave got the Distinguished Service Cross and a Purple Heart. I lost my team, and he gained a general's star in his future. I didn't see him again until I drove up to his house at Fort Devens.

I had been angry at him. For a time, I had been angry enough to fight him but by the time I got out of the hospital, he had rotated home stateside, and I got a front row seat to the war in a Covey. After a while, I stopped being angry. Recon was dangerous. If Dave had proposed the mission straight up to me, I would have taken it. It was no different from being told to draw fire. After a while, I stopped thinking about it except at night when my dreams would drag me back to that day in the jungle. Ger's head exploded over and over again in front of me for almost fifteen years. The others too, but it was Ger's face that came back most often. He had turned back to smile at me, to tell me the trail was all right. It wasn't. He never felt a thing. Years later, I still find myself unconsciously rubbing the spot on my cheekbone that some of his brain matter spattered on. That wasn't the type of stuff I could tell Leslie, or anyone, about.

FOUR

The next morning, I pulled up in front of the provost marshal's building at nine fifteen, which was early by private detective standards, but by Army standards the day was three and a quarter hours in. I found a spot that wasn't reserved for a commander or sergeant major. I didn't have much use for sergeant majors. Billy Justice had raised the bar high, and most I had come across were pale imitations. He didn't care much about the garrison bullshit about haircuts and uniforms. He was a fighting sergeant major whom I had personally witnessed fighting the NVA in the field. I would have followed him to the gates of hell and through them.

The building, unlike the sea of red brick that infested most Army bases, was made of tan brick. It looked like a two-story shoebox with square windows and doors. There was a sign that told me it was the home of the 624th Military Police Company. It had the usual crossed pistols MP logo, and below that it listed the name of a captain who was in command. I forgot it before my foot hit the first step up to the door. I wasn't there to see the company commander, but I was there to see the provost marshal. The company commander oversaw the MPs who were responsible for law and order on the base. The provost marshal was an MP, but he was a colonel who answered to the post commandant. If the company commander was the chief of police, then the provost marshal was akin to a public safety director.

In a normal town, I wouldn't check in with the chief of police right away. I might not at all if I could avoid it. An Army base was a different beast. It was federal property, and my license wasn't worth the paper it was printed on. I couldn't legally carry a gun, and if I got stopped with one on me, it could result in a trip to federal prison. MPs lacked the discretion that cops have. The fact that the Intelligence School and Special Forces were on post and everyone was worried about

Soviet spies . . . I didn't want to go poking around without clearing it with the provost marshal first.

The private first class at the counter was young and, unlike ninety-nine percent of the MPs I had come across, was a woman, and a pretty one at that. She had blond hair that was cut shorter than was currently fashionable, but that was the Army for you. She had a pistol belt with a holstered .38 revolver and a white-painted billy club on the opposite side. She looked up and, with a voice that seemed more suited to the 4H club than the Army, said, 'Can I help you, sir?'

'My name is Roark. I'm a private investigator from Boston. I was hoping to speak to the provost marshal.' It was pronounced 'provo,' like the city in Utah, not 'pro-vost.' It was apparently French in origin. I had found that out one night in Saigon while cooling my heels in a cell. The duty sergeant had objected to my expressing the opinion that he, the provost marshal, and MPs in general, were a form of deviant so bad that I was ashamed to be called deviant myself. I also pointed out that I would rather be in the Air Force than be lumped in with their lot. The straight jab had positioned my jaw for the hook. I went down faster than a box of rocks. I came to with an annoying, repetitive pain in the tip of my nose. The Saigon Commando was hitting the tip of my nose repeatedly, with just enough force to hurt but not do any damage, with his white-painted billy club. It was insidious, and I forgot about the knot in my jaw. I heard that if they really didn't like you, they did it to the bridge of your nose. Must have been my winning personality that kept it to the tip.

'Now, asshole. We don't mind when drunk GIs fight with us. We have come to expect it. We don't mind being called names. That is part of the job. We don't mind when people disparage the Military Police Corps in general, but we do draw the line at ignorance. There is no such thing as a pro-vost marshal in the entire United States Army.' Each syllable high-lighted by an eye-watering tap on the nose. 'The term is French in origin and is properly pronounced "provo marshal."' I'd never forgotten that lesson. It had done little to change my opinion of the MPs, but he had made his point.

The PFC's name, if her black plastic name tag was to be

believed, was Collins. She picked up a phone and after a few seconds said, 'Yes sir, there is a private investigator from Boston here to see you. No sir, he isn't wearing a Hawaiian shirt. No sir, no Ferrari either.' For the record, I was wearing loafers, pressed khaki pants, white button-down shirt, and a summer weight blue sport coat with gold buttons. My mustache and hair were trimmed, and I looked about as respectable as I ever did. PFC Collins hung up the phone and beckoned me to follow her down the hall. I did so, admiring the fit of her uniform slacks as she walked in front of me. The view was more fascinating than the standard issue black-framed chain of command photos on the wall.

She stopped in front of a door that had a small name plate that read 'LTC Wardron.' She knocked, and went in when the voice inside told us to come in. The man seated at the desk was skinny. The short sleeves of his pistachio green Class B shirt billowed around brown arms that looked like ropes. He was tan and bald with brown eyes that reminded me of a Saint Bernard.

'Sir, this is the private detective from Boston.' She about-faced and walked out. He stood up, and I was not surprised to see that he was tall and thin. His fingertips bore the stain of someone who smoked more than I did. He stuck out his hand, and we shook as I introduced myself.

'We don't get a lot of private eyes here on post. What brings you here?' His accent was from somewhere like Kentucky or Tennessee, and the Army had done little to soften it.

'I'm working on a divorce case. My client thinks his wife is having an affair with an enlisted man here on post. They meet in Boston on weekends. I was hoping to check it out, maybe talk to him.' Just because I was checking in didn't mean that I had any intention of telling him who my client was or what it was about. 'I was in Vietnam with Dave Billings, and he told me to reach out to you.'

'You were in Vietnam with Colonel Billings?' I assured him I was. We talked about Vietnam for a bit. He had missed out. Most of his duties had kept him in Germany or stateside. He talked about Dave Billings like he was the quarterback who had just won the big game. It seemed that was how people always talked about Dave. Dave, who had the Ivy League education, the pedigree and breeding. Dave, whose family could have gotten him a deferment, but who had gone to Officer Candidate School, gone SF, and volunteered to go to Vietnam. Dave wasn't exactly a legend, but people always seemed to treat him as though he was.

'OK, Mr Roark, I think we can accommodate an old Army buddy of Dave's. The only things I ask are that you stay away from the Military Intelligence School, and no guns on post. This is federal property, and we can't have civilians running around armed.' I didn't bother mentioning that I had more experience with guns and gunfights than most of the soldiers on post.

'Of course, sir. The man I'm interested in I believe works in the motor pool as a mechanic. I completely understand about the gun. I don't carry them if I can help it. Got plenty of that in 'Nam.' I smiled at him as the butt of my .38 dug into my right kidney, and I hoped my having been there when he wasn't was enough to get him to change the subject.

'Good, good. If you need anything, contact the duty NCO.' He picked up the phone and punched some numbers. 'Collins, give Mr Roark a pass for the post for one week, one of the purple ones.' He covered the mouthpiece of the phone with his hand. 'Y'all can get another one if you need more than a week to do your job.' He said it in such a way that I couldn't mistake the fact that he thought he was doing me a favor. He showed me to the door of his office, and we shook hands again.

'Mr Roark. We don't want any issues here. You get that, right?'

'I do, sir. I do.' I was pretty sure I didn't like him, but I understood him. He didn't mean to be chickenshit; it just came to him naturally. He was close to retirement. He had no promotions left in his future if he was the provost marshal at a small post like Fort Devens. Now he was looking out to make sure nothing could derail his retirement or even slow it down. He didn't want anyone making waves, especially a civilian he had no authority over. He didn't want to end his career at some miserable place like Fort Polk, Louisiana. Fort Polk was so deep in the middle of nowhere the Army euphemistically referred to it as a 'sportsman's paradise.'

'Good, good. Thank you.'

I walked down the hall and found Collins at her desk by the door. She handed me a piece of laminated purple construction paper with all the usual warnings on the back. On the front, it let the reader know they were restricted to main post and that the provost marshal's office expected the pass returned at the end of seven days. Collins instructed me to have a good day, and I assured her I would. I thought about winking at her, but she had been at her senior prom just a couple of years ago. It made me feel old. When I got into the Maverick, I put the purple piece of paper in the glovebox next to some napkins from a fast-food place. At least the napkins were useful.

Dave Billings had given me the kid's name. It was Derrick Page. He was a mechanic down at the motor pool. The building was a giant hangar type structure that handled all sorts of vehicles. There weren't any armor units at Devens, which meant not too many tanks or armored personnel carriers, just trucks and Jeeps. I had spent most of my time on foot, in helicopters, or jumping out of planes. Tanks and armored personnel carriers were foreign territory to me.

I parked in the large parking lot in front of the massive tan building. There were a lot of new cars that young GIs were led to believe they could afford by the local dealerships. I could almost hear the ad on the radio: 'E-1 through E-4, Echo Zulu credit, no money down.' Car dealers loved junior soldiers, because they knew that if a GI fell behind on his payments, the dealer could go to the Army and have the payment taken directly out of the soldier's check. There were other cars and motorcycles in the lot too, but there were a lot of Mustangs and Camaros.

I got out of the Maverick. It was not new or flashy, but I would stack it up against anything in that lot. My mechanic friend Carney had taken a good car and made it a lot better. One night after the gunfight in a Chinese restaurant, I had the needle on the speedometer pegged all the way on a stretch of empty highway. I had been a little drunk, sad for dead friends and my war that had slipped away. I was mildly curious as to what would happen if a deer stepped in front of the Maverick at a hundred and twenty miles an hour. All that happened was that I got back to Boston a little sooner and dumber.

The motor pool building had rows of windows up near the roof but nothing on the ground floor. They were there for ventilation and light, not for the view. It was a little quiet, but that might have to do with it being a good time for a coffee break. The Army's day had started at 0600 with PT. By nine thirty, it was coffee break time. There was an office to my left with country western music twanging from it. Before I could get to the door and knock, it was opened by a barrel-chested man shorter than me but thicker through the chest and neck. He looked back over his shoulder and in a thick Spanish accent said, 'You fucking fuckers better figure out where that shit is. Otherwise, I'm gonna come back here and put my Panamanian boot so far up your fucking ass you will need toilet paper to blow your nose.' He slammed the door, and the building seemed to rock with the force of it.

He turned and saw me. Then stopped. I was an anomaly in his carefully controlled world. He was a first sergeant according to the diamond in the chevrons and rockers on his collar. He was a god in the enlisted world, one step below a sergeant major and a hell of a lot more immediate. I was a civilian with non-military hair and a mustache that only I thought looked good. The bottom of my left earlobe was an angry, itchy, pink mass of flesh. I clearly wasn't an officer, and I clearly wasn't someone who belonged in his motor pool.

'Who are you?' His name tape said his last name was Rosario.

'Hey, Top, my name is Roark. I'm a detective from Boston.'

'You a cop?' He was looking at me with the eye of someone who had been put up against a wall by cops his whole life. Had orders barked at him, got patted down, his dignity taken before he was even old enough to know what it meant. His was a face that had one emotion for cops: hate. It's funny how many guys like him end up in the Army, funnier still how many climb the ranks to give orders themselves.

'No. Private. I'm looking for a kid. He isn't in trouble or anything, but I need some help with a case.'

'My ex-wife send you?' He fixed me with one eye, and he seemed very serious.

'No, this isn't that type of thing. I'm just trying to help out an old buddy from 'Nam.'

'You were in 'Nam?'

'Yeah. Special Forces. You?'

'No. I enlisted in 1970. They sent a kid from Panama to Fort Greely in Alaska. That was the worst three years of my fucking life.' He shook his head. There were a lot of Panamanian NCOs in the Army. We had been in Panama since the canal, and our countries were close allies. A lot of Panamanians ended up in our Army by some sort of geopolitical osmosis and our desire to have close friends in southern places.

'That's the Army for you.'

'No shit.' His accent was thick enough that it sounded like 'chit' instead of shit.

'Top, the kid I'm looking for is Derrick Page. I think he is a PFC. I just need to talk to him for five or ten minutes tops. That's all. I'm not looking to jam him up.' He thought about it for a second or two.

'He isn't in trouble?'

'No, Top. No one is looking to get him in trouble, least of all me.'

'OK, but if the kid doesn't want to talk to you, he doesn't have to.' He gave me the hard look that first sergeants all have if they're any good. It conveyed authority backed up by the possibility of having your ass kicked.

'Absolutely, Top.'

'OK, go have a smoke. I will get the kid and send him out to you.' The Army wasn't keen on anyone smoking around oil and fuel, so I went outside to something that looked like a bus shelter but had butt cans tacked to the walls. I shook a Lucky loose from the pack, got it in my mouth, and lit with my Zippo. Halfway through the Lucky, a tall black soldier in olive drab green coveralls and camouflage cap came out of the motor pool and made his way toward me.

'You the private eye?' He was a head taller than me but skinny. His name tape said 'Page' and he was light skinned. He took his cover off and he had a flat top haircut.

'Yep, Andy Roark.' I stuck my hand out and tried to be charming. It is part of a multi-part self-improvement plan. It hasn't been going well lately, so I was making extra effort. He looked at me and reluctantly took my hand in his. I got the feeling that life had made him weary of detectives coming by unannounced.

'What do you want, man? You aren't CID.' CID was the Army's Criminal Investigation Detachment – Army detectives.

'No, I'm not one of the specialists in ill-fitting suits.' Page smiled. CID agents usually dressed in off-the-rack suits from department stores. Their clothing allowance only went so far, and they had to look detectively. They bought the cheapest ones off the rack and pocketed whatever was left from the clothing allowance. Army issue black low quarters were the shoe of choice.

'What do you want, man?'

'I understand you used to go with Judy Billings?'

'Yeah, we dated for a while, but then we stopped.'

'How come? I mean, was it for any reason or just one of those things?'

'She was young and her daddy the colonel didn't like the idea of her fooling around with a brother from the motor pool. He didn't have to worry; it wasn't going to last. She wanted to party Thursday through Sunday. I couldn't afford her style.'

'Tough on a PFC's wages.'

'That would have been tough on a captain's. She likes to go to clubs in Boston. She likes coke, she likes champagne. I can't afford that financially, and I can't afford to get busted. The Army is a chance for me to go to college. I wasn't gonna wreck that shot.' His brow knitted as he thought about it.

'Do you have any idea who she is with now?' That was what we in the detective profession call a leading question.

'No. After her father came by to talk to me, we broke up. I haven't heard from her. She hangs out with another dependent, this skinny girl named Cindy who works at the bowling alley after school every day. I can tell you what clubs she liked when we were going out.' He named some clubs in Boston that were popular with college kids, not the scholarship ones.

'Colonel Billings came and talked to you?' I was curious as to what was said. I couldn't imagine Dave being happy that an enlisted man was taking up with his daughter but had a hard time picturing Dave as a racist. Or even threatening the kid. On the other hand, it had been a few years, and I didn't know what it was like to have a daughter on an Army post.

'Yeah, he did.' Page's voice rose and he was leaning toward me. 'We done?'

'Take my card in case you remember anything.' He walked off without a word and without my card. I was curious about the discussion between him and Dave. I don't think it was a fond memory for PFC Page.

I got back into the Maverick. It started with a low, throaty rumble that reminded me of a lady I once met. I listened to the WBCN out of Boston while I jotted down some notes. Then I put it in gear and pulled out of the lot. I drove three hundred yards and turned around in a parking lot. I went back to the motor pool and parked in a spot in the rear where I was in the shade and could watch the door. I had these cute little binoculars that were small and let me see the people who came and went.

Detective work is not like it is in fiction. On TV, PIs seem to have an old buddy do a favor or break in someplace. No real PI zooms around in a cool helicopter. No one drives a flashy sports car, let alone a red Italian one.

Most detective work is about sitting, watching, and waiting. It isn't glamorous and sitting in the Maverick during the warm June morning I was reminded of that. I sat slumped with the windows open and the car off as the morning warmed up. As the sun chased the shade away from my car, I was thankful that it was June and not July or August. June is warm, manageable, but later in the summer, the heat and humidity would have been brutal.

I yawned and lit a cigarette. It wasn't good practice on a surveillance, but neither was falling asleep. Plus, it discouraged the large fly that kept buzzing in and out of my window. I waited and watched and tried to keep my eyes mostly open. A little bit before noon and a few Lucky Strikes later, troops came streaming out of the motor pool. Most of them got into

cars in twos and threes and went off to find lunch. The majority
would head toward the bowling alley, but plenty would head
for the McDonald's outside of the gate or something in town.
Derrick Page came out and went to a two-year-old black Ford
Mustang with a lot of gray primer down the passenger side.

I followed him at a distance. His half-primer car wasn't
easy to miss. He drove a couple miles under the speed limit,
and it was probably the dullest tail job in all of history. He
parked and hopped out. I generously let a few cars pass so
that I pulled into the parking lot as he was making his way
toward a low-slung building with a line of camouflage soldiers
waiting outside. The chow hall. Page stopped at a phone booth,
and through my cute binoculars I watched him fish coins out
of his pocket and feed them into the payphone. He stabbed
his index finger in a series of short jabs at numbered buttons,
but I was too far away to see which ones. It wasn't a long
conversation and didn't seem particularly animated. He hung
up and went to go wait in line for his turn in the chow hall.

I figured that I had at least half an hour to go find a cup of
coffee. I eased the Maverick out on to Lafayette and cruised
slowly toward Vicksburg Square and the main gate. The nice
thing about Fort Devens was that main post was small by
Army standards. There were bases in the south and southwest
where you could drive for a couple of hours and still be within
their confines. Even crawling at two miles below the posted
speed limit, I was outside the main gate and on my way to
Ayer in five minutes. I found a Dunkin' Donuts not far from
the post.

I parked and went in. I ordered the biggest black coffee that
they would give me. After the ritual exchange of bills and
coffee, I took my Styrofoam cup outside. In New York City,
coffee comes in blue cups with a Greek theme and the words
'We are happy to serve you.' In New England, it is a Styrofoam
cup with orange and pink letters saying 'Dunkin' Donuts.' I
still hadn't figured out if it was supposed to be a gerund or
not.

I leaned against the Maverick and smoked a Lucky while
the coffee cooled. The day was sunny, and a little breeze
pushed the treetops and long hair around. I wasn't sure what

Dave was hoping I was going to be able to do. Teenage girls have been worrying their fathers since time began. Plenty of kids party and stay out late. This was the eighties, electronics were replacing musical instruments, punk rockers were putting safety pins in their faces, and rich kids put coke up their noses instead of drinking it. Also, this was 1985, not 1965. Who cared anymore if Judy Billings was dating a black enlisted man?

I smoked, watching the good people of Ayer, Massachusetts go about their business. The cars that drove by were mostly American and mostly not very new or old. The haircuts tended to be GI short or just a bit longer, current and retired soldiers. There weren't many high fashion hairdos in Ayer, and I was pretty sure most people here drank their Coke instead of snorting it.

My coffee tasted better than battery acid but not as good as Mr Marconi's espresso corretto. I was sure any coffee would taste better with a belt of sambuca. Maybe I was turning into a Back Bay yuppie? What would be next, fruit frappés at Café Florian's? Or a sudden craving for crêpes? Maybe I could convince Brenda Watts to go out for an almost romantic sushi dinner.

I finished my musings and my coffee. The Styrofoam cup went in the trash, and I went back in the Maverick. I turned the key and listened to the low rumble of the engine. I had loved my VW Karmann Ghia, but it had died a hero's death. All that style and almost Porsche elegance replaced by short-bodied, stocky American might.

I drove back to the main gate past the litany of Korean restaurants, tattoo parlors, and pawn shops. I stopped at the check point at the elegant wrought iron main gate, which stood open. I showed the MP – who didn't look old enough to shave, much less have a loaded .38 revolver on his hip – my pass from Dave Billings. He did that combination salute and wave forward that MPs do, one fluid motion of impersonal courtesy and an order to move the fuck out!

PFC Page's half-primer Mustang was still parked in the chow hall parking lot. Even without the side of primer it wasn't as elegant as the earlier models. The fuel crisis in the late seventies and boxy styling hadn't done much for a once proud car design. At least my Maverick had some curves to it.

Page came out and stopped at the phone booth again. He put a coin in it, dialed, waited, and then hung up. Somebody wasn't answering. He got in the Mustang, and I followed him back to the motor pool at a distance. I parked in my spot and waited, watching, and slowly working through my pack of Luckies. At 1600, or four in the afternoon if you weren't in the Army anymore, men started streaming out of the motor pool. They went to their cars and drove away. Page was no different. I followed him to Vicksburg Square.

The square was comprised of four brick buildings, each several hundred yards long and four stories high. They housed battalion and company offices with enlisted barracks above. They were built in an era of elegant construction between the two world wars. I watched him park in the parking lot at the center of the square. It was a grass-covered parade ground in the thirties, but the proliferation of private automobile ownership had meant the grass was paved to make way for parking. I watched Page go to a building and, through my binoculars, saw him appear on the open second and third floor landings.

I sat and waited for a while, but I had been sitting and waiting all day. It didn't take long for the boredom to get the better of me. I hadn't eaten anything since morning, and food seemed like a good idea. The bowling alley had food and cold beer, and a friend of Judy Billings' worked there.

FIVE

The bowling alley was near the Commissary and the PX. Like them, it was made of red brick and concrete blocks. The architectural style wasn't brutal or even ugly, it was just extremely functional . . . and about as exciting as the back of a box of Wheaties. I found a spot for the Maverick, resisting the urge to park in spaces reserved for the post commandant, sergeant major, soldier of the quarter, and NCO of the quarter. My humbler parking spot was fine, even though it meant having to walk a few more yards.

I walked up the steps and inside the bowling alley and entered a time machine. The music was a radio station out of Boston that was playing The Cars. The décor was a mix of 1950s space-themed sparkling stars and rocket ships. In front of me was a counter where you could rent shoes; behind and below that were the lanes. Off to the right were rest rooms and to the left a bar and half a dozen tables. There were booths with brightly colored Formica-topped tables that were nestled against the low wall separating the snack bar from the lanes.

It didn't take a great detective to spot Cindy. If her name tag didn't give it away, she was the only woman working in the bowling alley who was under forty. The other lady was behind the bar wiping glasses with a white rag and not much enthusiasm.

'Hey, can I help you?' She was looking at me with skepticism. I was too young to be a retired twenty-year veteran on post to get a cheap meal, and my hair was too long for me to be a soldier.

'Yeah, I was looking for something to eat . . . maybe a beer.' I wasn't just a clever detective, skilled at spotting the lone teenage waitress in the place, I was hungry too.

'Sure thing.' She wore too much mascara the way teenagers do, and a little too much makeup trying to cover some acne.

She was skinny and her brown hair hung down to her shoulders in a cascade of permed curls.

I smiled disarmingly at her and she told me to sit anywhere. I found a booth that was in the middle of the bunch. There weren't many people in the bowling alley, and it was far enough from the bar to offer some privacy from the lethargic bartender. I watched Cindy drift off. She was wearing a blue, sack-like uniform dress made of polyester.

She came back and handed me a laminated menu. Burgers, hotdogs, and fried chicken were offered with a choice of French fries or onion rings. Other than lettuce, onion, and tomato on the hamburger, coleslaw was the only vegetable offering. On the way in, I had seen a chalk board offering specials.

'Can I get you anything to drink?'

'Do you have Löwenbräu?'

'Sure, if you don't mind it in a bottle.'

'Nope, as long as it is cold. How are the specials?'

'They're OK. I mean, everyone acts like the Schnitzel is sooo good, but it is hit or miss.'

'Is today a hit or a miss?'

'Definitely a miss. It was made the other day and Willy on the grill overcooks it. It comes out dry.'

'How is he with burgers?'

'Pretty good.'

'OK, can you get me a cheeseburger and French fries?'

'Sure. Coleslaw too?'

'Yes, please.'

'It comes with lettuce and tomato. Do you want chopped onions? They're the sweet kind.'

'Yes, thanks.' She wrote down my order on one of those green pads while chewing on her lower lip. She whisked off in a polyester swirl to get my beer. She came back and put it on the table. I had taken my business card and my license out of my wallet. I slid them over to her.

'What are those?' She was suspicious, as any teenager should be, of anyone too old to be in college.

'Cindy, I'm a private investigator from Boston. Judy Billings' dad is an old friend of mine and he is worried about her. She hasn't been home in a few days.' It had been a long time since I was a teenager, but things hadn't changed that much. I was sure that she was going to tell me to pound sand.

'Huh, a real private eye?' She spared me the obligatory *Magnum* jokes.

'Yes. I was in Vietnam with Judy's father. He is worried that she is getting into trouble. Drugs, that sort of thing.'

'What could you do about it?' Her eyes flashed, pupils narrowing a little.

'I don't know. But the first step is trying to find out if she is getting into trouble. Then talking to her to see if she is getting in the type of trouble that she can't grow up out of.' A bell rang, and she turned on her heel and walked to the kitchen. She came back with my food and put it in front of me. She took silverware wrapped in a paper napkin and put it next to the plate.

'Is there anything else, sir?' Her voice was colder than my Löwenbräu.

'I'm not a bad guy. I'm just trying to help out an old friend who is worried about his little girl. You are the only person who knows her who might talk to me. Point me in the right direction. That is all I'm looking for.' It seemed to be a better idea than trying to find her diary. I wasn't even sure teenage girls kept diaries anymore. When I was a teenager, I certainly didn't know any who did coke.

She walked away, leaving me with my food. Fortunately, the food was more than I was expecting. The cheeseburger came wrapped in wax paper and was cooked medium, with melted American cheese on it. Not the orange stuff but its paler brother. The bun was a potato bun that had been buttered and grilled before the cook had put mayonnaise, iceberg lettuce, and a slice of tomato on the top. I could smell the onions mixed with the smell of grilled beef but couldn't see them.

I found them when I bit into the burger. They had been pressed into the top of the patty and when the burger was flipped, they were on the bottom, where they cooked in the juices from the hamburger. The burger wasn't too big or too small and was moist. It was a far cry from the gray discs of factory meat served at the big fast-food places. It was one of the best cheeseburgers, and juiciest, I had ever tasted. The

French fries were crisp outside and steamy inside. The coleslaw was southern style, chopped green cabbage and carrots in a tangy sauce that was so tasty it had to take years off my life.

While I was contemplating the unexpectedly excellent meal I had just eaten, she came back and sat down. She had a thin sweater thrown over her shoulders like a cape. She had a glass with ice and cola in one hand and a packet of menthol cigarettes in the other. I noticed an orange Djeep plastic lighter had been slipped between the cellophane and the cigarette box.

'I'm on my break. I have to wear this sweater over my shoulders so that everyone knows I'm on break and not just being lazy, sitting down on the clock.' She took out a menthol and lit it. Had she been older I would have raced her to light it for her.

'Even in a bowling alley, the Army has rules.' It was still the Army, even if she wasn't actually in it.

'Are you, like, looking to narc on her?' She had managed to light the cigarette and now the glowing tip was facing me like a third accusatory eye.

'That depends.'

'Depends . . . on what?'

'Well, if she is doing normal teenage stuff but stuff her dad doesn't approve of, dating a guy from the wrong side of the tracks or partying a little, then no. No, I'm not looking to narc on her.'

'If she is into other stuff . . .?'

'It would have to be hard drugs . . . and the things teenagers might do for money for drugs. Anything dangerous or unhealthy . . . then, yeah. Yeah, I would have to tell Dave.' I looked her in the eye as I said it.

'Why? It's her life.'

'It is but it isn't. She isn't an adult yet. Dave has an obligation as a father, and frankly under the law, to raise her safely. And on top of all of that I owe her dad.' There was no way to explain to a child that I owed Dave for saving my life. That we had been in combat together, survived it, and were brothers.

'He's an asshole.'

'That may be, but he is her father.'

'He treats her like she is always fucking up.' She jutted her chin out at me with teenage defiance and anger at an unfair world ruled by parents who were, at best, capricious tyrants.

'Is she?' That was me, a master conversationalist, lulling people into giving away secrets by asking simple, leading questions.

'Kind of, but it isn't her fault, not all of it, you know?' She inhaled and then let out a cloud of menthol-tinged smoke. 'She isn't stupid, but school isn't her thing. She has that thing where she gets things backwards.'

'Dyslexia?'

'Yeah. Colonel Daddy treats her like she is dumb or isn't trying. Her mom is two or three vodkas deep by lunch, and she gets up at ten.' That explained Palm Springs . . . the Betty Ford clinic was out there, and rich no longer-socialites can't take the cure anywhere else. 'He acts like just because she parties a little she is just like her mom.'

'I'm sure that was a tough way to grow up.' Me asking questions by making statements.

'Were you an Army brat?'

'No, my dad got out when he got home after World War II. We lived in the same apartment until I left for college. College didn't take and the Army did.' I lived with my father, who consoled himself with my mother's having left us by drinking whiskey and reading poetry. He was a good father, but he had eventually succumbed to the pressures of a world that had been unkind to him. Or maybe he had been injured by his own expectations. Expectations of surviving jumping into Normandy, bloody fighting, wounds, and dead friends, and then a marriage that had ended as suddenly as those dead paratrooper friends had died in the war. Or maybe he had just used up his lifetime. I didn't have answers to any of those questions. He had been my father, he did the best he could, and that was it.

Until I went to the University of Rhode Island for a few months, my whole world was a few square blocks of South Boston and trips to Fenway Park. Fenway, Boston's real cathedral, that was where my father was happy and untroubled. Then I shipped out for Fort Benning and Fort Bragg and a few years in Vietnam. There were times when I went on leave and I traveled in Europe a little and then home to Boston . . . not Southie. I had been to see the elephant, had been to the other side of the world, to a war, and I couldn't fit in a few square blocks anymore.

'My dad, he's a supply officer. We move around a lot. Every couple of years Dad gets a new assignment. This one is pretty good. This isn't some shithole in Texas, Louisiana, or Missouri, places where the snakes outnumber the people. Where the radio plays more talk about Jesus than music. I have been to places where the nearest big town that isn't all strip clubs and pawn shops is hours away. No, this is OK. Every couple of years you are the new kid in class, but everyone has gone through it. Nothing seems permanent, though . . . but for Judy, well, between Colonel Daddy and Martini Mommy, she is a little more at sea than the rest of us.' It hadn't occurred to me that parents are important to a teenager.

'Well, he is her father. He should be worried about her if she is partying too much, missing school, and not coming home for days at a time.'

'He's just worried about his next command and chasing a general's star.' Her voice was a little bitter, and I wondered how much she and Judy had talked about this.

'I'm sure he isn't perfect, but he loves her, and he is worried. Maybe he is a little out of his depth?'

'What do you mean?'

'Well, he is an Army officer; he is used to being in charge. He plans for every contingency and every possibility. I have to imagine that is hard to do with a teenager. I'm sure he has spent a lot of time away from home, more so than most other types of officers.' Guys in SF spent a lot of time in the field training, then they spent a lot of time going on missions that they couldn't talk about. Dave probably hadn't actually spent a lot of time with his family. There was a reason why the divorce rate was so high in the service.

'Maybe . . .'

'Look, he is an old friend, but his daughter might be in trouble. Maybe she isn't. I'm just trying to find out. Can you help me?'

'She doesn't like school and hasn't been going much. I keep

trying to tell her that college is the best way to get away from all this. She skips school or cuts class a lot. She goes to Boston a lot and she is partying a lot with an older guy.'

'Derrick Page?' I liked the kid but if I had learned anything in the cops or as a private eye, everyone lies to you. Everyone.

'No, not Derrick. They went together for a while, but she ended that. Derrick couldn't keep up with her, and he was definitely worried about Colonel Daddy.' One of the funny things about the Army was that the wives, not so much the kids, tended to act as though their husband's rank was theirs as well. It was quite common to see officers' wives in the PX or Commissary bossing around the wives whose husbands were junior in rank. I was wondering if the Billingses were worried about having an enlisted son-in-law. 'This guy is in Boston . . . he's not from a nice neighborhood.'

'Are they involved?'

'Involved . . . yeah, she sleeps with him, stays over at his place.'

'Do you know his name?'

'Kevin. People call him K-nice.'

'People?'

'Yeah, I went out with them once to a club. He was wearing an open shirt showing off his chest and his gold chains. People kept coming up to him, buying him drinks and giving him money. Judy was wearing this dress and heels he bought her – there wasn't much to the dress. She sat next to him and he kept feeling her up in front of everyone, like she was his. Not like a girlfriend but like something he owned.' K-nice sounded like exactly the type of trouble that Dave was worried about.

'Derrick was older but not a bad guy. K-nice . . . is.'

'OK, tell me what club or clubs you went to with them. Restaurants, bars, anything. What type of car he drives, anyone you remember, and I will write it down and then go see what there is to see.' She named the clubs that they had been to and gave me a couple of names of other acquaintances as well. She told me that he drove a four-door blue Jaguar with tan interior and tinted windows.

'Mr Roark . . . he is scary.' She picked at some fingernail

polish that was starting to flake. It was a shade of red that only teenagers and women over thirty-five can get away with.

'Andy. Call me Andy. Scary how?'

'He carries a gun. It is shiny and flat with grips like pearls.' The line from the movie *Patton* pushed into my mind, and I smiled. I also thought of a friend of mine who once told me that I carried a gun that looked like it belonged to a pimp on Tu Do Street in Saigon. 'He carries one of those old-fashioned razors, you know, the kind that folds up and is really flat.'

'A straight razor?' It was an old-fashioned weapon in an era of automatic pistols and switchblade knives, but it was a good one. I had seen firsthand the damage they could do, and in the right hands it could be impressive. I remember one night when I was a beat cop trying to get information from a college football player who had gotten into a fight with the wrong person. He was holding his right cheek to his face with his right hand while waiting for an ambulance. The slice had been clean, and when the shock started to wear off the kid was going to be in unbearable pain. I had a healthy respect for anyone who knew how to wield a straight razor.

'It isn't just the gun and the razor, but it is his eyes . . . they get small and mean when he is angry. It is really scary.' She shivered. 'The night I went clubbing with them, this guy pissed him off. He had been looking at Judy. K-nice knew him, but it was clear he didn't like him. The guy came over and K talked to him for a minute and then offered him some blow. When he bent down to snort it, K broke a bottle on his head. Then grabbed him by the hair, smashed his head into the table a bunch of times. There was blood everywhere, it was gross.'

'It is a good thing I don't do coke.' I said it in my best deadpan, and she smiled.

'Mr Roark, be careful. He is dangerous.'

'Yeah, they always are.' Maybe someday I will get to investigate people who aren't dangerous. If that were ever the case, I would be out of work. Clients wouldn't need me if they could deal with things themselves.

Her break ended and I had finished my food. I left a twenty-dollar bill for a five-dollar tab. She was a nice kid and seemed genuinely worried about Judy Billings. I headed back out into the late afternoon sunlight of a beautiful June day that was sliding toward early evening. I shivered and told myself it was caused by going from air conditioning to the warmth outside. It might also have had a lot to do with not liking the thought of Judy Billings with a violent man who carried a straight razor. In my mind, Judy was a picture of a cute toddler that my Army buddy showed me in Vietnam one night. Now he'd asked me for help in protecting her, and I thought he might need it.

SIX

I pulled up in front of Dave's quarters on Walnut Street. I didn't really want to talk to him, but he had asked me to stop by and let him know what was going on. Normally clients got written reports or phone calls. Normally I delivered not-so-good or bad news with a level of professional detachment. Normally the client wasn't an old Army buddy who had saved my life. This time, I had to tell him that his teenage daughter was doing all the things any father would be worried about. Worse, if you included the fact that she was sleeping with a drug dealer or pimp, but neither option was good.

I got out of the car and walked up the front steps. It was early evening, but the sun was still a long way from setting. Maybe Judy would be home, and we could all hash this out together. Or maybe I could talk some sense into her. Maybe it was a phase she was going through . . . a cry for attention. Maybe I was still suffering from the aftereffects of having my car blown up in front of me three months ago. It had knocked out a lot of windows in my apartment building and rung my bell pretty good. If my neighbors gave me a wide berth before, they really avoided me now.

I pushed the doorbell and heard chimes faintly on the other side of the door. I waited a minute and pushed the doorbell again. Dave's orange BMW was in the driveway, and somewhere in the neighborhood kids were playing catch. I could hear their voices but not the words as the ball slapped into the catcher's glove. There was something wholesome about it all, the 1950s all-American small town. Except this one was surrounded by fences and armed soldiers. There were Russian spies who would love to know what was going on here. But that was part of what made Army bases feel like tight-knit communities.

I was about to walk back to my car when I heard footsteps

coming down the hall. The lock turned and the door opened. Dave was standing there wiping his hands on a dish towel.

'I'm sorry. I was doing the dishes.' He stuck out a damp hand and we shook. I was amused at the thought of the future commander of one of America's elite commando units, probably a future general, washing his own dishes. I was sure he hadn't learned that in boarding school.

'No worries. Got a second?'

'Sure, come on in. Do you want a beer?'

'Please.' Maybe a beer would help me deliver the not-so-good news, or at least wash some of the taste of it out of my mouth.

'Löwenbräu OK? If not, I might have some Beck's.'

'Löwenbräu is perfect.' I had been drinking it successfully for years.

'Good, c'mon.' He started down the hallway past the antiques and family pictures. Everything was still tasteful and spoke of Dave's success both in marriage and life. He directed me to his office and kept going to get the offered Löwenbräu. I whiled away a minute or two looking at framed pictures from his time in Vietnam. He had put up one of my team and himself that hadn't been there the first time I was in his study. We were posing for posterity, with our weapons and gear. We were young, bristling with grenades and weapons. We looked like happy, dangerous, all-American kids. Take away the weapons and change the uniforms and we could just as easily have been posing after the big football game. It was taken right before the last mission, before the Arc Light strike to end all Arc Light strikes.

There was another picture in a small frame. Dave and me, filthy, faces streaked with camouflage paint, dirt, and that type of grime that you can only get in the field. We had thrown our arms across each other's shoulders, CAR-15s in one hand, tape shot off the muzzles, and beer in the other. It had been a hairy mission, the second to last one we went on together. I couldn't think of a mission with Dave that hadn't been hairy. It had been a prisoner snatch, and we had managed to bring out the prisoner, an NVA officer, and we hadn't lost anyone on the team. Dave had left in a bird for Saigon with his prisoner after that. I went to the Head Shed for debrief, then a shower and a steak dinner. The steak and the drinks after a mission, those were always the best steaks and drinks I had ever had. Being alive after the NVA had done their best to kill you somehow made each meal seem like a banquet and every paycheck, a fortune.

'Here you go.' Dave stepped into the office with the beer outstretched to me in his right hand. He had one of his own.

'Thanks. Cheers.'

'Cheers.' We touched bottles and drank. 'Well, what happened? Did you find out anything?'

'I met and talked with the PFC she had been going with, the one from the motor pool.'

'Did that little asshole tell you anything? That kid is bad news, Andy, bad news, I know it.' Dave had moved a half step closer, his eyes boring into mine.

'No, he didn't. I don't think he knows anything. He said that after you read him the riot act, they broke up.' I took a pull on the bottle of cold beer.

'He's lying. They're still sneaking around, I know it.'

'Dave, he told me about a friend of hers from school. I went and talked to her. She said that they had broken up a while ago.' Cindy's earnestness was still fresh in my mind.

'She is covering for him, for them, they're lying to you. I know she is still seeing that spade from the motor pool.' He was getting worked up. His free hand was on my bicep, and the pressure wasn't comfortable. Dave's life involved a lot of skiing, rappelling, parachuting, some judo, some karate, and a lot of tennis. His grip was strong. I flexed my arm to counter the pressure of his fingers digging into it. It wasn't enough to distract me from his use of the slur.

'Easy there, mister.' I said it in my best imitation of John Wayne, which wasn't very good at all. 'Even if I didn't believe the PFC, I believe the girl. She is worried about Judy.' Dave let go of my arm and stepped back.

'If she isn't with the kid from the motor pool, then what is going on? She's never here. She comes by when she knows I'm at work. She takes money . . . some of her mother's jewelry is missing. Andy, what is going on?' He was upset and I had never in all the months of combat seen him agitated or upset.

'It isn't good. According to her friend, Judy has gotten involved with a man in Boston.' I didn't want to tell him too much about K-nice. I didn't want to scare him. Dangerous men who are scared for their daughters can do a lot of irrational things. Dangerous and irrational things. Also, I didn't want to take away that last sense of his little girl. 'He is older than her.' I was stalling for time with details that were not important. 'It sounds as though he is a lowlife criminal.'

'Jesus.' It came out hoarsely. 'Andy, how bad . . . how bad is it?'

'I don't know, Dave. He sounds like a drug dealer, maybe a pimp. He has a reputation for violence.' Which sounded silly because both Dave and I were violent men, very skilled violent men at that. But the type of violence that K-nice was a practitioner of was hugely different from our violence. His was a tool, used for controlling his stable. Protecting his drugs. Ours had been used in a secret, brutal part of a war that everyone wanted to forget about now.

'Jesus Christ, I will kill him. I will fucking kill him.' Dave would, too. He was experienced, smart, and extremely well trained. I had no doubt that he could kill K-nice. It was the getting away with it part that worried me. Dave was a soldier, an SF officer, but he wasn't a criminal. He was used to avoiding East German soldiers and Stasi agents, setting an ambush, and then fading into the woods. He wasn't used to dealing with the boys from Homicide, the Crime Lab or the District Attorney. At the very least, Dave could fuck up his brilliant future. He could flush that general's star right down the crapper. I wasn't about to let that happen.

'You don't know what you are dealing with, and you don't know where to find him. You are good in the woods, Vietnam, East Germany, wherever you go over the fence, but you aren't skilled at the city, the Combat Zone, my jungle.' I was pretty sure that Dave had never even been to Boston's little patch of misery, sex, drugs, and violence.

'Andy, this is my Judy we're talking about.'

'I will find the guy and have a talk with him.'

'What if that doesn't work?'

'Then I will persuade him.'

'And if that doesn't work?'

'It will.'

'If it doesn't, what then, what if he doesn't care about you or Vietnam? What will you do then?'

'Then I will put a bullet between his eyes.' I hadn't really considered it until I said it but, in that moment, I knew it was true. That was something else that I had learned in Vietnam; sometimes a bullet was the only answer. All those bumper stickers saying 'Violence isn't the answer' had simply never been asked the right question. Maybe that was a gift that the war had given me?

'Andy . . .'

'We aren't there yet. We simply don't know enough.' We didn't know anything except that Judy was involved with a bad dude. She might be in love with him, she might be in trouble, but it was too soon to do anything other than try and find out more.

'Well, then, you're the detective. What is next?' He was worried, and I couldn't blame him.

'I know some of the clubs she goes to. I know what this guy looks like, what he drives. I have contacts, and he isn't exactly in the business of being anonymous. I will find them and bring her home.' I said it as though I had some sort of plan. Like I knew what I was doing.

'OK, I'm counting on you.' He didn't say I owed him for saving my life in Vietnam. He didn't have to. There really wasn't much to say after that. The beers were finished and neither of us was in the mood to drink more, to reminisce about the old days. I told him I would call him, and he walked me to the door.

Outside the sun was still out. The Maverick was furnace hot inside. I took off my jacket and would simply have to chance being stopped by the MPs with the .38 in the small of my back. I wound down the driver's side window and leaned over and half rolled the passenger side one down. The car rumbled to life, and I made my way out of officers' housing, down the main drag, and out of the main gate. I made my way through Ayer, my back damp, making me wonder how bad it would be in July and August. I turned on to Route 2 and, with wind screaming through the car and the radio blasting rock and roll, I headed to Boston. Mick Jagger told me about the condition of his feet and Fleetwood Mac explored their relationship issues. Me, I just drove the car.

The Maverick powered its way over the hills and down Route 2 back to Boston. The engine designed to compete with Ford's own magnificent Mustang had been finely tuned and benefited from a Holley carburetor. The car had lots of horsepower ready to respond to my driving whims. It had been lovingly tended to by Carney at his garage in Boston. He knew some unsavory people who paid him to provide cars for unsavory acts. Carney liked me because he had been a paratrooper in Korea and had a daughter who had been in a jam. I had helped him out.

Now, driving back to the city in the waning light of a June evening, I was struck by the fact that a few years later I was trying to help another man whose daughter was in trouble. Carney's daughter had been hooked on heroin and was living with a guy who was half boyfriend and half pimp. He was a junkie too. He had pulled a knife on me and ended up at the bottom of a flight of stairs with some broken bones that had been fine when we had first met at the top. He didn't know what he was doing with a knife and tried to stick me with it like he was fencing. I had pivoted one foot on the step, the other hanging off into nothing. The knife shot past me, and my right hand had wrapped around his right wrist. I squeezed it hard, pulling my right side back toward the wall while slamming the palm of my left hand against his elbow. Three things happened: his wrist broke when I sheared it, his elbow dislocated when his face smashed into the wall, and my left palm became a fulcrum. His nose flattened, exploding into a fountain of blood and snot when it hit the wall. I snaked my left hand up over his neck, cupping it as I moved down a few steps, pulling his right arm. My weight took him, he launched into space, and I did a little jig to keep my balance on the edge of the step. He landed with a sickening crunch on the landing. He was moaning as we stepped over him with Carney's daughter between us.

Carney's daughter had been high and woke up in a private clinic in New Hampshire. She didn't remember anything or maybe she didn't try too hard to. Later, I had heard a rumor that a dealer Carney had done business with was found floating in the harbor. The indents from the wrench were still visible on his face, and even after being in the water you could still clearly read the word 'Craftsman.' Carney and I didn't talk about it, and I hadn't been impolite enough to ask him about it, but in the years since, he had done me several good turns. The Maverick had been the latest one.

I parked in my parking spot. It was easy to find because the tar was a different color from the other spots. It was too early to go to the clubs looking for K-nice, and I wasn't sure that I had the energy to go prowling through the Combat Zone looking for Judy. The Combat Zone was Boston's own five-acre patch of sin. It had burlesque clubs, nude dancers, and theaters that played dirty movies in color. If you wanted books where the editors were more concerned with different ways to reference genitals than with grammar, the bookstores in the Combat Zone were for you. If you were looking for a peep show or wanted to buy sex – boys or girls – the Combat Zone was your spot. The liquor was watered down in the bars, and the heroin was strong. If you liked your cops dirty or wanted to fight with sailors from the Charlestown Navy Yard, then the Combat Zone was your amusement park.

It was a whole lot of human misery that I couldn't stomach right now. The prostitutes calling everyone 'honey' or 'baby' only depressed me. It was made all the worse knowing that Judy Billings' future with a man like K-nice was, at best, dancing on stage at a place like the Pussycat Lounge or, worse, selling her ass on LaGrange Street. The high rise buildings, sleek and glassy, were encroaching, and the Zone wasn't what it used to be, but there was still plenty of sin to be found in 1985.

Prostitution had been rife in Vietnam, and I, like most GIs, had partaken. In Vietnam, it didn't seem to have the same stigma it did here. There it was just a fact of life and a way for women to earn money. It didn't seem that bad, or maybe I just didn't care about things as much. I was young and certain that I was going to die every time I went 'over the fence,' across the border into Laos or Cambodia to spy on the Ho Chi Minh Trail. It wasn't that I wasn't confident in my skills or my teammates. They were the best men there were. It was so dangerous that I simply accepted my death as a fact, and that allowed me to do my job without overthinking my own mortality.

I never stopped to wonder if the girls were there by choice or if they were forced into it. The right and wrong of it was lost on my twenty-year-old brain. Now, years later, I felt about it like the way I felt about calling the Vietnamese 'gooks' at the time. It didn't occur to me that the fact that everyone else was doing it didn't necessarily mean it was the right thing to do. I'm not sure I thought about much other than doing Recon work or having a good time when I wasn't getting ready for or being on a mission. I had done some growing up since then.

When I came home and I was a cop, my perspective changed. I remember vividly the first working girl I met. She had been standing on LaGrange Street. I was the junior man and was covering an empty patrol car because someone had called out sick. She was skinny and looked about seventeen going on thirty-five. On TV she would have been older, sexier, and classier. Not on LaGrange Street.

She was wearing hot pants, a tank top, and Keds. Her clothes, such as they were, hadn't seen a washing machine in days. She was missing an eye tooth, and her other teeth were yellowish. Her skin was pockmarked. She had track marks up her left arm near the elbow, and her eyes were unfocused the way that good shit makes your eyes go. She was nothing like TV and the movies.

'Hey, officer . . . you're cute.' It wasn't the first hint I had that she was high.

'Thanks.'

'Wanna party?' She tried to cock her hip and look sexy. She didn't. She wasn't really selling sexy, she was selling instant gratification and a quick exit.

'No, thanks . . . I'm all set.' Even if it wasn't a July night in the Combat Zone and she hadn't been a few days gone from a shower, the answer would have been the same. This was worlds different from what was offered in Vietnam.

'Come on, officer . . . you're cute . . . have one on the house.'

'No, girl. I'm good.' I left her on LaGrange. She was too pathetic looking to roust. I wasn't so green as not to realize that if she didn't reach her quota that night, she wouldn't be able to score heroin. I also knew enough to be aware that if she didn't bring home enough cash, she would get knocked around by her pimp. She would end up dead sooner rather than later, one of the Street's disposable people.

The Street ate up young girls and boys and left behind human wreckage. They usually started down the path of addiction by being involved with someone like K-nice. That party boyfriend who had the good drugs. That older guy who convinced them that he loved them. Then love would turn into a beating, each one punctuated with the question, 'Baby, why'd you make me do that?' Conditioning them to believe it was their fault and training them to want to please. It was sick and Pavlovian. Eventually they ended up standing on LaGrange Street or a street like it selling their ass. I didn't want Judy Billings to join their ranks.

Judy was fortunately still at the 'making bad choices' stage of things. She could still walk away if she wanted to. I could hit the streets looking for K-nice tomorrow. Tonight, I could have a drink and see if there was anything good on the Movie Loft on Channel 38. There might even be some food in the refrigerator.

The apartment was still and quiet. I could hear sounds of traffic outside and wondered if Brenda Watts was home. If she was, would she answer the phone? I still wanted Sir Leominster back, and it would be nice not to have her mad at me. I was running low on friends, much less pretty ones who liked bourbon. I called, but when her voice came on telling me to leave a message, I didn't. Instead, I poured whiskey over some ice. I turned on the TV and sat down on the couch. The Movie Loft was playing *The Third Man*, and Dana Hersey was explaining about Graham Greene's script. I took the .38, holster and all, and put it on the coffee table in front of me. It was a relief not to have the hunk of steel and wood digging into my kidneys anymore. I watched Joseph Cotten and Orson Welles play their parts in black and white. I drank whiskey until the movie ended, then went to bed with a James Crumley novel, the .38 on the nightstand, and the promise of sleep.

I was in the jungle. The heat and humidity pushed against my face. I was running toward a bomb crater. No matter how fast I ran, it felt like I was running through molasses. My chest was heaving, and my lungs were burning. I made it to the bomb crater and dove in, rolled on my stomach. I shouldered my CAR-15, but when I pulled the trigger a flag with 'BANG!' on it popped out of the barrel. Somewhere a bugle sounded, and wave after wave of NVA rushed at me. I tried to shoot them again, and again the flag popped out. The NVA just laughed at me, advancing with bayonets. The bugle sounded again and again until I opened my eyes, not in the jungle, but in Boston.

I picked up the phone by the bed and with my other hand found my Seiko dive watch on the nightstand. The luminous dial pointed out that it was five in the morning. A voice down the wire from the handset said, 'Andy! Andy, are you awake?' Last time I had heard Dave yell those words at me I had been getting ready to die in the jungle.

'Yeah, what's up?'

'Andy, it's Judy. She's run away!'

'Huh?'

'We had a fight last night. An argument. Someone told her I hired you. When I got up this morning to go to PT,' – he was referring to Physical Training, the Army's version of gym class – 'she was gone. There was a note and some of her clothes are missing.'

'OK, OK . . . I will be there as soon as I can.'

'Hurry, Andy. Please.' I had never heard Dave sound scared or desperate before . . . now his voice was a mix of both.

'I'm on the way.'

SEVEN

skipped the shave and just showered. I wore Nike running sneakers, faded blue jeans, and a navy blue polo shirt with an alligator sewn on the chest. My little .38 with its slim wooden grips went in a waistband holster on my right hip. It had five hollow points in it, and I put a speedloader with five more in my left front pocket. I had my Buck knife with the big lock blade in the right-hand pocket. It was sharp and broken in enough that I could open it with a hard flick of my wrist. It was equally good as a weapon or a B&E tool.

The Maverick started with its usual throaty rumble. I made my way out of town, stopping only for a black coffee and doughnut to take on the road. Neither was anything special, but I needed caffeine and some calories. It was an hour's drive to Fort Devens, even with the Holley carburetor carbureting the whole way. There wasn't much that a Holley carburetor could do about the traffic in and around Boston.

I couldn't get much out of the Maverick until the city streets had turned to suburban roads which turned into highway. It was on the highway that the Maverick shone. I pushed my right foot down, and the car ate up the miles. I had the sensation of cruising over hills, almost surfing instead of driving. In the fall, it was an especially beautiful drive with trees turning into a riot of red, orange, and yellow. It was still pretty when they were lush and green, speckled with dots of color from flowers and bushes.

I pulled up to Jackson Gate a little after seven in the morning. Dave had called me sometime after five. I showed my pass to the tired MP who was already bored less than an hour into his shift. He waved me through, and a few minutes later I pulled up in front of the house on Walnut Street.

Dave's BMW was in the driveway, and cars were working their way through the neighborhood. Commissioned officers and senior NCOs on their way to their jobs like everyday commuters, except these commuters were in starched camouflage fatigues. I walked up to the door and it swung open before I could ring the bell. Dave must have been watching and waiting.

'Andy, Jesus, I'm glad you are here.' While most of the Army wore reversible black and yellow PT uniforms, no self-respecting Special Forces soldier would be caught dead wearing them except for rare occasions like a run with the post commander. Dave was no exception; he wore a t-shirt from a Dutch paratroop unit and Adidas running shorts that were so thin they could best be described as 'grape smugglers.' He was wearing Adidas running sneakers which were nearly silent on the floor as he padded behind me. His shirt was damp, and he must have gone to PT with his men after calling me. Maybe he figured that there wasn't much that he could do until I got there. Or maybe he needed to burn off some nervous energy. People do weird things when they get stressed out.

'I put a pot of coffee on. Do you want some?'

'Sure, that would be great.' The stuff that I had in the car had provided caffeine but not much in the way of flavor. 'What happened?' We walked into the neat kitchen. The big appliances provided by the Army were dated but in good repair. Everything else was purchased with Billings' money and not the Army's. If the Army had paid for the furnishings and kitchen gadgets, then they would have had to make do with one less tank or helicopter that fiscal year. Dave poured me a cup.

'Cream? Sugar?'

'Black. Thanks.' He handed me a heavy ceramic mug. This one was from the officers' mess in Kleber Kaserne, Kaiserslautern, Germany. Kaiserslautern was home to one of the largest US military garrisons outside of the United States. Dave must have filched it on an away game from Bad Tölz where 10th Group was headquartered in West Germany. I sipped the coffee. It was good, imported, and dark.

'I got up at five. The house was quiet as always. I came into the kitchen to get a glass of water and found that she had left me a note.' He gestured distractedly at the kitchen table.

There was a folded piece of paper and I picked it up. It said, 'Daddy, I don't want to be here anymore like this. Tell Mommy I said goodbye. Judy.'

'I went right to her room. Her bed was empty. Her school bag was missing. You know, one of those backpacks from L.L. Bean's. I think some of her clothes are missing. She took all the cash from my wallet, about two hundred dollars. Also, some of her mother's jewelry is missing. Jesus . . . what do I tell her mother?'

'When did you see Judy last?' I had no idea what he should tell his wife, so I asked him one of those questions you are supposed to ask in cases like this. It meant I didn't have to answer his question.

'Last night, after you left. She came home around twenty hundred, maybe a little after.' Twenty hundred hours was eight p.m. Dave had been in the Army so long he forgot that the rest of America used a twelve-hour clock. 'She came home, I think she was high – you know, weed. We had a fight. I told her she was ruining her life. She accused me of spying on her. I told her I was worried about her running around with drug dealers. She told me to go to hell. Me, her father. Can you believe that?' He was shaking his head in disbelief.

'What happened then?'

'She stormed off to her room and slammed the door. I knocked and knocked, but she didn't answer. I could hear her crying. After a while I decided we both needed some space, and I went to pour myself a big scotch. She stayed in her room, and I eventually went to bed. When I woke up, it was just like I told you, there was the note, and she was gone. Do you think she went to Boston to that man?' He spat the end of the question like it was vinegar in his mouth.

'How would she get there?'

'There's always the bus.' The Greyhound bus terminal in Boston was a mecca for teenage runaways coming to the city.

'She doesn't drive?' He shook his head. 'Does she have any friends on or off post she might stay with?' I asked.

'No, not really. We haven't been here that long.'

'Does she know anyone in town?'

'In town? In Ayer?'

'No, Boston . . .' I was born in Boston at the Lying-In, and my whole life everyone referred to it as 'in town.'

'Not that I know of . . . just that man you mentioned. Oh god, is he . . . do you . . . I heard a lot of these drug dealer types also . . . also pimp young women. Do you think . . .' His voice was getting hoarse as he trailed off.

'Let's not get ahead of ourselves. We don't know for sure she is with him. It's possible she is just trying to shake you up. Scare you a little.' It wasn't likely, but offering an old friend a glimmer of hope wasn't the worst thing in the world either.

'No, Andy. I think she is serious this time.'

'Has she run away before?'

'Yes, but not like this. She never took clothes or stayed out too long.'

'OK, we don't know for certain she is with K-nice.' Not for certain, but it wasn't unlikely. Guys like K-nice appreciated runaways who were angry with Daddy.

'Do you think she is with that asshole kid from the motor pool?' I was starting to get the impression that Dave didn't like Derrick Page.

'It is a possibility, but I don't think so. He was believable when he told me it was over. Also, the friend I talked to was even more believable.'

'Come on, Andy, they could be playing you, lying to you.'

'Thanks, Dave, I didn't know what you meant by playing me.' I was so used to people lying to me throughout the course of my day that I didn't know if I should be surprised or disappointed when they didn't.

'Well, you just don't know.'

'I'm a pretty experienced private investigator. I was a cop before that . . . if that isn't good enough for you, I can recommend some guys in the business who are good. Really professional. They wear fedoras and trench coats too.' It irked me having my judgement questioned, even by old Army buddies.

'Jeez, Andy . . . I'm sorry . . . I didn't mean to . . . you know. It's just scary . . . she's my daughter.'

'OK, we should call the MPs. They will need to take a report and they will want a recent picture of her.'

'Why call the MPs?'

'That way they can file the missing persons report and contact the State Police, Boston and the other city departments. It can go out on the telex.'

'No, Andy . . . I don't want the MPs or the police involved.'

'Dave, it's the best chance to find her. They have a lot of resources.'

'NO. I don't want the police involved.' His voice was firm. 'If anyone can find her, you can. Andy . . . you owe me.'

'I know. I will find her.' I shouldn't have said it. You never made promises in this line of work. Never.

'Thank you, man. I know you will.' He gripped my forearm, fingers digging in hard enough to leave white marks. 'Bring her home to her mother and me.'

'Can I take a look at her room?'

'Sure. Let's go.' I took a sip of coffee and followed him, mug in hand, to the hallway and up the stairs. There was a door at the top of the stairs that, by the look of the open door, was Dave and Barbara's bedroom. To the right was a bathroom. There was another door down the hall. Dave pointed to the one closest to me on the left. 'This is it. Feel free to look around while I hop in the shower.'

I had heard stories of Army households where the kids' bedrooms were always inspection ready. Just like the troops, the beds were made with hospital corners and the shoes were lined up neatly in a row under the bed. Clearly the Billings household wasn't one of those. Judy's room had a bed that was made but not neatly, not so much made as the covers pulled up hastily. Piles of clothes were on the floor and on one of those weird papasan chairs. There was a desk that had books and teen magazines on it. There were posters on the wall for Duran Duran, Wham!, and Madonna. While Judy and I may have shared a philosophy on making the bed, we would never have the same taste in music.

There was a closet by the bed and a bureau on the other side. I opened the closet to find clothes on hangers, shoes in a pile on the floor, and a shelf above the clothes. The shelf held hats, shoeboxes that seemed to hold pictures of friends from other Army posts, and things she had outgrown like ceramic horses. There was nothing in the pockets of her clothes and nothing under the mattress or pillows. The only things she was hiding under the bed were some of the biggest dust bunnies I have ever seen. There were more teen magazines and an empty bag that used to have potato chips in it.

The drawers in the bureau contained things like blue jeans, skirts, t-shirts, and sweaters. The top drawer held her underwear and bras. In the back, there was also a plastic clamshell case. Inside were pills in a wheel-shaped blister pack. Based on where I found them, I was fairly certain that Judy didn't want her parents to know she was taking birth control pills.

The top desk drawer held cassette tapes, school supplies, and nothing exciting. The next one down held makeup, nail polish in disturbing neon shades, and a double-sided mirror with a little metal stand. There were a couple of compacts and several tubes of lipstick in different colors.

Her schoolbooks were tossed in a pile on the floor next to her desk. On the desk was a lamp and a small boombox to play tapes or get the local radio stations. There was a series of books by S.E. Hinton and a coming-of-age book by Judy Blume. There were a couple of trashy-looking romance novels and a hardbound copy of the collected works of Shakespeare.

I picked out the Shakespeare from the stack of books. It felt light, and when I opened it and flipped through a few pages, I found out why. Judy had hollowed out the book and glued all but the first thirty or so pages together to form a hide. There was a pack of menthol cigarettes in it, a small bag of weed, and a couple of pills. Dave definitely wouldn't approve. There was also a small makeup mirror with just the faintest bit of white powder stuck between the glass and the plastic frame. Judy liked to party. That fit with what Derrick Page had told me.

Next to the bottles and tubes of makeup was a diary. It had a flowery cover and leather tab that ended in a lock that was supposed to keep prying eyes out. I used the Buck knife to pop the clasp. I skimmed through the pages. It was the usual teenage stuff: boys she liked, boys she thought liked her, friends who were loyal, people who weren't nice to her. She talked about her parents. Mom was a drunk and Dave was an absentee authoritarian who was home just enough to ruin her life. Her tone grew angrier toward the last few entries. Dave was apparently ruining her life by not letting her do any of the things she wanted to do. Based on what she wrote in the diary, Dave shouldn't let her do any of it. She was a woman, why did he have to treat her like a child? She was free to date whomever she wanted to.

Dave was out of the shower and was moving around in the master bedroom. I slipped into the bathroom. It was still steamy from Dave's shower as I closed the door behind me. The medicine cabinet had the usual things: Band-Aids, aspirin, creams, and ointments. There was a bunch of pill bottles in Barbara Billings' name. There was one filled with Valium and another that seemed to be for pain. I closed the medicine cabinet and went to a small door in the wall. It was a closet that had some first aid stuff, more Band-Aids, bandages, burn cream, hydrogen peroxide, and things like that. The other shelves held monogrammed towels. I had never known anyone who had their own monogrammed towels. That was strictly for hotels that I couldn't afford to stay in. I flushed the toilet that I hadn't used and washed my hands. I didn't want Dave to think that I was snooping.

Dave was on the landing in a camouflage uniform. His left shoulder bore the Special Forces patch with a sword bisected by three lightning bolts, Airborne tab centered above that, Ranger tab above that, and the Special Forces tab on top of that. In my day we just had the patch, no fancy tab. Tabs were just for Rangers. Maybe I was starting to show my age?

On his left breast he wore the Combat Infantryman Badge (CIB) above his Jump Wings and above the piece of cloth with 'U.S. Army' embroidered on it. The Jump Wings had a star in the canopy so that the world would know that Dave was a master parachutist. Below the US Army on the pocket flap, was his Air Assault Badge, a helicopter with birdlike wings which meant he was officially qualified to rappel out of helicopters. Sewn on one collar was the black oak leaf denoting his rank as a lieutenant colonel, and on the opposite collar was sewn the crossed arrow insignia identifying him as a Special Forces officer. He had a pair of foreign Jump Wings sewn above his right breast pocket. On his right shoulder he wore the SF patch showing that he had served with SF in combat. That was one of the things about Army uniforms, they were meant to be a visual resume for the wearer. My time in the Army had been just the opposite. We wore sterile uniforms that were made anywhere but in America. We never wore unit patches, rank, or any other insignia if we were out on a mission. When we were in the rear, we wore enough to let people know we were Special Forces, Green Berets, and not much more.

His uniform was starched, and the pockets were so flat I wondered if he'd had the buttons removed, as I had heard of some officers doing. They cut the buttons off and either sewed the pockets shut or sewed in Velcro closures. It made for a nice, sharp-looking uniform. The leather of his jungle boots gleamed with black polish. Seeing Dave in his Battle Dress with all its patches and sewn-on badges reminded me of the first time I met him, fresh up from Saigon. Dave was showing a little mileage, but he was mostly the same.

'Nice shine on the boots. Did you drop them off at the Korean barbershop?' It was well known that most officers couldn't put a decent shine on their boots if their lives depended on it. The barbershops outside of post had a cottage industry shining boots for officers. Dave laughed. 'The guy at the barbershop works some sort of magic.'

'Probably uses a buffing attachment and an electric drill. You look sharp.'

'Thanks. I have to brief some brass today, so I have to look sharp.'

'I'm sure you will be fine.' Dave, like most senior officers, earned his pay these days not in the field but instead wielding a pointer in front of a map or slide presentation.

'It can't be avoided, or I would be out with you looking for Judy.'

'Of course. I will call you as soon as I know anything. Call me if she comes home or touches base. If I'm not in the office, leave a message on the machine at home or with my service.'

'What are you going to do now, Andy?' We had made our way downstairs.

'I will go into town and head to all the places that kids go when they run away.'

'What types of places?' He was curious.

'The Greyhound station, South Station, Back Bay. I will check the streets and fast-food restaurants, convenience stores, shopping centers, places like that. Record stores, Faneuil Hall, the Common, and so on. Can I have a recent picture or two to show around?' I left out the fact that I would call around to the hospitals and the police. No point scaring Dave.

'Sure, give me a second.' He left and came back a couple of minutes later with two color prints of Judy.

'This one is a month old and the other is from a few months ago.'

'OK, thanks. Does she take any medication that she would have filled?'

'No, nothing. Why . . . oh, yeah, you could check the pharmacies.' Dave was sharp – maybe too sharp to be an officer?

'Something like that.'

He went out to his little BMW, his green beret rolled into his clenched fist instead of on his head. I got in the Maverick and aimed it for Boston. I didn't want to tell Dave that I had been through this before with Carney's daughter. That a couple of years before I had plunged into it headlong. I had known that she was with a heroin dealer and that had narrowed the field a little. He hadn't been hard to find, and he was not tough. The hard part had been getting her back to Carney and to a rehab hospital in New Hampshire. That had been a long ride for everyone, but compared to Carney and his daughter, I had it easy.

EIGHT

I didn't rush driving back to the city. It was a stunning June morning, and I had the windows down. Driving out of Ayer on my way to Route 2, the air was clean and perfumed with pollen. As I got on the highway, I was struck by how beautiful it was out here. Everything was green, and the rolling hills gave the landscape a dramatic texture. The city seemed grimy and litter-ridden by comparison. I didn't hammer down on the gas pedal the way I had been doing on this drive lately.

It wasn't about saving gas or money. I was procrastinating. Every mile toward home was a mile closer to plunging into a part of the city that was depressing, filled with forgotten people. It might have been lit with neon lights and bright marquees, but the Combat Zone was grim if you were looking for a teenage runaway. There would be a lot of women and some men who were out selling the only commodity that they had. They were doing it to make the money to buy drugs, to keep the pain of their lives manageable. The fact that they had a pimp willing to hurt them to squeeze money out of them was a heck of a motivator too. It was a cycle: trick, cop, use, and repeat, except they had to turn a lot of tricks before they could cop drugs. Usually it was heroin, easy, cheap, and addictive. If they were having a special occasion maybe they would get some coke, but it was heroin that they needed. They would do it day in and day out until they got clean and got out or until they ended up dead. There were no vacation days from the cycle. Usually, it was death that offered an exit from their pain.

Judy probably wasn't there yet. She was probably just at the introductory stage with the boyfriend who told her he loved her but used her and gave her drugs. If he hadn't already, he would hit her one day soon. Then he would ask her why she made him do it. He would act like it was a one-off. Beg her for forgiveness and buy her something nice. Then it would

happen again, and then again. Then instead of some weed or
some party coke, it would be heroin. He would hit her more
often and she would shoot up more. Eventually she would be
selling herself and giving him the money out of love or fear
or both. She might be convinced that she loved him, but she
would become a slave to the heroin. She would do anything
to be able to keep shooting up. It usually worked that way, or
near enough.

When I was a street cop, I had gotten pretty good at not
thinking about it too much. Each story was a series of tragedies
that were distilled down to chasing the next high so as not to
feel the pain. Like looking at a bad car accident, you couldn't
let it get to you. Couldn't let yourself feel, because this accident happened every night in the Combat Zone. It might end
the same way, but it would take years and a lot of pain. Being
a street cop down in the Zone meant watching the girls and
boys die little by little, millimeter by millimeter. They were
always young. There weren't a lot of old addicts in the game.
Sometimes it would be quick, a beating gone too far, being
stabbed or maybe strangled, but usually they died slowly. I
found that I didn't like watching them die on the installment
plan. There was nothing I could do to help other than look
the other way on the occasional warrant or buy them something
to eat once in a while.

This time it was different. It was a friend's daughter. She
wasn't the little girl in a picture wrapped in a plastic sandwich
bag tucked into the breast pocket of his jungle fatigues, but
she was Dave's daughter. I owed it to him, to them, to find
her. Like the tag line in a bad movie, this time it was personal.

My first stop was the print shop near Carney's garage. They
made copies of the photos, and they rushed it for me.
They also made a bunch of flyers with Judy's picture, her first
name, and my number on it. The flyer said people should call
me, but I put the number that would go directly to the answering
service. It took an hour, and they took twenty of my dollars.
I took that time to call Captain Johnson of the Boston Police
Department.

'Roark . . . what shit are you getting into now? I have
enough stuff blowing up in this city, I don't need you adding

to it.' There was a rash of Irish and Italian mobsters blowing each other up lately. Johnson had felt that my exploding car, the late, great Karmann Ghia, had been an unnecessary trouble to add to his investigative woes. He probably would have been happier if I had been in it.

'No, this case is a runaway teenager. No explosions.'

'With you involved, I will believe it when I see it. You piss people off. The kind of pissed off that results in people trying to blow up your car.'

'But not you, Captain.' I tried to sound charming, but the telephone is not my best medium, and I'm not really all that charming to begin with.

'Roark, the way you do things I will be surprised if you live long enough to get on my nerves. Who is the teenager?' He did have a point.

'Judy Billings. She is seventeen.' I gave him her height, weight, hair color, and date of birth. 'She is the daughter of an old Army buddy, and she ran away from her home at Fort Devens last night. If anyone turns up, will you let me know?'

'Absolutely. The Boston Police Department would be more than happy to do your job for you. Maybe you would like me to have a couple of my detectives look through some keyholes for you?' His sarcasm was not the subtle kind.

'Captain, come on. She's a kid and her dad saved my life in Vietnam.' I knew that to him she was just another runaway and that he couldn't care about them all, or even just her. That was my piece in the whole thing.

'OK, Roark. No need to buy me a ticket for the guilt trip. I will call you if she turns up in the system.' His voice had softened. Guys like him understood what it was like to owe someone for saving your life. It was part of the currency that came with having a badge and gun on your hip, or a tour in Vietnam.

'Thank you, Captain. I would appreciate it.' He grunted and hung up. When he wasn't telling me what an asshole he thought I was, he was a man of few words.

It seemed a little too soon to start calling the hospitals. I called a detective I knew on the Cambridge Police Department and had a conversation similar enough to the one that I had with Captain Johnson to make me wonder if I was as much of an asshole as people were saying. It was still too early to go find K-nice. The city's finer criminal elements were rarely awake before late afternoon.

I headed over to the Greyhound bus station on Saint James Avenue, near Arlington Street. The Greyhound sign stretched up into the sky with its Art Deco design. The building had a prominent circular window and a Burger King inside. Litter was strewn around the place, drifted up against the walls where the wind had blown it.

I parked the Maverick a block up and walked back. I hadn't been inside in several months, but nothing had changed. The stalls in the men's room still wanted you to pay a dime to use them. There were banks of black hard plastic chairs in the middle of the waiting room with small black and white TVs that you had to put a quarter in to watch. The rows of seats without TVs were also made of hard plastic and were orange or white in color. The bus station still smelled of piss, stale cigarette smoke, and diesel exhaust. The whole place was more depressing than a book of Raymond Carver short stories.

It was the usual mix of travelers who couldn't afford to fly, college kids, service members trying to save a little money on leave, and people who were on the margins but had scraped together Greyhound's ticket fee. There were a couple of young men, you know the type, short hair and button-down white short sleeve shirts, black ties, trying to spread the lord's word to any who would have it. There weren't any takers at the Greyhound station on Saint James Avenue. There was a cop walking around twirling a nightstick. He moved, seeing everything and trying hard not to see anyone. There were a couple of disheveled-looking homeless guys leaning back snoring in a couple of the TV chairs. They smelled of cheap wine and stale sweat and days without a shower.

I went into the Burger King, and after spending money on a burger and a Pepsi I didn't want, I was able to talk to the manager. He hadn't seen Judy. He thought she looked familiar, but he saw teenagers come off of busses day in and day out. For ten dollars he agreed to call me if Judy came in, and he would put up the flyer by the time clock. I left the soda and the thing masquerading as a cheeseburger behind and went back to the terminal.

The cop wasn't super excited to talk to me and didn't have much to say. He reluctantly took a flyer and moved off with a twirl of his nightstick. The two missionaries were only too eager to talk, but they wanted to talk about Jesus and not about Judy. They refused to believe I was beyond salvation, even if I knew better from personal experience.

I went to the ticket counters and showed the ladies working behind the counter her picture, but they didn't recognize her. They took a flyer and said they would keep an eye out. I thought about asking the homeless guys flopped in the chairs, but something told me they wouldn't appreciate my waking them up.

I walked out on to Saint James Avenue and checked with the taxi drivers parked in front of the bus station. They looked at Judy's picture but neither had seen her. I walked a box around the bus station, Arlington to Stuart, Stuart to Berkeley, and then Berkeley to Saint James. Then I walked over to the Public Garden and then across Charles Street to Boston Common. I would stop and check with anyone who looked like they were a park fixture, people selling flowers out of plastic buckets, a guy selling roasted peanuts out of a cart, three hotdog carts, and four or five homeless guys. No one had seen her and no one I talked to had much interest in talking to me.

I made my way out to Beacon Street and walked down to Government Center. Boston City Hall still looked like some sort of architectural revenge on an otherwise pretty city. City Hall Plaza was filled with a mix of tourists with their brightly colored clothes and their cameras and office workers in muted colors with no cameras. They were all enjoying the beautiful June sunshine. Mixed in here and there were pockets of teen-agers sitting, smoking cigarettes, and enjoying their freedom from parental tyranny. A smaller group of teenagers were doing tricks on skateboards. None of them seemed to be Judy, and it was all I could do to get the briefest 'no' when I asked if anyone had seen her.

The John F. Kennedy Federal Building was on the other

side of the plaza. I wondered if Special Agent Brenda Watts
was at her desk. Would she stay on the phone long enough
with me to convince her to have lunch with me at the Union
Oyster House? Probably not. I made my way to Faneuil Hall
and walked through the rows and rows of stalls. No sign of
Judy. There were plenty of teenagers. No one who worked
there had seen her, and no one really wanted to talk to me.
Story of my life.

I stopped for two slices of New York style pizza. I shook
garlic powder and red pepper flakes on them. The slices were
so big the ends hung over the paper plates, pointing down at
the ground like Salvador Dalí's take on pizza, dripping orange
pepperoni grease on the ground. I washed it all down with an
RC Cola and managed not to get too much of any of it in my
mustache. It was a lunch meant for a king.

I made my way back through the streets to Downtown
Crossing, stopping at every fast-food place I could find. I went
into the Macy's on Summer Street. No one had seen her. I
was able to hand out some flyers and walk off the pizza.
I skirted around the Combat Zone and headed over to Copley
Place. I wanted to tell myself that I was just being practical,
that a teenager would be attracted to a shopping mall more
than the Combat Zone. I wasn't ready to face the thought
of Judy Billings there.

Copley Place was built above the Mass Pike; before there
had been the Mass Pike it had been the South End Armory.
Drilling state militiamen had been replaced with blacktop and
cars whizzing through the city only to be covered by a shopping mall, condos, and offices. It was designed by Howard
Elkus and funded by Pritzker money out of Chicago. I wish
they had collaborated on Government Center too. Copley Place
was gleaming, clean, and beautiful. Government Center was
something that should have been designed by the Soviets to
deter their citizens from seeking civil services.

I went in and took the escalator up to the main shopping
area. I was struck by the sixty-foot-high waterfall and sculpture.
It was a mix of granite and marble shapes. It was the type of
luxury statement that went along with Neiman Marcus and
Rizzoli's Bookstore. There was a Loews movie theater and a

Legal Sea Foods. There were a bunch of other stores and restaurants, all too high end for someone who makes as little money as I do. My idea of luxury is scotch so affordable that I can pronounce the name easily.

Beautiful people were walking around me in their nice clothes and Italian leather high-heeled shoes. Their hair was well coiffed. Men and women alike had manicured nails. They were leaving their offices in the upper floors or coming in from the street outside. There were no hard-hatted construction workers here. I felt out of place in my faded jeans, old polo shirt, and running sneakers. There was a spot of pizza grease on my shirt, and I was certain it was the only one in all of Copley Place. I was also sure, after walking through the stores and food court, that Judy Billings wasn't here either.

It was still too early to check out the clubs or the Combat Zone. I wasn't hungry, but I wanted to get off of my feet. Harvard Square was a mecca for teenagers, and I didn't want to drive. The Green Line was the answer, and there was a T station right there. I went down the steps, traded some coins for tokens, and went through the turnstile.

At Park Street I switched to the Red Line. I always thought there was something classy about the Red Line. The train came up out of the ground by Mass General Hospital and the Suffolk County Jail. The jail had housed German POWs, infamous Boston mayor James M. Curley, Malcom X, and Sacco and Vanzetti. It had also housed legions of unknown criminals and innocents too. It should have been closed years ago, but it was still open for business, and celebrity and common folk alike were welcome. Jail in Boston was a very egalitarian affair.

My fellow riders and I rode across the Charles River on a bridge. We ignored each other, and I enjoyed the late afternoon sun on my face. We were swallowed up by the earth again on the other side of the river. After a few stops and one sharp turn, I was at Harvard Square. I got off the train and made my way up the steps into a station that looked like something out of a science fiction movie. More *Blade Runner* than *Star Wars*.

I emerged into the daylight. There were groups of kids

clustered here and there, some smoking, some riding skate-boards. It was a smaller, better-looking version of the action at Government Center. I went to the oversized kiosk that sold newspapers and magazines from all over the world. Occasionally I would get a newspaper or magazine in German, if only to remind myself of how rusty mine had grown.

The first six years of my life, it was almost all that I spoke at home and the only language my mom spoke to me. Even my dad would use his Occupation Army German at the table. Then thirty years ago, my mother kissed me goodbye and left. When Dad got home from work, I was eating cookies from a box because there had been no lunch. When he realized Mom was gone, he forgot to be mad. We had stew from a can that night for dinner, and my dad had a second, then a third helping of scotch. He eventually figured out how to make decent stew not from a can, but he never figured out how to lay off the whiskey. If he had, maybe he would have lived a little longer. Who knew?

No one in the news kiosk had seen Judy, nor had any of the kids. The stores around the square didn't offer any more hope. The Wursthaus was nearby, and I was tempted to get a stein of real German beer, but it didn't seem the responsible thing to do. I was tempted to go into the Harvard Cooperative, affectionately known as 'the Coop' to one and all. Their book selection was first rate, but that would be as irresponsible as getting a beer. I get lost in bookstores.

After an hour and a half, it was clear to me that no one had seen Judy in Harvard Square. Why would they have? She was probably in Boston with K-nice. But I had to do my due diligence. I had left flyers with everyone who would take one, and now it was time to ride the T back to the city. I got off at Arlington, which was close enough to where I had parked the Maverick.

The sun had gone down, and the sky was a shade of purple that was between day and night. The French have a term for it, but they have a term for everything. *L'heure bleue* – the blue hour; it is said with all of the implied romance that the French language can convey. Boston wears it particularly well, like a lady who puts on just enough makeup. Soon it would be dark. The Combat Zone would be flooded with men looking for sex priced to move at a discount. I was hoping that Judy wouldn't be for sale.

The bus station was a short walk from the Combat Zone, no doubt making it easier for scores of teenage runaways to find their way there over the years. I walked the few short blocks up Saint James Avenue. I took a left on Charles Street and walked by L.J. Peretti's, where I liked to buy pipe tobacco when I could afford it. From Charles, I picked up Boylston Street and followed that one block right into the heart of the Combat Zone.

The Combat Zone is Boston's five square acres of sex, sin, and prostitution, had allegedly been on its last legs for almost a decade now. If the Combat Zone was being driven out of business, I couldn't see much sign of it. There were still plenty of places that were looking to separate a man from his money: the Naked i, the Pussycat Lounge, and numerous theaters where you could watch porno movies, or if you liked your sex more immediate and more alive, there were plenty of peep show booths. The fun lasted as long as you had quarters to put in the till. If you wanted the types of books that Rizzoli's wouldn't dream of carrying, the Liberty Book Shop was there to meet your needs. There were hawkers and bouncers, and sex was for sale cheap, in print, on film, and live.

When I was a teenager, it was taboo, forbidden fruit, for good Irish Catholic boys and not nearly far enough away from Southie for our parents' and priests' liking. I knew more than one guy whose dad had brought his son to the Combat Zone to 'make him a man.' I was thankful that my own father hadn't felt the need. When I got home from Vietnam, the Combat Zone earned its moniker because of all the soldiers and sailors floating around it in their Class B uniforms. They were still there when I was a cop in a different uniform. The problem for me was that by then the Zone just made me feel tired, old, and dirty. There was just too much human misery for sale too cheaply for me to feel good about.

I managed not to work in the Zone much, and then I had ended up in the Special Investigations Bureau. I spent my time dressed as a hippie, war veteran type, making street buys or

doing decoy work walking around waiting to get robbed. I
had a few bottles broken over my head and got cut a couple
of times. All of that was a lot better than watching people sell
themselves for the cost of a score.

The lights, both neon and bulbs, were bright above the
marquee that offered such things as 'Live, Nude Girls!' It was
hard to believe that this was part of the famed City on the
Hill, the beacon for the Puritan world. If this is what the city's
founders had wanted, they wouldn't have exiled Roger
Williams to Rhode Island. Providence was probably the only
place that made the Combat Zone look classy.

I walked around the Zone. I talked to every hawker, doorman,
bouncer, and stall owner who would listen to me. Some were
friendly and helpful. Some looked at the flyer. Some didn't
care, and I didn't have enough cash to rent their interest. There
were a lot of glassy-eyed stares and more than a little hostility
behind some of them. In the end, I went back to the Maverick
feeling dirty and disappointed, with feet that wanted a rest. I
opted for a hot shower and cold whiskey. The Combat Zone
would still be there in the morning. Maybe Sue Teller would
still be there too. I didn't want to see her, but I was short on
options.

That night I fell asleep thinking about Sue. At some point
I was dreaming about sitting with her at a café. At first it was
in Paris but, as happens in dreams, it switched to New Orleans.
Then she was leading me down a dark alley by the hand. She
turned back to smile at me, except now it was Ger smiling at
me. Smiling at me someplace near the Ho Chi Minh Trail.
Smiling at me to reassure me that everything was safe, everything was cool. Then his head exploded when the machine
gun round hit it. I was running for my life in slow motion,
shooting a CAR-15 that had turned into a blue plastic toy.
Then a man named Colonel Tran shot me in the face.

I woke up feeling my ear for the earlobe that Colonel Tran
had surgically removed with a bullet a few months before. I
got up and padded to the kitchen for a glass of water from
the tap. I went back to bed and lay there trying to sleep.

NINE

I woke up and went for a long overdue run from my apartment, along Storrow Drive and the Charles River, past the Hatch Shell. I crossed the Longfellow Bridge into Cambridge, by MIT and around Kendall Square, down by Memorial Drive and back across the Harvard Bridge which carried Mass Avenue across the Charles. I ran almost four and half miles. I stopped a block away from my apartment and walked back past my charred parking spot. My chest heaved, and it occurred to me that maybe I should cut back on the cigarettes. Not only that, but there had been too many pizza lunches lately. It felt good to be moving, and I knew that the rest of the day I would feel loose the way you do after a good run.

There were no messages on my machine in the apartment. Sir Leominster had not magically reappeared, and I was beginning to wonder if I was going to have to offer Special Agent Watts a ransom. I hadn't much wanted a cat; Sue Teller had brought him home one day when she lived with me. He was miserable, but I had gotten used to him. He had grudgingly accepted me on the basis of my feeding him regularly. He was a very practical cat.

'See, Andy, you two are perfect for each other. You are both miserable.' Her hand was scratched from an attempt to pet him. She had said it with a smile, but it was the type of smile where her lips were tight across her teeth. The cat had hissed at me and clawed at my hand to prove her point.

I was working a case in the Quincy shipyard, down on the Fore River. It wasn't a great case. Long, cold hours of surveillance in the back of a little Subaru BRAT with a cap and the rear jump seats taken out, lying in the bed on a sleeping bag that was too thin, with binoculars and a camera. Smokes and a Thermos of lukewarm coffee my only luxuries. If it was a

good day, I would stop for Chinese food at a place called the
Blue Lotus in Quincy. The cat had won me over by insisting,
that cold winter, on sitting on my lap if I was watching TV
or reading a book. Once or twice, I woke up in bed with the
cat snuggled against me after Sue had left to save the world.
Saving souls was early work in her mind.

Then one day after one fight too many Sue had stormed
off after telling me, 'You are just miserable. You and that
cat deserve each other.' She had rocked the door on its
hinges when she slammed it. I couldn't remember what the
fight had been about, but the cat had stayed and proved
good company as long as I didn't overstep my bounds. It
was his apartment, I just paid for it and kept the litter box
clean.

I showered and dressed more or less as I had the day before
except the polo shirt was dark green today and didn't have a
pizza grease stain on it. The .38 went in my waistband on my
right hip, speedloader in my left jeans pocket, Buck knife in
the right. Instead of going to the office, I called the service
and there were no messages. I hadn't seen Mr Marconi in a
few days and would have loved one of his espresso correttos.
Instead, I made do with an espresso from my little pot on the
stove. I called Dave. The conversation was short and to
the point. I had checked the places I thought she might be and
struck out. More to follow. Roark out.

Then there was no more avoiding it. I drove over to the
Combat Zone and found a place to park on Knapp Street.
The Maverick looked beat up enough I was sure that no one
would have any interest in breaking into it. Sue's office had
been a storefront on LaGrange around the corner from The
Glass Slipper. Even though it was mid-morning, there were
men out hawking, trying to get me to go into a peep show or
a club. The Zone wasn't as alive as it was at night, but there
were still quarters and dollars to be had, just not as much
effort went into acquiring them. This was the junior varsity
version of sex work.

Sue's storefront was where I remembered it, plate glass
windows with 'Anthony's' painted on them in gold. They had
been rubbed down with soap so no one could look inside.

'Why Anthony's?' I had asked her. 'It sounds like a pizza joint.'

'Have you ever heard of Susan B. Anthony? Did you sleep through that part of US history? Or didn't they cover the Suffragettes between World War II and John Wayne, tough guy?' Sue was petite and compensated with a fierceness that she wore like a medieval knight wore armor. It was just as subtle too. She could switch from happy to angry with the speed of a drunk combat vet. Being with her, making love to her, had been intense. I also had a lot of bruises. I rarely took a beating on the street, but often at home she would lash out with tiny angry fists. She said she was passionate. The punches never did any damage, and I had been raised to believe you didn't hit women. Instead, I just weathered the blows from her small fists.

I took a breath and pushed open the door, and a bell tinkled above my head. It was a narrow storefront that when I was a cop had sold dirty books, dirty magazines, pills, and pot. Now there was a desk up front furnished with a phone and awash with papers. The place was cluttered and smelled of a mix of mothballs and scented candles. There were boxes stacked up against one wall and rolling garment racks lined up against one another. Then Sue's voice came from somewhere in the back. I couldn't see her because of all the clothes and general clutter. 'Hang on, I'll be with you in a sec.' The clothes were donations, and Sue gave them to the girls on the street. A lot of them were semi-homeless, flopping where they could, exchanging sex for a place to crash. Their lives were extremely portable, and they didn't have a lot of possessions. 'If it means that a girl doesn't have to choose between another trick or clothes, or clothes or food, it is worth the effort.' I had heard her say that more than once.

'Sorry, I was just putting some stuff—' She saw me and stopped. She looked good; she always did. Her hair, which had been long, brown, and blown out, was now in a short bob. 'Roark. I always wondered when you would walk through my door again.'

'Of all the gin joints, that type of thing?' My Bogie

imitation hadn't been very good to begin with. She smiled and I smiled back. Then she shocked me by stepping in and hugging me. Her head fit somewhere just under my chin, and she was still slight in my arms.

'Jesus, Roark. I thought you would be dead by now or at least on the run.' She sighed, and her words weren't a vote of confidence.

'Nope, still here.' I didn't bother to mention that was despite several near misses since she had left. She squeezed me once around the chest and stepped back.

'You look tired.'

'Oh, you know me . . . sleep is an elusive thing.' She did. She had put up with months of nightmares and too many bad jokes to avoid talking about them.

'What happened to your ear?' She reached up toward my slightly mangled earlobe but caught herself before she touched it, as if it were too intimate a gesture.

'Oh, that was the good news. The guy shooting at me missed the rest of my head.'

'What's the bad news?'

'It itches like hell.' It did. There are a lot of nerve endings in earlobes, and once the pain died down, it itched. I was not looking forward to February in New England. She didn't laugh, but most of my jokes weren't that good.

'Same old Andy, laughing at people hurting you.' She hadn't particularly cared for the violence that seemed to come with my job. She had never liked the fact that sometimes I had to fight with people.

'Yeah, something like that.'

'What brings you here? I haven't seen you in, what, two years? No phone calls, no Christmas cards?'

'Well, you left me. I kind of figured that meant you didn't want to hear from me.'

'Ha!' Her laugh came out like a bark. 'You don't know much about women, do you?'

'Nope, I can't say I have been accused of that.'

'My guess is that you didn't come down to LaGrange Street out of some sense of romantic nostalgia. You're looking for help again.' She had been key to helping me find Carney's daughter. She had not appreciated my methods. I think she found them unsound.

'Don't get mad.'

'You didn't do enough damage last time. How many broken bones did that boy end up with when you kidnapped that girl?' She hadn't been there, but word on the street got back to her.

'Sue, a seventeen-year-old is missing, run away.'

'Around here we call that Monday or Tuesday . . . do I need to go on?'

'Her dad is an old Army buddy. He saved my life in Vietnam. He used to show me her picture when we were there.'

'And you came to good old Sue, good-time Sue, to help you out again?' Her fists were balled up, one pressed into each hip. Her voice was raised.

'I owe him a debt I can never repay.'

'You macho John Wayne types amaze me . . . there is no such thing. You just use that as an excuse for all the shit you are going to pull, all the things you are going to break. The people you are going to hurt. Last time was bad enough. Why should I help you do more damage?'

'Sue, she's a kid. She's dating a bad dude and she ran away from home. I'm just trying to get her back home before she gets into something she can't get out of.'

'Andy, she might have a good reason for running away. Even if you find her, you can't stop her from running again. You can't save her if she doesn't want to be saved. If she even needs it.'

'No, I can't, but I also can't say no to a guy who pulled me out of the jungle when I was too shot up to move. I was out of ammo and saving a fragmentation grenade to use on myself so the NVA wouldn't capture me. Dave ran through a hail of bullets and carried me to the helicopter and threw me on. I can't say no.' My face was flushed, and my chest was tight thinking about it.

'That is the most you have ever said about Vietnam to me.' She smiled at me, but it was a sad sort of smile. There had been a lot of conversations that we hadn't had because I didn't want to talk about any of it.

'Sue, I'm not asking you to find her. I just need to know if anyone has seen her or heard anything. I can find the boyfriend, but you know there isn't anything that says she will be with him. I'm scared she will get hooked on H and start hustling out here.' I couldn't let that happen to Judy, and I couldn't let Dave down.

'Do you have a picture?' She held her hand out. I handed her one of the copies and a couple of the flyers.

'Sue, I really appreciate it.'

'Sure you do. I'm sure you'll make it up to me somehow.' I wasn't sure if she meant dinner or if I would have to help her move a piano. 'Who's the boyfriend?'

'I only know his street name . . . K-nice.' One of Sue's eyebrows arched.

'K-nice. I know him. He is trouble, Andy. He's a real nasty guy.'

'Let me guess, a mid-level drug dealer and half-ass pimp?'

'You have heard of him.'

'No, a friend of Judy Billings' described him to me. Sounds like an asshole.'

'He is a world class asshole, Andy. He is mean and violent.'

'I know, I never seem to get to deal with accountants or peaceniks. Just once I would love to go up against a pacifist . . . maybe talk the case to death.'

'I'm serious, Andy. Watch out for him. He travels around with some muscle, a big guy. I don't know his name, but the two of them are a rough pair.'

'OK, that is good to know, and I will keep it in mind.'

'It is still early for the Zone. No one will be up yet. Why don't you come back around five, and we'll see if anyone is around who has seen her?' She was smiling again. Sue had a great smile, rows of little white teeth that shone like pearls. She had dark eyes and they crinkled at the corners, making her smile seem somehow brighter.

'That sounds like a plan. I did a lot of walking around yesterday, but nothing came of it.'

'I'm not surprised. Andy, you might think you aren't a cop anymore, but to people on the street, you are almost as bad.'

'Yeah, story of my life, all the blame, none of the perks. OK, I will be back around five.'

'Andy.'

'Yeah?' She had stepped close.

'It's good to see you.' She stood on her tiptoes and pecked at my cheek.

'You too.' I smiled at her.

TEN

I went back to my office. Marconi's pizza joint was on the first floor of the building. The doors were closed, and the lights were off. It was unusual considering it was around lunch time. I pressed my face to the glass window and peered in. At first, I thought the place had been robbed. There were a couple of chairs on the floor, tipped on their sides. There was a trail of paper napkins leading from the counter to the kitchen. Most of the tables and chairs had been pushed into a corner. The spot on the counter where Marconi's prized espresso machine had been, the one that he had shipped all the way from Italy, was empty.

I was confused until I saw a piece of shirt cardboard taped to the next window. Someone had written on it in spidery script, 'Thank you to our customers for twenty-five years of loyal patronage. Ciao, Marconi!' I hadn't been expecting that. Nor did I expect the next sign; this one was professionally done and not on shirt cardboard. 'Coming Soon: Super Video . . . video rentals and more.' No more pizza, no more correttos, just another place renting VHS tapes.

I walked up the two flights of stairs to my office feeling like I had lost something to progress and innovation. The world didn't need another video rental place. Or at least not at the expense of great pizza, espresso, cappuccinos, and correttos. In a world where most pizza places used sauce from a can, Marconi made his own from fresh tomatoes and spices. He got his cheese fresh from a place in the North End where all the best Italian restaurants are in Boston. I knew that he got his sausage and pepperoni from a small butcher somewhere in Rhode Island, one of the towns outside of Providence. He would never tell me which one. His mushrooms and other produce were fresh and wouldn't be out of place in Locke-Ober, one of Boston's oldest and fanciest French restaurants.

I would miss Marconi. He had a way of putting things in perspective whenever I was feeling put upon by the casual cruelties of the world. He thought my being a private investigator was juvenile. He couldn't understand why I wasn't still a cop or in the Army fighting the communists. He hated communists, and especially the Red Brigades, with a passion. I wasn't sure but I thought it had something to do with why he left Italy.

I unlocked the office door and opened it very slowly. For the last few months, I was worried about people booby trapping my office door. Just because I was paranoid didn't mean I was wrong. Back in March, someone had booby trapped it with a fragmentation grenade. Marconi had tipped me off to the fact that strangers had been sniffing around, asking about me. I couldn't see some clerk in a video store doing that. The door was fine, and the office was warm and dusty, still smelling faintly of the last pipe of tobacco that I had smoked a week or so before. More importantly, no one seemed to be trying too hard to kill me this week. That was always nice.

Sitting on the coffee table that I kept magazines and copies of *The Globe* on was Marconi's slightly battered espresso machine. There was an envelope of brown paper taped to it. I opened it, and there was a single sheet of paper with the same spidery script as the sign downstairs.

> *Andy,*
> *A video store chain offered me a lot of money for the store. I have the cancer and want to go home, drink wine from my hometown, and feel the Italian sun on my face again before I die. Every man should be lucky enough to go home to die.*
> *I hope that you make an espresso or corretto and you think of Marconi.*
> *Ciao,*
> *Marconi*

He had left me a big bottle of sambuca and a few tin cans of Italian espresso. I carried the machine from the waiting room into my office and cleared some papers from the table that was against the wall to set it up. The cans of coffee and liquor went next to it. He had also left me an instruction manual, but it was in Italian. There was going to be a learning curve before I could make anything as good as his.

I sat down at my desk, looking at the espresso machine and holding Marconi's note. Then I put it in the drawer in my desk, next to the big Ruger .357 Magnum I keep in there. It was there mostly to scare off angry husbands whose wives hired me to catch them cheating. I picked up the phone and called the hospitals and the cops I knew. No one had seen Judy Billings. There were no messages on my machine or with the service. Maybe she wasn't in Boston, or maybe she had come here and hopped a bus somewhere else. Greyhound went to a lot of places, not just 10 Saint James Avenue. After a lot of fruitless calls and a bad attempt at making my own espresso, it was time to meet Sue.

A little before five, I pulled up in front of Anthony's in the Maverick. Sue must have been waiting, because she was outside locking the door behind her as I got out of my car. She was wearing faded blue jeans that I couldn't help but notice fit her well across her bottom. She had on a white sleeveless blouse and carried a brown handbag with the strap running over her shoulder and across her chest. She wore white sneakers, and she looked good.

'You got a new car?'

'Yep.' I didn't know what else to say.

'What happened to the Karmann Ghia? I really liked that car.'

'It blew up.'

'Yeah. Right.'

'Nope, blew up right in front of the apartment a few months ago. The neighbors are still pissed about it.' That was true. It had knocked me on my ass, and I had picked up a ringing in my ears and some new scars.

'I thought Volkswagens were good cars. Well, at least no one was hurt. I mean, you weren't hurt?' She was looking at me. I didn't bother to tell her it had nothing to do with the good people at Volkswagen.

'No, I wasn't any the worse for wear.' I just left it there. I didn't see much point in telling her about the cuts and scrapes, or the dead girl.

'Good, I'm glad. Wait a minute . . . Did this have anything to do with your ear getting shot?'

'Same guy, first attempt.' I tried to say it casually like Steve McQueen would have.

'You do have a habit of pissing people off, Andy.' She said it quietly, and I knew she wasn't just talking about guys like the late Colonel Tran.

'It must have something to do with my personality.' I smiled at her.

'Yeah, you are a wiseass.' But at least she smiled back at me. 'Come on, Andy, let's go talk to some people and see if anyone knows where the girl is.'

We walked down LaGrange and turned on to Washington Street headed to Essex Street. The Zone was filling up with men in suits who, after a day trapped at jobs in offices, had their ties five o'clock loose, top button of their dress shirts undone. They were making their way to cold drinks and gyrating women who with each song would show more flesh. By the third song of their set, they would be as naked as the law would allow. The crush of office men forced us to walk close together, shoulders almost rubbing. Every now and then we would stop so Sue could talk to a girl, either to check on her or ask about Judy Billings. No one had seen her, and we would move on, slowly winding through the Combat Zone.

'Sue, why do you do it?'

'Work out here, helping the girls, you mean?'

'Yes, it seems pretty thankless. I don't remember a lot of girls leaving the life and living happily ever after.'

'Why are you a private investigator? Why are you willing to hurt people or get hurt?' She had asked me that question on more than one occasion. Sue had always worried that my hurting people hurt me as much as them. An 'injury of the soul,' she called it.

'It is one of the few things that I'm good at. I was good at being a soldier. I was OK at being a cop. Being a private investigator . . . it gives me a lot of freedom.'

'And you don't worry about getting hurt or killed?'

'Sue, I spent almost three straight years in Vietnam. I was almost killed on nearly every mission. If I wasn't on mission, they would mortar or rocket attack, and I knew guys who were killed in their sleep. I was almost killed once on R&R in Da Nang. I got shot or blown up . . . Here, in the cops, I was almost killed by drunk drivers, drunk wife-beating husbands, criminals who didn't want to go back to prison. Being a private eye is probably the safest job I have ever had.' There were exceptions like the run-in that turned my earlobe into scar tissue.

'I got into this because where I grew up was like a different universe. I was from a nice town in the Hudson River Valley, ninety minutes outside of the city. My parents are still married and were always very involved in my life. We did things like every Christmas my mother and I would go into the city; we would stop for tea and go to the matinee of *The Nutcracker*. It was a great childhood. Everyone assumed that I would go to Vassar, which was just up the road. Instead, I came here for college.' She paused. We had talked about all the things that new lovers talk about when we had started dating. She never explained it like this, just as I hadn't talked about Vietnam or much about my time in the cops.

'Andy, these girls . . . they didn't have that, or if they did, they also had a pervy uncle or dad or stepdad who molested them. A lot of these girls, they're running from abuse or rape. For them, choosing to sell themselves is better than having it taken. Or they started using drugs to escape from something that happened, and now they must pay for that habit.

'When I first got to Boston, it was this magical city. Fall in New England, the Faneuil Hall, the Charles River, the leaves turning in the Public Garden. Then my senior year in college, my boyfriend and another couple we were close to wanted to come to the Combat Zone. You know, for kicks. Like some sort of urban safari for middle class kids from the suburbs.

'I had never been in a burlesque club before. I had never seen a prostitute. To his credit, my boyfriend was horrified. He thought it would be fun, liberating, or exciting. Yet he saw what I saw, and I think he was a little ashamed of himself. We graduated and he went on to graduate school in Ohio. Me,

I was obsessed and wanted to know what made these girls' – she gestured at the girls on the street – 'so different from me. The more I found out about that, the more I learned about their lives and how different theirs were from mine, the more I was compelled to help them.'

'Sue, you couldn't help the family you were born into any more than any of us can. That is the lottery of birth.'

'No, I couldn't, Andy . . . but I was lucky, and I had it good. The least I can do is to help women who can't say either of those things.' She was looking up at me, chin tilted, and her eyes were bright. I had a flash, a moment, a memory of what kissing her had been like, and then it was gone. We weren't on a date; we were out in the Combat Zone looking for a teenage runaway.

We wove through the Combat Zone's five acres for a couple of hours, talking to anyone we could. The women of the evening looked at me with suspicion, but their faces softened when Sue pulled them to one side. I couldn't blame them. Their experiences with men had given them good reason to mistrust me, mistrust my half of the species in general. The girls talked to Sue. Most of the hawkers outside of the clubs were polite enough but not interested. Everyone else just went around us, going about their business like a human stream around rocks.

'Andy, I'm hungry. Buy a girl dinner?'

'Sure, it is the least I can do. Where do you want to go?'

'Do you like Greek food?'

'Sure. Anything you want.'

'House of Pizza makes the best gyros.' She pronounced it right, not like the rocket guidance system but like an exaggerated version of 'hero.'

'That would fit the bill.' We were outside of the Liberty Book Shop, and House of Pizza was about a block down on the other side of the street.

'Hey, Sue.' There was a man standing inside the alcove of the Liberty Book Shop. The hawker ignored him the way the bank tellers ignore the security guards. He was tall with dark, almost black hair on the sides of his otherwise bald head, and a black waxed mustache that ended in curls on either side of his upper lip, which seemed to have a permanent sneer. His eyes were heavy lidded, making him look drowsy.

'Hey, Sailor.' Sue was more polite than friendly.

'Watcha doin out here, Sue?' He had an accent that reminded me of New Bedford or Fall River. His arms had some muscle to them, and a blue anchor was tattooed on each bicep. He wore a purple short sleeve button-down shirt and blue jeans. He was running to fat around his middle, and when he crossed his arms across his chest, I could see that his knuckles were heavily calloused. He liked to fight. His skin was pale, the way that people who work at night have pale skin. Not quite prison pale but paler than Irish pale.

'Looking for a girl, Sailor. Have you seen her?' Sue held the flyer out to him.

'Yeah, I know.' He ignored the flyer in her hand and looked at me. 'You and the dick been out here for hours. He was out here all day. Kinda bad for business.'

'Sailor, have you seen her?' Sue was dogged.

'Seen lots of girls. Dancing on the Carousel inside.' The Carousel had been a revolving platform where women posed erotically for the men in the peep show booths. The Carousel broke, hadn't turned in years, and no one was going to spend the money to fix it. 'You know, Sue, you're pretty, you should take a turn on my Carousel.'

I took a step forward, or started to. Sue's hand was on my left arm, nails digging in, and she pressed her hip and bottom against my left thigh. Sailor's feet had started to shift, blading his body, his left side toward me. He had been in more than a few fights. I wanted to punch him, to break his nose, feel the ecstasy of violence. I couldn't because Sue was leaning against me, pushing hard and effectively. In other circumstances it would be nice to feel her hip and bottom against my leg.

'Andy . . . you were going to buy me dinner.'

'Yeah, Dandy Andy . . . you gotta buy the girl dinner. Carousel's still gonna be here when she wants a turn.' He was smirking and he knew I wanted to smash his teeth in.

'Andy, no.' Sue was serious, and I took a deep breath. Sailor would keep. I uncoiled my fists and took another breath.

'Yeah, Dandy Andy . . . listen to the little girl.'

'You know, friend, the lady and I are going to go.'

'That's a good idea.'

'I suspect you will still be here looking to dance later?' I was smiling at him.

'Any time, shitbait. Sailor's here all night, every night.' 'Shitbait' was a beloved insult in the Navy.

'Good. Be seeing you.' He kept grinning his shit-eating grin and I smiled back. He and I were going to dance; it was just a matter of when. Sue turned away still clutching my arm and dragged me off. My hands started to shake with the pent-up adrenaline I hadn't burned off when we didn't fight. Eventually they were still, and we were at House of Pizza. Her hand was on my arm, and I knew she could feel me shaking.

House of Pizza used to have a sign that was two stories high and half again as wide. It hung over Liberty Tree Park advertising 'Pizza, Hot Oven Subs and GREEK FOOD.' In the 1970s, some folks who worked at city hall wanted to class the place up and had the sign taken down in the middle of the night. The owner was angry, but what was true the world over was just as true in Boston: you couldn't fight city hall.

We didn't say much except to order a gyro each and a plate of French fries to share. We found a booth and sat across from each other waiting to be called for our order. We each had a Coke in those wax cups with ice and a straw. Sue picked at some of the faux wood-grained Formica top.

'Andy, you really wanted to hurt Sailor, didn't you?' Sue hadn't ever seen me when I wanted to fight someone. That was not a side of me that I was eager to share with any woman in my life.

'Yes. Did you know that there used to be an elm tree here, and a little over two hundred years ago, the Sons of Liberty planned their revolt against the English under it? Hard to believe how much it has changed.' Now the liberty involved here was dirty books, dirty movies, and strippers. I wondered what the city's Puritan founders would think of that.

'Yes, Andy. I had heard that. Everyone who lives in Boston for more than ten minutes knows that. Don't change the subject. You wanted to kill him. I could see it in your eyes.' She was leaning forward toward me, hands on the tabletop. Her hands were small, and her nails were painted with red polish.

'The British couldn't allow it to stand as a symbol, so they chopped it down.' The British knew a thing about symbolism.

'I haven't ever seen you like that . . . your eyes, I think of them as twinkling, like they laugh with you. Just then they were empty, cold, and just empty. I thought you were going to kill him.' She was right, I had wanted to beat him to death with my bare hands. Some people bring out the best in me.

'That guy's an asshole. He really needs a punch in the nose.' A few other places too, but this didn't seem like the time or place to bring it up.

'Sure, but that isn't going to solve anything. The Combat Zone is full of assholes. Beating him up isn't going to help find your friend's daughter.' She shivered. 'Jesus, were you like that when you threw that boy down the stairs? Were you like that in Vietnam?' I was spared from answering because the guy at the counter yelled out that our order was ready. I hopped up to get it. There is no way to explain violence to someone who hasn't had to fight. Not the hair-pulling, slapping tiffs on the playground or the wildly thrown punches between teenage boys after school, but a real fight. The type of fight where two people are trying their hardest to hurt each other. Soldiers, cops, guys like Sailor are used to violence. The relationship with it and application of it become very casual after a while. It is impossible to grasp if you haven't lived it. Vietnam . . . that was different too. We only lived because of our sudden ability to deliver violence to the enemy. To drive them with our fire and break away. Fast, violent action was often the only thing that saved us.

The gyros were half wrapped in tin foil and on paper plates. I brought those and went back for the French fries. There was a red plastic bottle of ketchup on the table and a small bottle of malt vinegar. Sue shook salt on the French fries, and then some vinegar, as soon as I put the plate of fries down. I never saw the need for more than salt and ketchup.

The gyro was great. Pita bread that had been slapped on the grill to warm it, then in went the fillings. Gyro meat, that mix of seasoned lamb and beef, shaved as it turned on a vertical spit, with shredded lettuce, tomato, raw red onion, crumbled goat cheese, and nestled in tzatziki sauce. It tasted fantastic.

'Andy?' She was poking a French fry into some ketchup.

'Sue?'

'Sailor's an asshole . . .' The French fry went into her mouth.

'Well, we can agree on that.'

'But you wanted to hurt him because he was saying rude things to me.'

'Yes.' It was mostly for that reason.

'But I don't want you to hurt someone because of me. Not even an asshole like Sailor.'

'I know. The thing of it is that guys like him kind of need to be hurt occasionally. It reminds them that they can't just act with impunity. He is the type of guy who stands too close to women on the T or a crowded elevator trying to rub against them. Enjoying the feeling of them trying to pull away more than anything else. You're right that I didn't like what he said to you, but I also didn't like that he was trying to degrade you into not looking for a girl who is in trouble. If it weren't Judy Billings, it would be another girl, another time.'

'Guys like him will always exist. Out here they're the majority. Pimps, dealers, johns, mob guys, street guys, criminals, he is just one more drop in the bucket. Why should it matter to you? Why should you get your hands dirty?'

'It's kind of like you trying to help the girls. It doesn't have to be you, but someone should be trying to help. Maybe it is the only way I can get my hands to be clean?' I took a bite of my gyro; the gamey lamb sandwich was a masterpiece of its own. The tzatziki was tangy Greek yogurt mixed with cucumbers, garlic, and lemon juice. I could drink it by the shot glassful.

'You think you're helping, but violence isn't the answer.' She was looking at me over the top of her sandwich.

'Sue, that very much depends upon what the question is.'

We finished our meal, and I walked Sue back to her storefront operation.

'What are you going to do now?'

'I will go to a couple of clubs and try to find K-Nice.'

'OK, but no going back to fight with Sailor.'

'Only if the case takes me there.'

'Good, and Andy, be careful. If Sailor is an asshole, K-Nice is an asshole who is dangerous.'

'The best kind.'

'Andy . . . seriously.'

'Sue, I'm looking for Judy Billings, not trouble.' That was strictly the truth . . . the reality of it was that trouble was inevitable. I wasn't looking for Judy in a nunnery.

'OK.' She put her hands on my arms and stood on tiptoe to give me a peck on the cheek. 'It's good to see you, Andy.' She opened the door, turned, and let herself into her storefront before I could say anything.

'You too,' I said to the closed door.

ELEVEN

I tried to keep my word to Sue. I really did. I went to the Channel and a bunch of other clubs where I thought that K-nice might be. I went from club to club, and when I got sick of walking, I rode the T around the city, stopping at clubs only to find nothing and no one. There wasn't much point in driving just to fight for parking. Boston is a great city with a lot of great features, but available parking isn't one of them. No one had seen him, and no one had seen Judy. No one had seen anything. It was like the city was having an epidemic of not seeing nothing, man.

I had left my car parked near Sue's storefront operation, but a little after midnight I found myself across the street from the Liberty Book Shop. I was tucked back away from the street in the doorway of a boarded-up storefront. Businesses were slowly leaving the Combat Zone as the city's real estate market kept driving prices up. Developers were holding on to properties and not renewing leases. Someday this would all be condos and glass-fronted office buildings. The mayor and the city council didn't mind, and the good people who owned businesses and lived in Chinatown didn't mind. They wanted the Combat Zone to go away, to die a quick death. Instead, it was dying by inches at a time. One of those inches was the former dirty bookstore whose doorway I was standing in.

I wanted a smoke, but I wasn't going to give my position away with a lighter or the glowing tip of a cigarette. Running Recon, we would stop smoking seventy-two hours before a mission. It sucked, there was no way around it. The smell of a cigarette in the jungle would carry for hundreds of yards and give your position away. The smell of cigarettes on your clothes would stay with you and give you away days after you had smoked them.

The NVA didn't have a big PX filled with soda, candy, booze, and American tobacco. They had rice and tinned fish if they were lucky. If they did have Pall Malls and Luckies, they were few and far between. Instead, the NVA would chew on toothpicks that had been soaked in peppermint oil. We would do the same while we were in isolation during our mission preparation. We would chew on the peppermint-soaked toothpicks on missions when we felt the urge to smoke. It wasn't the same, but it helped. Now I didn't even have one of those toothpicks.

I watched Sailor. He would call out to men passing on the street. He would take their cash and usher them into the theater where they would spend more money. He put their money in his left pocket. People came up to Sailor, usually working girls or street people, a few office types, but they were rare. He would pull his cupped hand out of his pocket, and they would slap five. Their hands would linger for a half beat, clasping, then they would move on. They would slide him some money, and he would put it in his right pocket. He was doing hand-to-hands, dealing out of his pocket. Every now and then he would duck back inside the bookstore, probably to replenish the supply of what he kept in his pocket: pills, small baggies of coke, maybe some angel dust. I didn't think he was dealing weed; it didn't seem to have a high enough profit margin for him.

I'm sure whatever he was doing, he was kicking a percentage back to the bookstore. It was owned by mob guys, and he would be long dead if he was earning on their property and not paying taxes. That also meant that there might be some heavies inside who might object to my becoming a nuisance in front of their business. I was struggling to come up with reasons why I would actually give a shit about that. That was the downside of playing tag with the best that the NVA had to offer; the local boys pale in comparison.

I was growing impatient and decided to go talk to Sailor. So far, he was the only person in the Greater Boston area who hadn't denied seeing Judy Billings. I stepped out of the doorway and managed to cross Washington Street without getting hit. I wasn't trying to be subtle, and his eyes tracked me the whole way until I was standing a few feet in front of him.

'Hey there . . . it's Dandy Andy . . . the shitbait from Southie.' He sneered and I took a breath through my nose. Sailor was annoying and I was feeling itchy for a fight.

'Hey, man. I'm just looking for a runaway girl.' A decade ago, I would have just ambushed him. No talk, just speed and violence of action. I would have broken some bones with some kicks, some punches in his kidneys, and if he wasn't passed out, asked him some questions. That was what I had learned in Vietnam: hide, ambush, and hit hard; violence and speed, speed and violence would save you. Not talk. Not negotiation. I was mellowing with age.

'Got lots of girls, plenty to look at, plenty to touch if you pay. Most of 'em were runaways once . . . could be anything you want them to be if you have the money.'

'She's the daughter of a friend I served with in Vietnam.'

''Nam, 'Nam, sing a song. Who cares, man, girls are cheap out here. Pay your money, touch the honey, pay your money, dummy.' His singsong tone was mockery raised to a high art. I had to force myself to focus rather than giving in to the urge to knock out his teeth.

'Have you seen her?' The code of silence among runaways, prostitutes, street people, and in the Zone was almost unbreakable. The CIA should take lessons from them on how to keep secrets.

'I've seen lots of girls, prancing, dancing on my Carousel . . . wanna see pretty little Sue there too.' He sang a little off tone, and he was flying high on some uppers or some coke.

'Yeah, I was wondering when you were gonna bring that up . . . I appreciate you reminding me about your bad manners.' My face felt hot, and my fists were balling up.

'Tough guy, are you? Nope, just shitbait.' He had shifted his weight to the balls of his feet and bladed his body away from me. He brought his fists up but he was just out of range to punch me. He snapped his right fist out. It wasn't even close enough to hit me, about ten inches short. At first, I thought he was mocking me. Shadow boxing or something. He wasn't.

I'm not sure why, but at the last minute I brought my left arm up, palm to my temple, and leaned down to my right.

Pain exploded just above my left elbow. It should have hit me in the jaw. His hand snapped and fire erupted in my ribs on my left side. The breath was knocked out of me, and my side hurt. He stepped back and cocked his arm to strike at me again, and I stepped in to close the space between us. My left arm was not good for much. When he threw again, I felt something hard thud against my back. He wasn't able to get enough force because I had stepped in close.

I wrapped my numb left arm around Sailor's right, trapping it. I pivoted at the hips and threw my right elbow into Sailor's chin. It connected with enough force that I felt it in my fingertips. He started to backpedal, and I went with him, driving him back into a wall. He was starting to go all jelly legged. I grabbed the back of his neck, slipping my right palm over his shoulder, grabbing his long greasy hair, tucking his head under my arm. I moved back two steps, dragging him on clumsy feet with me, then pivoted on the balls of my feet to my right and smashed his head into the opposite wall. The top of his head hit the wall with a hollow thumping sound, and he collapsed to the ground. My left arm felt as though it was a mass of fiery pins and needles, and my ribs felt like someone had hit them with a baseball bat. I didn't want to fight with his colleagues with my left arm not working and some sore ribs if I could help it. Back in March, I had been shot in that arm, and that probably wasn't helping matters. My breath was starting to come back as I forced myself to walk away.

I stumbled on something hard on the ground. It was a small ball of cord, black cord, about ten inches in length with a hard rope ball at the end. It was a monkey's fist, a rope or cord tied in a monkey's fist knot around a steel ball, an old sailor's tool for throwing line. It made it easier to throw a painter to shore or to other ships, and then the big hemp lines could be hauled in. They also made great weapons if you knew what you were doing. If he had connected with my head, I would have woken up in the hospital if I had woken up at all. If he had hit me in the jaw, it would certainly have broken it or knocked out some of my teeth. I like my teeth. I have had them my whole life.

I stepped into the river of humanity that was flowing toward sex for purchase or rent. Mostly men and some women, and then there were those who were selling sex. It was a river that made the Charles River look clean. My left arm throbbed, and when I found the Maverick, I was glad that it wasn't a stick shift. No one had booby trapped it, no one had tried to break into it. That was the advantage of a ten-year-old Ford Maverick, it didn't look worth stealing. I half collapsed against the seat-back and gritted my teeth because of the pain coming from my ribs.

When I got back to the apartment, I let myself in, noting that Sir Leominster was still on sabbatical with Brenda Watts. He was not the most loyal of cats. Maybe that is why he has survived so long, he values pragmatism over loyalty. I had never learned that lesson.

I made my way to the kitchen where there was ice and, more importantly, whiskey. My left arm still wasn't cooperating, so I had to bash the plastic ice tray on the counter a few times, which made my side ache. But I was able to get enough cubes to go in my glass. Whiskey followed and by the time I had taken a big slug of it, feeling was coming back into my arm, angry pins and needles. Sailor must have hit the nerve cluster above the elbow. That would explain why my arm was reluctant to do anything other than throb. At least he hadn't hit the elbow itself. I could only imagine how much that would have hurt or how long it would have been before I could use my arm again. I gently probed my ribs with my functional hand between sips of whiskey. I didn't think they were broken, but the bruise would look pretty fantastic in the morning.

I topped off the whiskey, replacing the larger than normal first belt that I had taken. Then I took the glass to the couch, took the .38 out from my waistband, and put it and my feet up on the coffee table. I turned on the TV, and the late movie on WSBK-TV 38 was *Ice Station Zebra*. I sat there watching Rock Hudson and Patrick McGoohan glower at each other in the tight confines of a nuclear submarine. I took sips of whiskey to kill the pain and flexed the fingers on my left hand to try and get some of the use of the hand back. I was able to time refilling my glass with the commercials and, by the time the

Russian paratroopers landed on the ice in the movie, I was feeling no pain. As a precaution I washed down two Anacin just in case the whiskey wasn't painkiller enough.

I drifted off on the couch and woke with a crick in my neck. It was late. I took the .38 and went to bed. I put the gun on the nightstand, peeled off my clothes, and crawled into bed. I should have taken a shower, but I was too tired and too sore.

I slept, sort of. My dreams carried me back to Vietnam and the war. I was sitting in the door of a Huey, my feet dangling out above the skid. Ger was sitting next to me, close. He was smiling, happy to be whizzing above the ground. We started to come in to land, and I was standing on the skid. Ger was behind me. The anti-aircraft guns opened up on us with a steady pounding. It was heavy stuff, bigger than the usual 12.7mm, and it was punching through the aluminum skin of the helicopter. Rounds kept punching through the helicopter, removing bits and pieces of it. Erasing it one bullet at a time until I was plunging, with my team that I couldn't save, spiraling toward earth.

I woke up twisted in the sheets, sweating, and wondering who was pounding on my door. I pulled on my jeans and polo from last night and put the .38 in my back pocket. You never knew who was knocking on your door. I was sure it wasn't the cops. They used a nightstick or a flashlight. They worked just as well on doors as they did on people's skulls. No need to bruise the knuckles that they might need to punch someone with later.

I stood to the right of the doorknob and said, 'Who is it?' The door doesn't have one of those peephole things, and the way things have been going lately, I wouldn't stand directly in front of it if it did.

'Andy, open the door!' It was Sue, and she sounded mad. I wasn't sure if a .38 would be enough gun if she were angry. I took the chain off the door, threw the deadbolt, and let her in. She pushed by me like a small, angry tornado that smelled nice. Flowers or expensive shampoo, that type of nice. She was wearing blue jeans and a t-shirt that had a print of an album cover for The Police that came out a couple of years ago. Sue wasn't the type to wear perfume with blue jeans.

'Was it you? Was it? Did you go back there?' Sue was angry, and I was confident that she was going to add to my growing collection of bruises.

'I went back to talk to Sailor. He was the only person in the city of Boston who didn't tell me outright he hadn't seen Judy Billings.' That much was the truth . . . I also had wanted to knock that sneer off his face. I never had a high tolerance level for assholes. He was a special sort of one.

'You beat the shit out of him. He is in the hospital.' She was shaking slightly.

'Good. He is an asshole.' I didn't feel that my position needed to be defended with more eloquent discourse.

'Andy, you are an asshole. He is a bottom feeder, but that is his pond.' She was almost yelling but not quite.

'So, what, he is a scumbag.' He was, and I was not going to feel bad about what transpired.

'He is, but he is also someone I can pay to help me. And he is someone who sees everyone and everything. He sells drugs. Most of the girls buy drugs. He might be an asshole, but he is a useful asshole. The problem is that I was seen out there with you for hours. I was seen with you when you had words with him. Now my job just got a lot harder.' She was shaking with anger.

'Sue, he is—' I didn't get far because she started to hit my chest with her small, angry fists. She wasn't doing any damage, but I can't say that I was enjoying it either. I started to turn away when a small fist connected in the same spot on my ribs as Sailor's slungshot had. I cried out and did a quick shuffle step back, air whistling out between my clenched teeth. Even though my ribs were bruised and not broken, it hurt a lot. I don't recommend being punched in bruised ribs by a petite true believer who thinks you have made her life's calling that much harder.

I kicked the door shut and then retreated into the living room. Sue followed me, but I was spared punches or insults. I dropped the .38 on the coffee table and sat down abruptly on the couch. I winced as the pain radiated outward from my ribs and arm. I wanted a cigarette, but the pack was in the bedroom.

'Andy, what's wrong?' Her anger seemed to be gone . . . or like a good adversary, she was probing for weakness.

'Sailor hit me in the ribs and arm with a thing called a slungshot. A weighted ball at the end of a cord – hurt like a bastard. I don't think he broke any ribs but getting punched there didn't help matters any.'

'Oh, Andy, I'm sorry . . . I didn't know.'

'There is no way you could have. But you could find a better a way of expressing your anger.'

'Or you could just not piss me off so much.' She had a point. 'Is it bad?'

'I've had worse. I'm bruised but not broken.' Story of my life.

'Let me see.' She moved around the coffee table and was sitting next to me on the couch.

'I'm OK. It's fine,' I protested feebly.

'Take your shirt off and let me see.' Her small hands started tugging my shirt up. I did my best to take it off, but the bruises weren't helping. Sue pulled it up and over my head.

'Jesus, those look bad.' She was running her hand over my ribs and then my arm. Then she leaned in and kissed me hard on the mouth. Then we were an increasingly naked tangle on the couch. Trying to kiss, undress, touch, and make love with the urgency of teenagers. After a time, we moved to the bedroom and made love with a little less urgency. Later, a little sweaty and breathless, we lay on the bed with her head on my chest. She was tracing scars and wounds trying to determine which ones had happened since the last time we had been in bed together.

'What is this one?' She was poking my left bicep.

'Bullet wound.'

'No kidding, but there must be a story.'

'Some Vietnamese gangsters shot me off of a ship.' That wasn't entirely true. I was jumping off the ship when I was shot. But that was only because I didn't want to get shot on board.

'Ouch. It is smaller than your other wounds.'

'Yeah, different bullets or shrapnel. This one was going pretty quick and just punched through my arm.'

'And your ear, was that the same time too?'

'No, that was a couple of weeks later. Different Vietnamese gangsters.'

'But still someone was shooting at you?'

'Uh huh.'

'How many Vietnamese gangsters did you piss off?'

'A few less now.'

'Andy . . .' Her tone was mildly scolding.

'Sue, they blew up my car. I really liked that car.' This didn't seem the right time to mention the girl that had been in it. Sue's hand had made its way to my face, where the faint scars were.

'Where did these come from?'

'Glass from the Ghia . . . I was standing closer to it than I should have. I was hit by some flying glass. My eyebrows have mostly grown back.' The ringing in my ears only happened every few days or so.

'Jesus . . . was it worth it?'

'No. It wasn't.'

'Then why do it?'

'I was hired to investigate a murder.'

'You could have walked away from it?'

'No, I couldn't. It doesn't work that way.'

'Bullshit!'

'OK, I don't work that way. If I start walking away from cases because they're dangerous then I may as well stop taking cases. I may as well look for a job selling insurance.' There was more to it than that. I had to know. Maybe that was my fatal flaw, I couldn't walk away from a case until I had the answers to the important questions. It would get me killed someday. It almost had a few months ago.

'You are stubborn. I will give you that.'

'It is one of my finer qualities.'

'It is one of your worst qualities.'

'But I come by it honestly.'

'Yeah, from where?'

'Oh, from my dad. After my mom split . . . he never stopped loving her. He just wrote his poems, drank his whiskey, went to work, and did his best to raise me. Then, a few years after

I came home from Vietnam, he stopped. Stopped writing, stopped drinking, and stopped loving her.' The wake at O'Boyle Brothers Funeral Home had been a grim affair. Dad was laid out in an open casket. There had been a few distant cousins of his and me. That was it. He hadn't been a bad father, and I could have done a lot worse. After I was on my own, his sense of purpose ebbed away on a tide of Irish whiskey. There are worse ways to go.

'Do you miss him? You don't sound like you two were close.'

'I do. He was good company. He was a good dad in his way. He just wasn't a Little League, work in the woodshop with me kind of dad, but he was my dad. I had been away in Vietnam for three years, away from home for five. When I got out of the Army and got home, he had withdrawn deeper into his books and poems. He died a couple of years later.'

'Andy . . . that is just . . . just sad.' She wrapped her arms around me and pulled herself close to me. I slid my hand along the smooth skin of her back, then put my face in her hair and breathed in the smell of shampoo. Soon her breathing was even and deep. She had fallen asleep and soon after, I did too.

TWELVE

Sue had left promising me that she would keep an eye out for Judy Billings. She would call me if she saw her or had word that she was in the Combat Zone. She said she would call me even if she didn't have word of Judy. Then she made one or two suggestions about what we might do next time we were together. The suggestions could be described as unladylike, and I had no intention of trying to convince her to act any other way.

I had finally managed a shower and some coffee. The afternoon had been spent making the usual calls to my answering service and to cops I knew who still talked to me. I called the hospitals and anyone who I thought might have any idea about a teenage runaway. No one had seen Judy. Nobody had heard anything. A vice cop I knew on BPD told me what clubs K-nice had been going to lately. Now it was a little after ten p.m., and I was parked in an alley near Shawmut Avenue.

I was parked by a dumpster, and I had a view of K-nice's Jaguar two blocks down. It was a blue XJ6 with a tan interior. It was parked near an exit from the club. The license plates matched what the guy in Vice told me that K-nice was driving. I made a mental note to send him a bottle of good scotch, the type of thing that I would only buy myself on my birthday or Christmas, but not the really good stuff that was reserved for wakes and funerals.

It was a sharp-looking car with its double headlights, stubby grill, and lines like a woman's thighs. K-nice must have been doing well at selling drugs and girls. The running joke about Jaguars is that you have to have the money to afford two of them. One to own and one to drive when the other one is in the shop. That is why I drive a ten-year-old Maverick. I can't afford one expensive English car, much less two of them.

I had taken one of the magic pain pills my friend Chris had given me when I was shot in the arm a few months ago. The pain in my ribs and arm had quieted to a very dull throb. I got out of the Maverick knowing I had dressed for success. I was wearing old penny loafers, an older pair of jeans, and a dark green button-down, short sleeve Swedish Army shirt. It had a little Swedish flag on the left shoulder, a Swedish Army patch on the right, and it screamed of college kid chic. It was the type of thing cool art school kids picked up in the Army/Navy surplus store. I liked it because it was loose fitting and comfortable. I had the .38 on my right hip, a speedloader in my left front pocket, my Buck knife in my right front pocket. After my run-in with Sailor and his slungshot, I had a black-jack stuffed in my back right pocket too. The Swedish Army shirt fit loosely, and I could easily get to all the tools if I needed them.

I sat in the car waiting. Listening to Loggins and Messina sing about the Same Old Wine. It was perfect to listen to while sitting in a darkened car in a dark alley, smoking a Lucky and thinking about the task ahead of me and the past that had led me here. Mostly I thought about a drunken night in Nha Trang sixteen years ago.

Dave and I had met up after a prisoner snatch. I didn't know it then, but it was the second to last mission we would run together. The CO told me to go to the beach for a few days. 'Don't get into any shit and don't fall in love with any nurses or Doughnut Dollies.' The nurses were commissioned officers who wanted nothing to do with a guy like me and the Red Cross volunteers had plenty of officer types to choose from.

Instead, Lieutenant Billings showed up and we got epically drunk. We toured the bars and drank a lot of cognac and beer. We ended up sitting on the sandy beach listening to the waves roll in and drinking beer. The bottles of '33' brand beer were warm, but we had stolen a fire extinguisher somewhere and would blast the beer to cool off before we would drink. Off in the distance red and green tracers did an odd dance on the Marble Mountains. The VC were probing our Observation Post again. Over the sound of the waves there was the distant crackle of automatic weapons.

Dave had been reciting poetry, Shelley maybe, and speaking to me about literature as though I had read the same books he had. Every time he opened another beer he would switch poems and start reciting 'The Charge of the Light Brigade' by Tennyson. Even I knew that one. Dave was good that way, he always acted as though I was just as educated as he was. Or as though I could sit next to him at the country club.

'Andy . . . listen to me . . .'

'Yeah.'

'Andy, you . . .' He paused drunkenly, formulating the words he was trying to say. 'You . . . are . . . you should do more.'

'More?'

'Andy, you are a natural leader. You could be an officer.'

'No, not me, man. I'm not officer material. I just want to run Recon. Do my time.'

'Then what?'

'I dunno. Go to college. Get a normal job, a normal life. Settle down.'

'Fuck that, man. I have seen you out there, over the fence . . . you are too good. You can't just . . . leave.'

'Maybe. Maybe not. Look at you. You are married to a great girl. You have a daughter, man; you have a family.'

'Yeah . . . yeah, man. But man, you are good at this. You saved my shit on this last one.'

'It could be you saving my ass next time out.'

'Who knows. Maybe.' He had taken out the picture wrapped in plastic. 'Look at my little Judy.'

'She's beautiful.'

'Yeah. Hey man . . . you know what we should do?'

'What?'

'When we rotate home, you should come stay with us in Maryland. You should meet Barbara and Judy. You are as close to a brother as I have ever had, man.'

'I would like that.' I didn't know when either of us would rotate home. The war was like that: people came and went, each on their own personal schedule. Dave must have been thinking the same thing.

'Well, you come when you can. Meet my ladies. My ladies meeting my brother. That would be something.'

'Yeah, it would.' I was flattered. Dave's house and Dave's world were a strange world for a kid from South Boston. I was fairly sure that Dave never had to settle for a hotdog wrapped in Wonder Bread because there wasn't enough extra in the budget for hotdog buns. Still, it was nice to be asked.

I shook my head to clear the memory and focus as I got out of the car. I walked down the alley to the street and the front door of the club. The bouncer took my money and stamped my hand. I went through the door and stepped into a crush of people in their twenties. The lights were low, and the music was loud. I pushed my way through to the bar where the bartender shook his head no at Löwenbräu but nodded yes at Rolling Rock. There were flashing lights, and the music made me long for the angry poetry of The Doors or just some hard driving Rolling Stones. The bartender put a Rolling Rock down on the bar, and I left a few singles.

I pushed my way through the crowd trying to get an understanding of the layout. It helped to know where the bathrooms were, the exits, that type of thing. There was a second level where the stairs were roped off and guarded by a big guy in black jeans and a black t-shirt. His arms were thick and looked powerful. He had a neck somewhere in the mass of muscle that rose up from his shoulders. I was betting that was where the VIP section was.

I worked my way around the club. The DJ was playing some sort of dance music or pop or something I wasn't interested in. The bathroom, when I went to use it, was the predictable sloppy mess that club bathrooms tended to be an hour after opening. I dropped a bunch of not-so-subtle hints that I was looking to party, and I heard that K-nice was the man to set me up. It wasn't subtle but I needed to talk to the guy. I went back to the bar and ordered a second Rolling Rock.

The bartender took my twenty and I told him to keep the change. He looked at me and I said, 'I'm looking to talk to K-nice. Can you help me out?'

'Who's K-nice?'

'A guy I need to talk to.' I slid another twenty on the bar.

'Yeah, he is up in VIP.'

'How do I get in?'

'You gotta square that with Luke.'

'The muscles with the head stuck on top guarding the VIP rope?'

'Yep, that's him. He isn't cheap like me, though.'

'Who says you are cheap?' I took my Rolling Rock and moved back into the rugby scrum set to music.

It turned out that Luke the Muscles wasn't expensive. I told him I had to see K-nice 'about business.' I tipped him a twenty and he lifted the rope up, saying, 'Take a right at the top.' I went up the stairs trying to see everything at once. The second floor was a carpeted mezzanine that ran the length of the club. There were booths and people drinking expensive bottles of champagne or imported Russian vodka. Here and there someone was bent over a glass-topped table snorting coke. The whole section of the mezzanine opposite the stairs was a room with large windows and louvered blinds. I was sure that was where the management/ownership hung out.

K-nice wasn't hard to spot. He was sitting at a booth near a door with a red exit sign over it, his back to the wall, surveying the room. Sitting next to him on either side were two girls. They were probably old enough to drive and maybe old enough to vote. Each was wearing a dress that looked more like a slip than a dress. K-nice was wearing a light blue silk shirt and pinstriped vest that was in need of a suit to go with it. He had straight dark hair and a pencil thin mustache. His skin was tanned, and he looked like his ancestors were from the Mediterranean. He had a scar under his left eye, and his hands bore the marks of someone who used to fight a lot before he took to getting his nails manicured. The nail on his right pinkie was long and lacquered, perfect for taking a bump of coke from. Leaning against the corner of the booth was a large black man who made Luke the Muscles downstairs look like he was the runt of the muscle-bound litter. As I got close, he stepped in front of me, blocking my way as effectively as a brick wall.

He was wearing one of those Adidas tracksuits, and the jacket fit his arms like a wetsuit would a normal-sized human. He was wearing sunglasses in the dim club and seemingly had no neck. I had to look up at him. He was packing a large revolver under his left armpit. His jacket was a third unzipped, and there was a bit of checkered wood poking out.

'What do you want?'

'I need to talk to K-nice.'

'Why?'

'That is business between me and him.'

'And my business is to be between you and him. What do you want?'

'I need to talk to him about a girl.'

'Wait a second.' He took a step and squatted down at the table so he could talk to K-nice and keep an eye on me. His thighs were huge, and I could see the outline of brass knuckles in his right front pants pocket when the nylon tracksuit stretched tight over his massive thigh. It seemed like no one was into a fair fight these days. After a short conversation he nodded and stood up, looked at me, and motioned me over with a nod.

'What do you want, man?' K-nice was looking past me at something on the far wall.

'I'm looking for a girl.'

'What makes you think I know anything about a girl?'

'Judy Billings ran away from home. Her father is a friend of mine.'

'You a cop? You have that cop look.'

I didn't think that I looked like a cop; my hair was too long and my mustache wasn't long enough. 'Nope, I'm a private detective. Judy's dad saved my life in Vietnam.'

'Not even a real cop. What makes you think that I give shit about Colonel Daddy and Vietnam?'

'I was trying to let you know how important it is to me. Have you seen her? Do you know where she is?'

'Hey, Private Dick . . . I haven't seen her, and I sure as fuck don't care how important anything is to you.'

'Hey, man, I'm just trying to find my friend's daughter. It's important.'

'I already told you I haven't seen her and I don't give a fuck how important anything is to you. You sure as hell don't have the money or the muscle to be important to me.' He motioned with his chin toward the muscles in the tracksuit. 'Now you need to be leaving, Mr Private Dick.' He emphasized the last three words in order to make each one sound like an obscenity.

I saw the muscles coming at me, and I raised my hands in front of me in the universal show of compliance. 'Hey, man, I'm not looking for trouble. I'm a reasonable guy. I'll go.'

'I guess Colonel Daddy was the only hero in Vietnam.' It came out of K-nice's mouth with brutal irony.

The big man stepped aside and watched me go downstairs. I paused three-quarters of the way down, counted to twenty, and then turned around. I walked up slowly until I could just peer over the landing. I could see K-nice's muscle. He was facing away from the stairs. After all, he was used to ending fights before they started. No sane person would want to fight with him. He had grown used to people leaving when he told them to. I wasn't smart enough to be sane some days. Today was one of them.

I stepped up the last few steps and walked with purpose toward the big man. As I got closer, I reached behind me and slid my hand through the leather strap and my fingers around the handle of the slapjack. I measured my steps like a place-kicker approaching the ball, and when my left foot hit the ground, I pulled the jack from my pocket and brought it up over my head in one fluid motion. When my right foot hit the ground, I brought it flat side down with a savage crash on to the big man's head. He was big, very big, and the first shot didn't seem to affect him, so I jacked him again. This time he staggered and started to go down, and I felt like I should yell, 'Timberrrrr!' Blood flicked off the jack on to the girl to the right of K-nice. The big man crashed almost on top of the girl on his left.

K-nice was a survivor. He was moving, trying to get out from behind the table where he was trapped by the big man pinning the girl on one side with his collapsed bulk. The girl on the other side had started to retch. K-nice shot across the table trying to get free. He didn't bother to try and pull his razor or a gun. He was going across it when the flat, leather-wrapped, ten-ounce piece of lead at the end of the spring steel in the jack connected with his forehead.

It opened up his forehead, and there was more blood, but it didn't knock him out. With my left hand I grabbed a handful of hair and dragged him over the table. He landed in a heap, and I kicked him in the stomach to wind him. While he was gasping for air and bleeding, I rolled the big man over and pulled a big Magnum revolver out of his shoulder holster. Everyone wanted to be Dirty fucking Harry these days. I jammed the artillery piece into my waistband and stepped over to K-nice. I grabbed a fistful of hair again and dragged him over to the emergency exit. I pulled him to his feet and smashed his face into the door and then shoved him into the push bar. The door opened on to a short landing. We went through, and it closed behind us. I didn't have much time and wasn't going to haul him down the stairs. I just kept walking and let go of him at the edge of the steps. He shuffled into space and gravity took over.

He bounced his way down, grunting and crying out when he would come into contact with a step here or there. He landed with a sickening crunch. I quickly went down the steps and kicked the exit door open, which set off a fire alarm. Good. More chaos, more confusion. I yanked the big Magnum revolver out of my waistband and panned it across the alley. No one. I dragged K-nice through the door into the alleyway.

I patted him down quickly and threw the razor under a dumpster. He also had a cheap Spanish-made .32 automatic, which I slid into my back pocket. He had baggies of drugs in his pockets, which I left where they were. Finally, I found what I wanted. Keys to the Jaguar. I opened the trunk and managed to get him up and then into it. He was moaning and I punched him, a short jab to the solar plexus. 'I told you this was important to me. I tried to be reasonable.' I slammed the trunk and got behind the wheel of the Jaguar.

I started the car and kept the lights off as I went down the alley, turning them on only when I turned into the street. The Jaguar was a nice, smooth ride, and I might have enjoyed it except for the big gun sticking into my side and the guy that I had just kidnapped in the trunk. I turned right and then left and two blocks later pulled into an underground pay-as-you-go garage. Parking in this town is a bitch. I pushed the button with my fist and took a ticket, then started making my way to the lowest part of the garage.

I pulled the Jag into a space, shut off the engine, and got

out. It was quiet in the garage. This time of night most of the cars parked here were long term or belonged to the people partying in nearby clubs. I put the key into the trunk and stood off to one side, then opened it. K-nice didn't have any tricks waiting for me, or any fight left in him. I rolled him out of the trunk and propped him up against the side of the car.

'K . . . K-nice . . . fuck, what is your real name?' His face was bloody from where the slapjack had opened up his forehead. His nose was in bad shape, and his right arm was hanging at a funny angle.

'Kevin.'

'Kevin . . . I'm going to ask you a question. It is very important to me that you answer me truthfully.' I was looking into his eyes.

'I don't know anything, man.'

'Kevin, where is Judy Billings?'

'I don't know, m—' His breath rushed out before he could finish the sentence, as I drove my knee up into his groin.

'Kevin . . . I told you this is important to me. I'm trying to be reasonable, man. Where is Judy Billings?'

'I don't know.' He grunted as I hit him in the kidney with a right hook. He cried out in pain.

'Kevin. Where is Judy?'

'Please, man, I don't know.' He moved instinctively to try and cover up. I swung the slapjack into the elbow that was protecting his side. The smell of urine assailed my nose. He howled. 'Please, man . . . please . . . I haven't seen her in a while.'

'Kevin . . . why are you making me do this to you?' I punctuated the question with a tap of the slapjack on his elbow. 'Kevin, just tell me where Judy is.' I could still hear the man from the Company who was teaching a class on advanced interrogation techniques. His bland, droning CIA voice in our classroom saying, 'You want them to feel powerless, that the only power they have is to end their discomfort, to help you. But you have to make them want to help you . . . not just through advanced interrogation, but through your delivery. Your personality has to shine through.' It was an absurd concept, like he was telling us how to be door-to-door salesmen.

'Please, man . . .'

'Kevin, I'm a reasonable man. I don't want to hurt you anymore. Don't make me keep hurting you. Where is Judy?' I felt hot and sweat had beaded up on me. There was a sour taste working its way to my mouth. I had hated those classes.

'I haven't seen her in a week. She was supposed to come by the club . . . she never showed. Please, man . . . I think my arm is broken. Please. Please, I pissed myself. Please.' The last bit came out in a whisper; blood was coming down his face in a slow rivulet. It wasn't just blood; he was crying too.

'OK, Kevin . . . OK. I believe you.' I felt the bile rise in my throat and managed to choke it back down. I eased K-nice into the driver's seat and opened the door behind his seat. I unloaded the guns, wiped them with my shirt, and threw them under his seat. I threw the bullets under the seat too. He was in no condition to get them out anytime tonight, let alone load and fire them at me.

'Kevin, I don't ever want to look over my shoulder and see you or your muscle man. Do you understand me? If I do, I will just kill you both, or anyone you send after me. You understand?'

'Yeah . . . Why? Why'd you do this to me? I'm all fucked up, man. You fucked me up.'

'I told you this was important to me.' I threw the keys in his lap and walked away. I took the stairs up to the street level and made my way back the several blocks to the Maverick. The fire engines had cleared out, and no one was around. I got in the Maverick and drove home.

I let myself in and for once was glad that Sir Leominster wasn't there to greet me. I knew that I wasn't up to his lofty moral standards. There was blood on my shirt, my left side hurt, and I was sweaty. I felt grimy, and it was only partially from the sweat and exertion. I went to the kitchen and poured some whiskey over ice. I took a big gulp and went to the bathroom. I wiped the slapjack down with a damp sponge, getting most of the blood off the leather.

My blood-spattered shirt went into the sink, and I got the hydrogen peroxide out of the closet. I poured it over my hands on to the shirt and then just over the shirt. It bubbled and turned the spots of blood white. I turned on the taps and rinsed it out. There was a spot of blood on my jeans and some peroxide went on that. I turned on the shower and went to the bedroom to drop the rest of my clothes in the dirty laundry basket. I put the .38 on the table next to the bed.

When I got in the shower, the water was hot, and it stung. I took my time lathering up and rinsing off. In Vietnam, after a mission, we were often covered in blood and dirt and god knows what else. The easiest way to get clean was just to get in the shower, gear and all. It would get the equipment clean, and eventually we would go back and take a real shower. It was never enough, though. It never could be. I turned the water from hot to cold and stood under the spray until I couldn't stand it.

After I had toweled off and pulled on some running shorts, I poured myself another large whiskey and sat down in front of the TV. My side hurt and I wasn't any closer to finding Judy. I had beaten a man, tortured him actually, only to find out that he didn't have her.

I could still hear the voice of a friend who had been in the Phoenix Program, as he said in his twangy, southern drawl, 'Torture is ultimately counterproductive. They might tell you what you want to know but they will definitely tell you what they think you want to know to stop the pain.' It might have been crude, but it had still been torture. K-nice wasn't a saint, not even close, but I couldn't claim to be one either. He was a pimp and drug dealer, and I had to know where she was. I just couldn't pretend that my hands were clean. But they hadn't been clean for a long time.

THIRTEEN

I slept late and woke up with the type of headache that comes from too much whiskey. I'm sure that Chris's magic pain pills didn't help. I hadn't slept well. In my dreams Ger kept turning to smile at me. Then his head would explode. Except right before it exploded, his face was replaced by Dave Billings' or, if the dream was really bad, Dave's face was replaced by Judy's.

I showered and dressed. I had my small arsenal in my various holsters and pockets. I drove over to the office. There were men hauling things out of Marconi's and throwing them into a dumpster. I went upstairs feeling like I had just seen a funeral. It could be a movie, *Death of Pizza Joint in Boston*. Out of habit I checked the office door, but no one had left any hand grenades or other nasty surprises.

There were no messages with my answering service. I opened a window and took a pipe out of the rack, packed it, and lit it with a match. The warm June air flowed in and mixed with the fragrant smoke from my pipe. I made all the usual calls: hospitals, cops, other contacts. Judy Billings was still in the wind. It was easy to run away and disappear, swallowed up by the streets. I had assumed she would go to Boston, but she could have hopped a Greyhound to any city in the country. I was pretty sure she wasn't in Boston or the surrounding cities and towns. I was also quite certain that she wasn't with K-nice. I kept making calls and kept getting the same answers to the same questions. No one had seen her. No one had heard anything. No one knew anything.

I did find out, from the same vice cop who told me where to find K-nice, that Sailor was at Mass General Hospital. His bottle of scotch was getting more expensive every time I talked to him. He even told me the room number. Maybe Sailor would be more cooperative if I reasoned with him?

I got up and went downstairs. The hospital wasn't far away,

and I knew of a florist nearby. I bought a bouquet on my way over and carried it a couple more blocks to MGH. I went into the lobby holding my bouquet wrapped with a large ribbon that had 'Get Well Soon' printed on it. With a Red Sox cap and sunglasses on, I was practically invisible. Just another Boston Irish guy. I walked by his room a couple of times to make sure that it was just him and there were no surprises. I had been pissing people off lately, or the cops might have taken an interest. K-nice could have made a complaint. I wasn't in the mood to risk it.

I doubled back and went into Sailor's room. His head was bandaged, and he was hooked up to a full IV bag and all the normal monitors. He was asleep, and there was no one in the other bed or in the small bathroom. I bent over the bed and took the combination control for the TV and call button for the nurse and dangled it over the side of the bed where he couldn't reach it. I sat down in the hard chair next to the bed and softly said, 'Hey, shitbait . . . wake up.'

It took a couple of tries, but he opened his eyes. They slowly focused on my face. I took my sunglasses off and his eyes widened. 'You . . . Dandy Andy.'

'Yep, in the flesh.' His hand was casually feeling for the call button, trying not to alarm me. 'I thought we might have a quiet talk. Civilized, even.'

'Sure . . . sure.' His hand wasn't finding what he wanted.

'The missing girl is important to me. Her father saved my life in Vietnam, and I can't ever repay that type of debt . . . but he asked me for help finding her. So that is what I have to do. You understand that, don't you? That this is an obligation . . . a debt that I can only try to repay.' His hand kept moving.

'You split my skull. You asshole.' He was starting to realize that the call button wasn't where it should have been.

'If you hadn't come at me with the monkey's fist, I probably wouldn't have needed to.'

'Hey, man, you can't blame me. It is rough out there. I can't just let guys walk all over me.'

'That's true. It is rough out there, but we're in here and I need your help. I don't want this girl to end up on the streets

or the Carousel.' I was speaking to him in my extra calm
voice.

'Hey, man, I told you I ain't seen her and I don't know nothing.'

'Sailor, last night I beat up a guy who told me those exact
words. I didn't just beat him, but I hurt him, hurt him quite
badly, and he didn't even hit me with a monkey's fist. I don't
like doing this shit. It's bad for my karma . . . you know what
I mean? But this is important to me . . . I told him that,
and I'm telling you. Now help me out.' I smiled what I hoped
was a nice smile, but it probably didn't work out that way.

'I don't know anything, seriously. I ain't seen her.'

'Maybe you know where a girl like that might end up?'

'I don't know nothing.'

'Sailor, were you in the Navy?'

'No, Merchant Marine.'

'So, you were never in combat?'

'No, man.'

'I was. Did you know that?' I said it conversationally. Just
two normal guys having a chat in a hospital room.

'No. What does that have to do with anything?'

'We learned how to give IVs. Guys would get shot up . . .
we'd have to give them an IV. Try and buy time for a medevac.'

'So?' He was getting annoyed.

'So, I injected your bag with some shit. Slow drip, it isn't
a problem. A little extra mellow over a few hours.' I stood up
and dropped the bouquet on his chest, partially in his face. I
put my left arm on his forearm and squeezed the IV bag from
the top with my right hand. 'But if I squeeze the bag like this
. . . well, that will speed things up a lot. This is pretty pure
shit . . . it hasn't been stepped on a bunch of times like the
shit you deal . . . a big quick dose . . . probably kills you.
You'll know, though, when you start feeling cold . . . then you
will know it is killing you.' I squeezed some more.

'Please . . . I don't know where she is. I ain't seen her.' He
was looking around, hoping for help.

'Sailor, look at me . . . this is important. You are just another
lowlife, half-assed drug-dealing pimp. Her father saved my
life . . . what do you think is more important to me?' I squeezed
again. 'Are you feeling cold yet, motherfucker?'

'Please . . .'

'Tell me something, anything. Give me a reason to walk away, to save your life. Come on, man. I don't like doing this shit. Give me a reason to help you, man.' I could hear the guy from the Phoenix Program, 'You have to convince them that you, only you, are their way out of the mess. In short, you have to convince them that you are their savior, not their interrogator.'

'OK . . . OK.'

'Tell me something, man . . . come on, give me something. Anything.'

'A few days ago, maybe a week, I dunno. I saw her, in the Zone.'

'Bullshit.'

'She was with a guy, in a car, she was looking to cop some stuff.'

'Guy in a blue Jaguar with a thin mustache?'

'No, a black kid, in a Mustang, with gray down its side.'

'Are you sure?'

'Yes, yes . . . please, man, I feel cold.'

'You'll live.' The IV bag was empty. I walked out leaving him with the flowers, feeling cold. I had squeezed all the bag's fluid into him. It was room temperature, about twenty degrees cooler than his body temperature. The sudden influx of colder fluid had made him feel cold but otherwise hadn't done anything to him.

The drive to Fort Devens was still beautiful. I should have felt elated about getting a lead, finding out that Derrick Page had lied to me and that he was seen with Judy in the Combat Zone recently. That was the first break I had gotten in the case. It should have felt good. I was pretty sure that if I looked in the mirror right now, I would recognize the face but not the person. Vietnam had been one thing; we were fighting a war and the stakes were the highest I had to wager with. My life and the lives of my men.

This was different. I wanted to find Judy to satisfy this debt to Dave. It felt like I was on some crusade. But what would happen if I found her, and she ran away again? If Dave asked me to find her again? What else would I do? How far was I willing to go?

I made it to Fort Devens in good time. I showed the gate guard my pass and drove over to the motor pool building where Derrick Page worked. I parked behind his primer-sided Mustang and waited. It was almost four p.m., or 1600 hours if you were in the Army. His workday would be ending soon. I waited, and at 1600 exactly by my watch soldiers started to stream out of the motor pool. I saw him coming, and I got out of the Maverick. I walked over to his car and leaned on the hood. I took out my pack of Luckies and lit one with the Zippo.

He walked up and looked at me with undisguised hostility. 'What the fuck do you want?'

'Hi, Derrick.'

'The fuck you doing leaning on my car?' Lately it seems like everyone is mad at me.

'Oh, I was on post. On my way to see Colonel Billings, but thought I would stop by and talk to you first.'

'About what?'

'Oh, the fact that you lied to me about Judy,' I said casually.

'Fuck you, man.' His brown eyes flashed with anger.

'How you and she were spotted in Boston, in the Combat Zone, a few days ago, trying to cop.'

'That's bullshit!'

'Naw, nope, no, it isn't.' I looked around at the soldiers getting in their cars and heading back to their quarters. I took a drag on my Lucky and said speculatively, 'How much trouble do you think the Colonel would make for you? Taking his daughter to Boston to buy drugs . . . and whatever else.'

'It isn't like that . . . she called me for a ride. Said she needed my help.' His anger now replaced by fear.

'Sure, she did. What type of help did she need?' He was shaking his head slightly side to side. It was an unconscious gesture. 'Derrick, where is she?'

'I don't know . . . I don't.'

'Derrick, don't fucking lie to me anymore. I tell the Colonel about you two in Boston, he will send you to the stockade forever. Goodbye Army, goodbye GI Bill, goodbye college, and goodbye dreams.' I slammed my hand down on the hood

of his car to punctuate the last sentence. I was a real tough
guy, bullying a kid who didn't have a chance of sticking up
for himself.

'Please, man . . . please.' I started to have that same feeling
in my throat that I did in the parking garage the night before.

'Don't piss me off. I only care about one thing . . . the girl.
I only care about where she is so I can bring her home.'

'OK, OK . . . I can take you there. Get in,' – he motioned
to the passenger side – 'get in and I will take you to her.' I
went around the back as he got in and started the engine.
I was almost at the door when the Mustang shot forward,
spraying me with dust as he bolted. I made it to the Maverick
in two big strides and was off in a shot.

I cursed myself for falling for it while I engaged in the
slowest car chase in history. He drove at exactly twenty-four
miles an hour on post and then did the speed limit when we
crossed into Ayer. We drove down Main Street. There was no
rush as long I could keep him in sight. Then Main Street
turned into East Main Street, and then we were at the rotary,
where each of the holy trinity of fast-food restaurants was
represented. He didn't stop at McDonald's, Burger King, or
Wendy's but took a hard right on to Route 111. It would lead
to Route 2 and back to Boston. I tapped the brakes to drop
the weight of the engine over the wheels and cut the steering
wheel to the right. My tires squealed a little and I pushed on
the gas pedal to power me into the turn.

Derrick put his foot down and the Mustang shot ahead of
me. I pressed my foot down on the gas pedal, pushing the
Maverick to catch up. The engine rumbled and the wheel was
a live thing in my hands. I could feel the road, every bump
and jolt radiated up into the wheel. The road was mostly
straight but there were enough turns that I had to pay attention. I watched the Mustang in front of me and just willed
myself to catch up to him. It was like some old primal hunting
instinct.

As I closed the distance between us, he would speed up.
He would slow for cars in front of him until he could pass
them. He would whip around them, and a couple of times
almost hit other cars coming in the other direction. The

countryside was flicking past in a wall of green, and I had to keep giving the Maverick more gas to keep Derrick in sight. He dipped out of sight around a bend and I almost missed him.

The road curved and he must have tried to pass someone where he shouldn't have. I passed a bit of twisted metal that could have been in a modern art museum. I braked hard and left a trail of tire on the asphalt. I turned the Maverick around in a clumsy K-turn and drove the thirty yards back up the road.

His car was on my right crashed into a tree. He must have crossed into the other lane and then lost control. I pulled ahead, turned again, and then pulled up behind what was left of his car. I got out and started to walk up to it. The smell of hot engine coolant and melting plastic was overwhelming. The smell was acrid; there's nothing quite like the smell of car crash. There was a loud hissing noise as the car's fluids leaked out on to the hot remains of the engine. The Mustang had hit an oak. The tree was old and huge. Derrick had gone through the windshield and the same tree that had stopped his car had stopped him, headfirst. He was dead. It wasn't pretty. It never is.

I got back in the Maverick and headed for Boston. I hadn't killed the kid, but I didn't want to talk to any cops right now. I didn't want to talk to anyone. There was no reason for him to be dead. He didn't have to run . . . he could have just talked to me and we would have gone our separate ways. I didn't have to chase him. I could have waited for him to come back to the post. It wasn't my fault he was dead, but I had been a part of it. His death was needless, and I had seen enough of that in my life.

FOURTEEN

I had gone home, stopping at the grocery store and liquor store to replenish my perpetually dwindling supply of whiskey. I had the urge to stay in. I didn't want to see anyone, and staying in, drinking whiskey, and watching TV was about my speed.

The next day found me in my office. It had been a quiet night and I had managed to get some dreamless sleep. When I woke up, I found that I was still thinking about Derrick Page. Did I have to chase him? If I was thinking about that, I was also thinking about K-nice and Sailor. I was doing things that I didn't like doing, but I was doing them to find Judy. To save Judy.

My thoughts were interrupted by the sound of the office door opening. I was about to get up and see who it was when the connecting door flew open. Derrick Page's First Sergeant, Rosario, was in the office looking around. He was wearing blue jeans and a black t-shirt with an eagle wrapped in an American flag on it. He was holding a sawed-off baseball bat in his right hand.

'You motherfucker . . . I'm gonna beat your fucking brains in.' He stepped forward raising the bat. I reached in the drawer in front of me and pulled out the big Magnum revolver. It was a Ruger .357 Magnum, and it was built like a Russian tank. I put the butt on the desktop and thumbed the hammer back. The click was loud, and he stopped in his tracks.

'Top, I'm too tired to fight with you right now. Put the bat down.' The revolver was leveled at his midsection and it would take some work to miss at this distance.

'Or what, you're gonna shoot me?' His hissing anger reminded me of a cobra I had once seen on R&R in Thailand.

'Yes. Right above your hip, close in. The pelvic bowl. Probably won't kill you, but you will hit the floor like a box of dropped rocks. It will hurt a lot. You'll never walk right again.' He thought about it and then lowered the bat. I motioned with the heavy revolver for him to sit down. He did.

'You fucking killed him.' It wasn't a question. 'You two argued and he left, and you ran him off the road.'

'I went to talk to him. I found out he lied to me about seeing the girl. He raced off and I followed him. He was driving like a maniac and almost got into an accident a bunch of times. He lost control of his car. That was it. I wish to hell he hadn't.'

'Yeah . . . sure.'

'Top, if I wanted to kill him there were a lot of better ways to get it done.'

He looked at me. 'Yeah, I guess there are. He was a good kid, you know. Hard working, and a nice kid.'

'Top, believe me. This is the last thing I would have wanted. I just wanted to talk to him. Why did he run? I only wanted to talk.' I almost told him that I felt like hell about it but he was too angry to believe me or want to hear it.

'Why do you think he ran? He's probably been hassled by white cops his whole life. I know what that is like, being hassled by cops. White cops, black cops, Panamanian cops. You're all the same.'

'I'm not a cop.'

'Maybe that's why, maybe he thought he had a choice this time.'

'Someone saw them in the Combat Zone trying to buy drugs a few days, maybe a week ago. I just wanted to ask him where he took her.'

'Fucking crazy *puta*!' He spat the phrase out. 'He was nuts about her. Even after she broke up with him, she would call him and get him to drive her places.'

'I need to know where he took her in Boston when he drove her down.'

'No. He didn't drive her down to Boston last week.'

'No?'

'No, he went down to pick her up. She needed a ride somewhere, so he drove down to get her.'

'He didn't drive her to Boston.'

'Sure, plenty of times, but not last week. He asked me if he could leave earlier to go pick her up. I thought it was a bad idea, but I let him go. He was nervous and jumpy about it later. Then you showed up asking about her. He was scared shitless. He thought her daddy Colonel War Hero was going to have him locked up forever. I guess he doesn't have to worry about that anymore.'

'No, I guess not.'

'I have had guys get hurt, but in fifteen years this is the first soldier of mine who has died. He is the first one I have lost on or off duty.'

'It sucks.' It was an inelegant explanation for something that there is no explaining.

'You were in Vietnam . . . you lost guys? Do you ever get used to it?'

'No, you don't . . . in the end you just think about it less.' That was almost true; I left out the bit about the dreams.

He stood up and tucked the bat under his arm like a British officer with a swagger stick.

'I'm leaving, *puto*. You gonna shoot me?'

'Nope, not unless you give me a reason to.'

'I don't like you, man. I see you out and about sometime . . . we're gonna dance. Just you and me. No big gun, no cops.' He left. He didn't do anything clichéd like slam the office door. He just walked out, taking his grief and anger with him, carrying it just like he carried his abbreviated ball bat, only it was a lot heavier.

I had taken the case as far as I could at this point. I had failed to find her, and I had chased the only good lead off the road and into a tree. I had failed. That was the type of news that I should deliver to Dave in person.

By the time I left the office, I had made a couple of not too bad espressos and eaten lunch. My head had mostly stopped hurting by mid-afternoon when I steered the Maverick away from the city and toward Fort Devens. I watched as the suburbs rolled by and gave way to green hills. The air seemed cleaner and cooler. My knuckles were bruised and scabbed, and my side hurt, but the scenery was beautiful. I took it all in and was struck by how different, how clean it was compared to the city and especially the Combat Zone.

I stopped at the gate and showed my pass to the MP, who

waved me through with the weird salute/wave thing that MPs do. I drove down Jackson Road past the golf course and made my way over to Dave's office. I parked and went to the door, which had push buttons to release the handle. To one side of the door was an intercom. I pushed the button on the intercom, and eventually a disembodied voice came out of the box.

'Yeah?'

'I was looking for Colonel Billings; my name is Roark.'

'Wait one.'

A few minutes went by and then I heard boots on the other side of the door. The door opened and a staff sergeant with aggressive sideburns and a mustache that was definitely not within Army regulations was there. 'Hey, sir, Colonel's down by the jump tower on the other side of post. He says you should head out there.' He told me how to get there and then disappeared back into the building.

I drove back the way I came, by the golf course, by the guard shack and the bored MP. I crossed over the highway and came to a gate in a large chain link fence. I rolled slowly up to the MP on duty and showed him my pass. He stepped back and waved me through.

I lit a cigarette and drove slowly down the road in the direction of the training sites. This part of the post was home to the specific training sites like the obstacle course, the rappel tower and, of course, the shooting ranges. Off to my right were the giant ammunition bunkers that contained everything from pistol ammunition to artillery rounds. I rolled slowly down the road past a stream and then took a hard left a mile or so further on. The occasional camouflage truck or Jeep would pass me heading back toward main post. If it weren't for that, I might as well have been on a country road in Vermont or New Hampshire. In the distance I could make out the crack of gunfire, volleys of it, as multiple shooters shot at their targets. Somewhere else they were firing machine guns, M60s. They were louder and fully automatic, so they were shooting faster.

On my left, the scrub brush opened into a field that was bordered by unkempt shrubs and short trees. There were a few trucks and Jeeps parked at the edge. There were men in camouflage fatigues milling about. No one was wearing any sort of headgear. Far off to one side was a thirty-four-foot tower with a metal box on it. There were more men in camouflage around it. The box was sand colored, and someone had halfheartedly tried to spray-paint a camouflage pattern on it. Lines were running off it to vertical poles on the ground, not unlike a zip line. The box itself was a mockup of an airplane used by paratroopers to practice exits and parachute landing falls.

I parked next to a Jeep that, given its extra antenna and radio, was probably Dave's. I spotted him over by the tower in a knot of soldiers. He saw me and waved me over. As I walked across the field, I watched a soldier stand in the door of the tower. Unlike most of the soldiers on the ground, he was wearing a helmet, one of the new lightweight ones that replaced the steel pot and was shaped like the World War II German Army ones. Also, he was wearing a parachute harness, but instead of being attached to a parachute rig, this was attached to the zip line. He put his hands on the outer frame of the door and stepped out, chin to chest, counting just as he would on a real jump to give his static line time to deploy. Then he reached up and grabbed the risers, lines he would steer a chute with. He hit the ground, feet and knees together, rolling into a perfect PLF. He got up, moved out of the way for the next jumper, and unhooked his harness.

'Hey, Andy, what do you think?' Dave swept an arm around to encompass the tower and the jumpers.

'Pretty neat.' It looked like good training. They could practice here, go to Moore Army Airfield at the other end of the post, and then jump for real.

'I'm really proud of this tower. The Army wouldn't build us one, so my guys and I scrounged the materials and did it ourselves.' He was grinning like a kid, and I was remembering how he would look after a mission.

'It looks pretty new. You guys haven't even cleaned up.' I pointed to a couple of large mounds of dirt behind the tower close to the railroad tracks that ran through this part of post.

'We were too eager to use it. We still have to paint it. Later, I'll get my hands on a bulldozer and those piles of dirt will go away. Still pretty neat, huh?' He was like a kid with a new toy.

'Yeah, man.' It wasn't like jumping out of a real airplane . . . nothing was. Nothing else would do. But for him, it would make it easier to train and save time getting training done.

'Come on, man, admit it, you miss it.' He punched my arm lightly.

'Jumping from the thirty-four-foot tower?'

'No. The Army. Special Forces . . . you miss being in SF, man.' He said it the same way other people asked me about missing ex-girlfriends. I hadn't thought about it, maybe intentionally. I had loved Recon. There I had found a home in an asylum with brothers who were just as crazy as I was. We had decided that you had to be insane to run Recon. But the Army, did I miss the Army? Did I miss the bullshit? No! Did I miss the camaraderie and the sense of purpose that I had found in Special Forces? I didn't think I could ever get that back, to have what I had when I was in Recon. That didn't exist anymore . . . but the downside of being a lone PI was that there wasn't a lot of camaraderie.

We watched a few more guys practice exits, which was about as exciting for the SF guys as a marathon runner going for a walk around the block. These were all guys who had made hundreds of jumps, and this was just proving that the new piece of kit worked. It was very laid-back, as stuff with SF tends to be, unlike the rest of the Army.

'Andy, let's go grab a beer.' He was in a good mood and I was about to ruin it.

'Sure, Dave.' A beer sounded great, and it would make telling him that I had hit the wall in the investigation a little easier.

'Good, we'll take your car.' He went off to tell his driver to take the Jeep back without him. He chatted with a couple of others while I waited, leaning on the hood of the Maverick smoking a Lucky Strike. He walked over and we both got in. We drove back to the post, enjoying the warm June air, late afternoon sunshine, and a radio station out of Worcester that was playing a lot of stuff like The Doors and The Rolling Stones.

We crossed on to main post, pausing so the MP could salute Dave and wave us through. I pulled into Dave's driveway and we got out. I left the windows down and the doors unlocked. Crime on an Army base was usually limited to theft from the Army or GIs getting drunk and fighting. The common form of theft was one unit stealing stuff from another to make up for something missing or stolen from them. The Army was good at making soldiers pay for things. I wasn't worried about anyone stealing my Doobie Brothers tapes.

We went into the house through the side door. It was quiet and still. Like Sir Leominster, Judy hadn't come home. Dave's wife was still away, resting her nerves in Palm Springs. We went into the kitchen, and Dave opened the refrigerator.

'St. Pauli Girl OK?'

'Sure, thanks.' I took the green bottle with the well-endowed lady on the label from him. He handed me a church key, and I popped the cap off and handed it back to him. We clinked bottles and drank. He took a long pull and wiped his mouth with the back of his hand. 'That's good. It was hot up in that tower.'

'I can imagine. It will only get worse with summer.'

'True, but not Fort Bragg hot or Vietnam hot.'

'Nothing is Vietnam hot.' It was true, the heat and humidity in Vietnam were almost living things. They had hit me like a giant hand when I first got there. Then the cold season arrived and it rained miserably, and we froze when we were on missions.

'What happened to your knuckles?' Dave was holding the beer bottle and pointing at my hand.

'I had a busy couple of days.' My left side and arm still hurt. I wasn't sure how I felt about my run-ins with K-nice and Sailor, and I wasn't about to bring up Derrick Page.

'Doing what? You are too old to fight with the MPs anymore.'

'Nope, no MPs in Boston. No, I found Judy's boyfriend, K-nice. He objected to my wanting to ask him questions. He was just one of two assholes I had to dance with this week.'

'Oh . . . and did he talk to you?' Dave raised an eyebrow; it was an art form that I was still trying to master. I was pretty good at the Gallic shrug.

'Yeah, after a bit he did. Judy isn't with him and he doesn't know where she is.'

'Bullshit, he is lying to you, Andy.'

'No, Dave, he wasn't lying. I'm one hundred percent certain of that.' I could still smell the blood and piss in the parking garage. I could hear in my head the sound of the sap hitting flesh, and I still felt like I wanted to be sick. The sound of him pleading with me to stop hurting him.

'She has to be with him.' Dave was pleading with me.

'Dave, she isn't with him. If she is in Boston, she isn't anywhere where runaways normally hang out. Dave, I couldn't find her anywhere. I looked everywhere.'

'What about the kid down at the motor pool?'

'That dog won't hunt.' My tone must have convinced him that line of questioning was going nowhere.

'C'mon, you must be missing something.'

'Dave, sometimes kids run away, and they come home a few days, weeks, months, even years later. Sometimes they don't. I don't know where else to look or what else to do.' I was dancing around it because he saved my life, and I was letting him down.

'Andy . . .'

'Dave, I don't think I can do much more to find her.'

'You're quitting.'

'I'm sorry, but I don't know what else to do.'

'Get out.' He pointed toward the door. I put my half-finished beer down on the table and walked out. The drive to Boston was not a happy one. I went over the case again and again in my head. Had I done everything I could to find her? Had I checked every place where she might be? I couldn't think of anything else to do. I could walk around the Combat Zone until my sneakers fell off . . . if she wasn't there, she wasn't there. It was the same everywhere else I looked. Sue hadn't turned up any sign of her, and Sue's contacts on the street were light-years better than mine. If she hadn't heard anything about Judy, then Judy wasn't in Boston. Not on the streets. I had walked them for hours and days, and she wasn't there.

When I got home, I parked in my bomb-damaged spot and got the mail out of the mailbox and made my way up to my apartment. I was greeted by a blinking light on the answering machine and Sue's voice coming out of the speaker. I picked up the phone and got it before she disconnected.

'Hi, Sue.'

'Hiya, Andy. I was calling to see if you were interested in some company tonight?'

'Company?'

'You know, takeout, beer, and the Movie Loft . . . making out on your couch . . . that type of thing?' Sue was not now (nor had I ever known her to be) shy.

'I would love that.' It would be a welcome relief after the last couple of days.

'Really?'

'Yes, really. I can't tell you how much that would be great right now.'

'OK, I will be by around six.'

'I'm looking forward to it.' I was. It wasn't just the obvious I was looking forward to, but also, I felt pretty low after leaving Dave's. Sue's coming by was a nice antidote to feeling low.

I took the .38 out of my waistband and put it in the drawer of the bedside table. I grabbed a yellow legal pad, a blue felt-tip pen, and a red felt-tip pen. I got a glass of water and sat at the table in the kitchen. On the first page, in red ink, I wrote down all the names of everyone involved. Then, in blue, I wrote out a narrative of what had happened to date in the case. I was intentionally vague about what happened with Sailor and K-nice. As for Derrick Page, I just wrote, 'Deceased, Motor Vehicle Accident.' There was no point in leaving a written record. I would know and would struggle with it. I hadn't killed him, but I was a part of it. When I was done, I had about ten handwritten pages of notes that said that I hadn't done very much.

At five thirty, I put it all away. There wasn't much more to say or do. Dave had asked me for help, and I had failed him. I would have to live with that. Just like I would have to live with the bad taste in my mouth from my time with K-nice in the garage. Not to mention Derrick Page's death. I had killed men in combat, I had gotten into fights with men, beaten some, been beaten by some . . . but the thing with K-nice wasn't that. It had been a one-sided affair. I had told myself that he would lead me to Judy Billings. That I could save Judy Billings from a life of drug addiction and prostitution – and beating a man who couldn't fight back was justified if it meant saving her.

While I was waiting for Sue, I killed time by looking through some old photos I kept from Vietnam. There were ones of friends and team members, clowning around. There were team photos, posing in two rows, bristling with weapons. Informal photos of us getting ready to get on the birds to go on a mission or just getting back from one. Exhausted, but happy to be alive. There were a couple with Dave too, smiling and happy. There was one of Dave and me, our arms around each other's shoulders, just back from mission. Dave had managed to go on three or four missions with us. Not a lot, but they were memorable.

'Andy, I like strap-hanging with your team. You are good in the woods, your team is good and your indig are fearless. You guys get it done.' That was at a bar in Saigon a few weeks before we went on our last mission together.

The doorbell rang and I buzzed Sue in. She came up the stairs with brown paper bags with handles and a six-pack of Löwenbräu. She was wearing khaki shorts and a white t-shirt with the logo for the London Underground on it, white sneakers, and white ankle socks. Her purse was thrown over her shoulder and across her chest. She had a pair of trendy French sunglasses pushed up in her hair, and when I leaned over to kiss her, she smelled vaguely of lavender. She kissed me back, then stepped back, handing me the six-pack.

'I got Chinese food. I hope you like either beef and broccoli or chicken lo mein?' She went into the kitchen as if she had never left. After all, she had lived here for months.

'How's Sir Leominster?' She hadn't much liked the cat.

'He is being held hostage by the FBI.' It would take too long to explain the odd relationship between Brenda Watts and myself.

'Good, maybe it will help his personality.'

'Chinese is great,' I said, changing the subject. I hadn't had it in a few months. She was already unpacking white cardboard containers of beef, lo mein, and rice. There was a bag of dinner rolls, plastic packets of soy sauce and Chinese mustard, as well as paper-wrapped chopsticks. And, of course, fortune cookies. Sue went to the cupboards and pulled down a couple of big bowls to put our dinner in. She pulled a couple of tablespoons out of the silverware drawer, and a fork for her. It was nice watching her move around the kitchen. It was as if she hadn't left, and I hadn't anticipated liking that feeling.

'Open us a couple of beers. I'm starving and thirsty.' I did what I was told and put the rest in the refrigerator. She made us each a bowl with rice and some of each dish. We sat at the table and ate in companionable silence the way we used to.

'Andy?' She was nibbling on a roll that she had ripped open and stuffed with a pat of butter and some mustard. I never understood dinner rolls with Chinese food.

'Sue.' I was trying to negotiate the lo mein with chopsticks and not end up wearing too much of it. I know how to impress the ladies.

'Are you making progress looking for your friend's daughter?'

'No, I have hit dead end after dead end. Have you heard anything?' I slurped the lo mein noodle from between the chopsticks.

'No. Nobody has seen her or heard anything.' She went back to nibbling.

'I don't think she is in Boston. Maybe she went to another city. Providence, New York, Omaha, someplace like that, but she isn't here.'

'I think you are right. Did you find K-nice?' She was looking at me intently.

'Yeah, I did. Why?' I took a sip of Löwenbräu . . . if this went south on me, I didn't want to be sober for it.

'He got arrested. He was in a car accident, hit a stop sign, and the cops found drugs and guns in his car.'

'Gee, that's too bad. He probably had a nice car.'

'Andy, people are saying that he was beaten up, bad. Broken bones and stuff like that.'

'Well, Sue, I heard he was a drug dealer and a half-ass

pimp. Many people told me to stay away from him as he was dangerous. He may have had it coming.'

'Yeah, but from you?' She had put the roll down.

'Are you going to be mad at me if I beat up a drug-dealing pimp?' It seemed like a fair question.

'No. I just want to know.'

'We had words. He made a move and I finished it.' That was a very charitable self-assessment of what had transpired. It wasn't exactly a lie. I was pretty sure that if I told her I was beating answers out of him after I had kidnapped him from a club she would have objections.

'OK . . . I'm not here to tell you what to do. I just wanted to know.'

'No, I can see that.'

We went to the living room to see what was on the Movie Loft. Tonight, it was a movie with Chevy Chase and Goldie Hawn. He's her flaky ex-husband who's wanted for a crime he didn't commit. He ends up hiding out at Goldie Hawn's house, avoiding her new man, and they fall back in love. Sue smoked a joint and I passed, opting for a big glass of whiskey. It wasn't long before we were making out on the couch, trying to see who could get out of their clothes faster. It was too close to call, and we missed most of the movie. Later, we sat naked eating Chinese out of the cardboard containers and watching TV. There was a movie on, but I don't think either of us paid much attention to it. Then, later still, she led me by the hand to the bedroom. I couldn't help but notice she was only wearing those white ankle socks and a mischievous grin.

The morning sun filled the bedroom, and the sounds of traffic and construction wafted up from the street. We had managed to sleep late. There were advantages to being self-employed, and most of her clients weren't up before late afternoon. It was Saturday, and for Sue it would be a busy night. We lay in bed for a while, just enjoying the lazy morning-after feeling. Then she got up to go to the bathroom, and I went to make coffee and see about breakfast.

Sue was in luck. I had eggs, bacon, and rye bread in the house. I put a bunch of bacon in the pan and turned on the heat. It didn't take long for the apartment to fill up with the wonderful smell of cooking bacon. The coffee started to percolate, and the smell of coffee complemented the smell of the bacon. I broke four eggs into a metal mixing bowl, added salt, pepper, a dash of cayenne pepper, some dried dill, and splash of cream. Then I beat them into an even mixture with a fork.

Sue appeared wearing one of my t-shirts and nothing else. It was a good look for her. She went to the cupboard and took out a glass and filled it with water from the sink. She went to her purse, which had spent the night on the kitchen counter where she had put it down.

'It smells wonderful.' Her hair was tousled, and she looked sleepy.

'Thanks . . . I thought you might be hungry.' My own stomach was rumbling.

'You mean after last night's events?' She grinned wickedly at me.

'Exactly.' I grinned back. As conspiracies went, it was a nice one to share.

'You are right. I'm starving, and I feel like I was worked over by a sex-starved maniac.'

'Funny, I feel the same way.' She might have blushed, but I doubt it. She rooted around in her purse and came out with a plastic case. She opened it and popped a pill out of the blister pack, put it into her mouth, and washed it down with a drink of water.

'What are you looking at? Haven't you ever seen a girl take the pill before?'

'No, sorry, spacing out. You planned to spend the night, so you brought them with you.'

'I didn't want to forget to take it. I wouldn't leave home without it.' She put the case back in her purse, and I put another pan on the stove, turned the heat on, and threw a large hunk of butter in. I put some bread in the toaster and shifted the bacon around to have it cook evenly. The butter melted slowly, and I waited for the white bits to start moving around on their own.

'Andy, do you want coffee?'

'Yes, please.' Sue reached around me for the now percolated coffee.

'Black?'

'Always.'

'Some things will never change.' She wrinkled her nose; she was a cream and sugar person.

'I am consistent.'

The toast popped up and I swapped two pieces of bread for the toast, poured the eggs in the pan, quickly buttered the toast, and went back to the eggs. I used a wooden spoon and started to stir them in the pan, working from the center to the side farthest from and then closest to me, in a figure eight. I paused to take a sip of coffee, then went back to stirring the eggs, watching them go from liquid to forming curds. It was slow, meditative work that was easy to screw up. There are few things worse than burned eggs. As they firmed up, I put another piece of butter in the pan with them. It would give them a very decadent buttery flavor as well as a nice sheen. When the toast popped, Sue went and took the pieces out and buttered them.

'Can you put the toast on plates, please?' I was heavily invested in my egg scrambling.

'Sure.'

I paused my egg stirring only long enough to stir the bacon and turn off the heat under that pan. When Sue put the plates down on the counter next to me, I lifted the eggs out of the pan and scooped them on to the toast. Then I lifted the bacon out of the pan and shook the slices a few times to get rid of any excess fat. I put a few slices of bacon on each plate next to the eggs on toast. I shook some salt and pepper over them and put the two plates down on the table.

'Andy, you know how to make a girl feel appreciated.' She smiled brightly at me.

'I try, plus I'm always looking to encourage repeat customers.' She took a bite of toast and eggs. So did I. The eggs were moist and creamy but not wet or underdone. They had just the right amount of salt and pepper.

'Andy, these are fantastic.' She picked up a piece of bacon and took a bite.

'Thanks. I should have had some fresh chives to chop up and sprinkle on them.'

'How come you didn't cook like this when I lived here?' I didn't have a good answer. Something was nagging at me, and I had begun to eat mechanically, not tasting, just pushing calories. Something was buzzing in my head.

'Sue, what was it you said about the pill? Your pill?'

'That I wouldn't leave home without it.'

'Why would a seventeen-year-old girl running away to meet her drug-dealing, half-assed pimp boyfriend leave her birth control pill at home?' I put my toast down.

'It doesn't seem very likely.' She kept on eating.

'No. No, it doesn't, does it?' Something wasn't right, and I had to drive up to Fort Devens to see Dave.

FIFTEEN

After Sue left, I showered and got dressed. I was dressed like any fashionable PI would be on a Saturday in June: jeans, sneakers, and a white polo shirt, my .38 on my hip, snug in its holster inside the waistband. With my aviator sunglasses on, I was too cool.

I steered the Maverick out of the city and the 302 rumbled as I headed toward Fort Devens. When I was up in the hills west of the city, the rain started, a slow heavy drop, followed by more drops, beating against the car. The windshield wipers swished back and forth, and I had to turn up the radio to hear The Doors sing 'Roadhouse Blues.' I had the window cracked to let the smoke from my Luckies out, and water made its way into the car. Not a lot, just enough to be uncomfortable.

By the time I pulled up in front of the house on Walnut Street, the rain had stopped. The air was humid and perfumed with the unmistakable smell of rain on warm pavement. I walked up the walkway. I was in luck; Dave's little BMW was in the driveway. I pressed the doorbell and heard the faint tinkling inside the house. I heard footsteps, and Dave opened the door. He seemed surprised to see me.

'Andy, what are you doing here?'

'Can I come in?'

'Sure.' He stood aside and let me in. He was wearing old faded blue jeans and a t-shirt from a German paratrooper unit. The *Fallschirmjäger* were part of the modern German Army, but they were formed under the *Wehrmacht*, not the *Bundeswehr*. When the NCOs got together for beers and wursts or whatever, they liked to sing the old paratrooper songs from World War II. They only did it when the officers weren't around, but NCOs doing stuff when the officers weren't around was what made most successful armies successful.

'Andy, I'm sorry. I lost my cool with you yesterday. I know you have been working hard on this. I'm just frustrated and worried about my daughter.' He hadn't shaved, and it was weird for me to see Dave that way outside of the jungle. His hair, such as he had, was a mess, and I was sure he hadn't showered yet.

'I know. I didn't take it personally. I can only imagine how worried you are.' He had bags under his eyes and looked like he had too much to drink last night.

'It's just . . . she's my daughter . . . I hate thinking of her . . . out there, alone . . .' He looked like he was going to cry. 'I'm sorry, do you want some coffee or a beer?'

'Coffee would be great.' It would give him something to do with his hands, simple repetitive work to keep his mind occupied. Also, I wanted him to be clear headed. I noticed my beer was in the same spot on the counter where I had put it down yesterday. Dave busied himself with his fancy coffee maker and coffee, his back turned to me.

'Dave, what is really going on?'

'What do you mean?'

'Judy didn't run away, did she?' He stopped moving and his shoulders hitched. He slumped over and a sob escaped his chest. I didn't say anything. I wasn't a parent and could only imagine what he was going through. Eventually the coffee maker started making coffee, and that seemed to snap Dave out of it. He turned.

'Why do you say that?'

'She is taking the pill. I found them when I was tossing her room a few days ago. If she was running away with her boyfriend . . . that seems like the last thing she would leave behind.' His face went through about a dozen emotional contortions at once.

'Oh Jesus, you really are a detective, aren't you?' He said it with enough conviction to make me wonder how much he had doubted it. He had lied to me. I wanted to yell at him, but I needed him to talk, not retreat into defensive silence. For now, I would have to swallow my anger.

'Well, that's what it says on my license.'

'You remembered one little detail . . .'

'It was stuck in the back of my brain and something jarred it loose. What is really going on?'

He handed me a cup of black coffee. 'Let's go in the study.'

We walked down the hall. Dave's feet were bare, and he made no noise when he walked. I had liked that about him in the jungle. He moved quietly for a big guy who spent so much time behind a desk in Saigon. He motioned me to the same chair I sat in last time. He went to his desk and rooted around in it. I couldn't help but notice a cheap imitation leather pistol belt with leather holster hanging from the arm of the captain's chair. The buckle looked like it was made from an old brass artillery shell that someone had hammered a star into, not original to the belt. The holster had a pouch for a spare magazine on it that all the Soviet Bloc stuff seemed to have. It was an idea that made sense if you didn't mind taking forever to reload. It was sagging with the weight of the pistol in the holster.

'Is that the old Tokarev you brought home as a war trophy?'

He looked up. 'Huh? Oh, yeah.' With one hand he grabbed the pistol belt and tossed it over to me. I unbuckled the holster and pulled out a Chinese-made copy of a Russian TT-33 Tokarev. The Chinese called it a Type 54, but, in my mind, it would always just be a Tokarev. It looked like the bigger brother of the old Colt 1903 I used to carry, except that it had a round spur hammer and no safety. It was obvious that Fedor Tokarev was not looking to invent a new pistol. It was a little smaller than a .45 caliber Government model. The Tokarev fired a high velocity, light .30 caliber bullet. It would punch through a GI issue steel pot helmet like a hot knife through butter. They were good pistols and were a great example of the Soviet design philosophy: crude but effective is better than pretty and not as reliable.

Dave had taken it off an NVA officer during a prisoner snatch. They were highly prized war trophies. You could tell Dave was an officer, because most self-respecting Special Forces NCOs would have sold it to finance a good time on R&R.

Out of habit I dropped the magazine. It was full of shiny brass bottlenecked cartridges. I racked the slide, and a shiny round popped out and landed at my feet. I bent over to pick it up, fumbled a bit, but got it eventually. When I sat up, Dave was holding some glossy pictures.

'Andy . . . I need you to know that I'm going to break about a thousand rules concerning the handling of classified materials. I could get in a lot of trouble if this were ever to get out. I need to know that I can count on your discretion.' He was looking intently at me, his face a mask of seriousness. This felt like some pre-mission briefing back when I was in Recon. I wouldn't have been surprised if he was going to have us synchronize watches.

'Hey, man, it's been a while, but I used to have a Top Secret clearance. I'm pretty sure I still remember how to keep a secret.' His underestimating me was starting to grate on me.

'OK, OK, my career is on the line, my daughter's life . . . I have to know that you . . . you know.'

'I get it, man. What is going on?'

'You know that I was in Germany for several years. First at Bad Tölz and then in Berlin.'

'Yeah, I saw the mugs in the kitchen. I get it.' Dave was about as bad at getting to the point as anyone I have ever met.

'Have you heard of something called "Detachment A"?'

'In Berlin?'

'Yes, in Berlin.'

'I have heard rumors and whispers. A secret Special Forces unit, guys who can pass for German or Eastern European. Guys like me who grew up speaking the language. Back in the early days, there were a lot of Lodge Act guys in it. Their mission is to stay behind if the Soviets attack the West, sabotage as much stuff as they can, and raise a guerilla army to fight the commies. Something like that?'

'That is pretty much it. They also do some intel stuff, collecting, spying, and a bunch of counter-terrorism stuff. The point is, they're super secret. Most people in our own Special Forces don't know they exist.'

'Dave, the funny thing about guys in Special Forces is that, while they're good at keeping secrets from everyone else . . . they talk to each other.' I had heard about Det A, as it was called, from an old Recon pal. We had run into each other in

1978 and got rip-roaring drunk. He told me about the unit and told me I would be perfect for it. Vietnam was still a recent enough memory that I didn't want anything to do with the Army. Whether I was perfect for it or not. No matter how cool the mission sounded. The next morning, he sheepishly swore me to secrecy. It was pointless, as I didn't have anyone to tell.

'Yeah, I can see that.' He handed me a series of black and white photos. They were all of the same man, all taken through a telephoto lens, and all were blown up to the size of notebook paper. The top of each one had been stamped 'TOP SECRET' in red ink. I flipped through them. They were all of the same middle-aged man with a slim, athletic build. He was bald with a Van Dyke beard and round metal glasses. He wore slacks, a jacket, and tie. The jacket looked like it was corduroy and had patches on the elbow. He had a trench coat thrown over one arm. The pictures were taken in Harvard Square by the T station and the kiosk that sold international newspapers and magazines.

'We know him as Dieter. He is an East German intelligence agent. Stasi – you know, their version of the KGB.' Dave's voice had dropped a conspiratorial octave.

'What does he have to do with Judy's running away?'

'Andy . . . Judy is hooked on smack. Heroin.' I didn't bother to point out to Dave that I knew what smack was. Like all Army officers Dave had a tendency to overexplain the simple stuff.

'She is with him. I think he paid her boyfriend in Boston to get her hooked and then paid the boyfriend to leave her with him. He keeps her supplied.' He was looking at me intently, and it must have been painful even to admit it.

'OK. Why?' It seemed a lot of trouble to go through. Most of the time spies wanted assets to work with them willingly. I had heard it likened to a seduction. Whatever Dave had, it must have been valuable for Dieter to coerce him into betraying his country. It was a risky way to go about developing a source, unless it was one that you didn't plan on using more than once or twice.

'My last two years in Berlin, I was the Commander of Det A. Dieter has Judy and wants me to give him all the names of the guys in Det A. Not only that, but all their contacts, their caches, and their safehouses. Their unit SOPs, codes, technical data, all of it. Everything I know. If I do that, he will give me back Judy. If I don't, he told me he will send movies of Judy . . . of Judy doing stuff . . .' He sobbed. 'He'll send them to my Command and to the security people. Then give her to a pimp.'

'Jesus!'

'Andy, he is a monster. She's my little girl. I don't care about my career; it is over once this gets out. But if I give him what he wants, he will give her back.'

'Except he won't, will he?' Blackmailers never willingly give away their leverage when they can still milk their victims. Dave had to know a lot of stuff and could potentially supply a wealth of valuable intelligence. Especially once he got promoted, he would be looped into all of the Army's most secret plans in Europe. 'Why didn't you tell me this up front? If I had known what I was looking for initially, I might have been able to find her. Jesus, Dave, think of all the time I wasted fucking around in Boston looking for a teenage runaway. I could have been looking for her in the right places days ago.' I was angry and it didn't matter if he saw it.

'When I first talked to you, I didn't know. Then you were out there looking, and I figured, who knows, you might find her, and everything would work out. I know it isn't rational, but I'm desperate. You were always good in the woods. No matter how bad the mission, you always managed to pull it off. You had this weird luck, they used to call it "Roark's luck" behind your back. I thought this time wouldn't be any different.'

'Well, it would have helped if you had been straight with me. You know I would have tried to find her no matter what. I wouldn't have wasted so much fucking time.' And I wouldn't have beaten a guy into confessing to me that he didn't know where she was. 'Now I'm behind the eight ball because you lied to me.'

'I know. I know. I'm sorry. I'm desperate. I'm trying to save my career, save the guys, and save her. I know you might not think much of a career in the Army, but it is almost all I have. Judy hates me, and Barbara and I are married in name only. Oh, god, Andy. I failed her . . .' He let out a long moan and was racked with sobs. I gave him a few moments to collect himself.

'OK . . . OK . . . what can you tell me about this guy, Dieter?' I tapped the topmost photo for emphasis.

'He is some sort of visiting professor at Harvard. We think he lives somewhere in Cambridge, but we don't know much more about him than that.'

'How does he make contact with you?'

'He calls me. The first time he sent me some pictures of Judy she was . . . she was with two men in bed. There were instructions to be at my phone here at a certain time.'

'When are you supposed to hand the intel over to him, and how?'

'He hasn't contacted me about that yet. But I only have a couple of days to get it to him.'

'OK, do you still have the original stuff he sent you? It might have some clues.'

'I couldn't keep that. They were pictures of Judy with two men . . . doing things . . . I couldn't keep those pictures, Andy. I just couldn't. I burned them in the fireplace.'

'OK. I will head to Cambridge and find Dieter.'

'Then what?'

'I will get Judy back.'

'Just like that?'

'More or less.'

'If you pull this off, I mean, if you bring my daughter back, I will owe you. I won't ever be able to repay you.'

'There is no need to. You saved my life in-country. If you hadn't come back for me and slung me on that helicopter, I wouldn't be here.'

'Andy, what I'm getting at is that you should come back in. We've had a few guys do it. You would either come in as an E-5, buck sergeant, or if you have your college degree, you could come in as an officer. The Army needs guys like you. Special Forces needs guys like you.'

'I don't know. I have been out so long that I don't know how I would take to taking orders again.'

'Everyone takes orders in life. It is just that the Army is more up front about it. You would be a shoo-in for Tenth Group. You could come work for me, and I would take care of you. I need a man I know I can trust.

'You know you miss being SF. You can't tell me you don't miss the camaraderie, the brotherhood?' He was leaning forward and looking at me intensely. 'You'd have a steady paycheck again, healthcare . . . the Army would take care of you. Andy, we could get the old magic back . . . just like Vietnam . . . but think of what we could achieve, both of us in Group, fighting the commies again.' I didn't have the heart to tell him that last time we had fought the commies together my team was decimated, and I was almost killed.

'It sounds tempting, Dave. It really does.' And it did. I missed all the things he said I did. The brotherhood, the sense of purpose, the feeling of belonging to something bigger than me. The feeling of being part of history, of being a player on the world stage. Not like Kissinger, but doing my part. 'Let's focus on getting Judy back and then we can worry about the rest of it.' My mind was already trying to figure out how to track down Dieter.

'Andy, I want you to think about it seriously.'

'I will.'

'Seriously, after you bring Judy back, then we will get you back into the Army. Back into SF where you belong. No more playing private eye. It's time for you to come home too.' I didn't have the heart to tell him that the bruises and scars didn't feel much like playing. It was a tantalizing prospect. I didn't have any family to speak of, and the Army had been a good substitute for one. That was the funny thing about the Army. I met a lot of guys in it who had been from dysfunctional families, broken homes. The Army drew us all in and offered us what we were missing.

I put the magazine back in the Tokarev, and the pistol back in its holster. I tossed the whole thing to Dave, then the loose round. 'Catch.' He caught it easily and hung it back over the chair arm.

'I want you to really think about it. You could have a home with SF again.'

'OK, Dave, I will, I will. Now let me get out of here so I can go find Judy.'

'Call me the minute you know anything.'

'Call me if you hear from Dieter,' I countered.

'I will. I swear.'

'And Dave.'

'Yes.'

'Don't lie to me again. Ever. I don't care how good the reason is. If you do that I will walk. Got it?'

'Yes.'

I stood up and we shook hands. I noticed that Dave's dollar bill was still under the ashtray. He slid the pictures of Dieter into a plain manila envelope and handed it to me. I walked out and he watched me from the door, raising a hand to wave when I started the Maverick and steered it toward Boston with a new sense of purpose. For the first time in a long time, a sense of opportunity too.

SIXTEEN

drove to the office. The only changes I could see since I had been out were not good ones. Marconi's was completely gone, and the video store was slowly taking shape. Good pizza and excellent espresso had given way to the tyranny of progress in the form of VHS tapes and videocassette player rentals. I wanted to believe that there was still the faintest trace of the smell of pizza sauce in the back stairwell.

I let myself into my office and dug a magnifying glass out of a drawer in my desk. I wanted to have a close look at the photos of Dieter to see if there was anything in them that would help me find him. They were good, high resolution pictures probably taken from a car or a restaurant with a 35mm camera and telephoto lens. The Army had spent some time teaching us Recon men how to use a camera. It came in handy for the few divorce or insurance fraud cases I took. Whoever had taken these photos knew what they were doing.

The photos showed me that he probably had light brown hair around the edges of his otherwise bald head and wore a signet ring on his left pinky. He went into the newsagent's and came out with a copy of *Der Spiegel* in his hand. The pictures followed him as he disappeared into the mouth of the T station. There was a clock visible in one of the pictures, and the hands were pointing to a little after four. It was daytime, so it had to be four in the afternoon. When I had looked at the photos through a magnifying glass to the point where my head started to ache, I put them back in the envelope and then locked them in the big safe that had come with the office.

The only thing that I could think of was to go hang around Harvard Square and see if he was around in the afternoon. I might be able to find someone to talk to at Harvard to see if they had a list of visiting professors. There couldn't be that many from Germany. But it was the weekend and the university's offices were all closed. If she would answer the phone,

Brenda Watts might be able to introduce me to the local counter-espionage agent at the FBI. If I could get her to answer the phone, maybe I could get Sir Leominster back.

I locked up the office and headed back to my apartment. There was a message from Sue on the answering machine when I got back. She wanted to know if I had plans Sunday. I called her back and told her answering machine that I didn't, and she should call me when she woke up. I called the answering service only to have them tell me that there were no messages. Story of my life.

There wasn't much in the refrigerator, but I was able to cobble together enough to have a grilled cheese sandwich with bacon and a fried egg in it. I found a Löwenbräu in the fridge to wash it down and sat down to see what was on the Movie Loft. Dana Hersey was showing *The Parallax View*, which was a moderately engrossing bit of post-Nixon era paranoia. Somewhere around the point where Warren Beatty uses a fishing rod to kill a man, I switched from beer to whiskey. The whiskey helped kill the pain of the slide montage set to music that is supposed to be some sort of psychological profiling test for Beatty's character. During another commercial break, I poured myself another whiskey.

I started to wonder what it would be like to be back in the Army. Would it be weird to put on a uniform again, to take orders, or would it be comforting to belong to something again? It might be fun to jump out of airplanes again. Or fly in a helicopter, standing on the skid getting ready to go into an LZ. It was probably all computerized now. Missions were probably approved or cancelled based on what some giant IBM monstrosity in the basement of the Pentagon had to say.

I got up and went to the closet where I kept a box of stuff from when I was in the Army. I took it back to the coffee table and the couch. I went to the kitchen to refill my glass with whiskey and ice, went back to the couch, and opened the box. On top was my old beret with its 5th Group flash, its diagonal yellow bar with three red lines in the middle on a field of black. There were a couple of the SOG beret flashes and uniform patches with the distinctive skull logo. There were patches from the teams I had been on. Also inside was an old set of my dog tags, taped together on their shiny metal beaded chain. In addition I found a Fairbairn-Sykes commando knife that Tony had given me in Vietnam. It wasn't practical to take on missions, but I wore it into town, tucked under my uniform shirt as part of my going-to-town kit. That usually included a .45 automatic or .38 snub-nosed revolver.

There were a lot of black and white pictures of me and guys I had served with on different teams. Most of them were taken in clubs or bars. In some we were clowning around out by the landing pads or the gun bunkers. There were pictures of me, Chris, and Tony goofing around. Pictures of me with my first team, then later some when I was the One-Zero. There were lots of pictures of men in uniform standing around with guns, bristling with grenades and weapons. Posing for posterity or for laughs.

Down toward the bottom of the box was a battered Zippo lighter. It was engraved with CCN, my team name, and something on the other side about fearing no evil. At the very bottom were some medals, a few paper citations, and my DD-214, which was the Army document that certified my honorable discharge.

Now Dave Billings was offering it all to me again. A team, a job, camaraderie, and brotherhood. That, and a steady paycheck. Maybe it was the only thing that made sense. As Boston got meaner, the pimps and drug dealers were the only ones who seemed to be prospering, while the Marconis of the world were leaving, their business bought out by chain stores and their health ruined by cancer. Maybe going back into the service was the only thing that made sense anymore. Maybe I had been wrong about leaving, maybe I needed the structure and the order of the Army. God knows, the chaos of civilian life hadn't provided me with much in the way of happiness in the last decade or so. I put everything back in the box and took my thoughts to bed with me.

That night in my dreams Ger and I were moving out from the landing zone as the helicopter pulled away. We started to move off the LZ when he stopped and looked at me. 'Welcome back, *trung sĩ*.' Then he frowned, looking at something in his hand I couldn't make out. 'The numbers are wrong.' Then he turned to smile at me, and his head exploded. Again.

Sunday late morning found me in Cambridge, in Harvard Square. I started with the newsagent's by the T stop. I had put a piece of tape over the TOP SECRET stamp and was showing the best picture of Dieter that I had to the people who worked there. No one recognized him. Then I went to the Harvard Cooperative – the Coop, as it is known – and showed it to everyone who worked there. Again, no dice. I tried the numerous bookstores and cafés that lined the area. No one in Cardullo's delicatessen recognized him either. They had been in Harvard Square since 1950 and were a fixture. If they hadn't seen him, maybe he hadn't been there. Dieter was proving as hard to find as Judy Billings.

I was hungry and thirsty and frustrated. This case seemed to be all dead ends. The only good thing of note to come of it so far was Sue coming around again. I looked across the street. Hanging from the third floor of a building was a six foot by six foot sign for Löwenbräu. It wasn't exactly a beacon. But it was a sign for the Wursthaus.

The Wursthaus was an institution in Harvard Square since 1917. Cardullo had bought it in 1942, a bold move during a time when we were at war with Germany. It did well enough that he was able to open his deli across the street. The Wursthaus had the best German food on this side of the Atlantic Ocean and a selection of German beer that was unparalleled. The food was so authentic that visiting German students and professors practically encamped in the place.

I walked up to the faux-Bavarian exterior and went inside. It was dark and cool compared to the warm, bright June air outside. I found a seat at the bar and the bartender came over. She was dressed in blue jeans and a black button-down shirt. After all, this was June, not October, so no dirndl dress.

'What can I get you?'

'Löwenbräu, please.' She went down the bar to a tap and pulled a pilsner glass full for me. After all, this was the stuff from Germany. She brought it back with a coaster.

'Menu?'

'No, thanks. I know what I would like.'

'Sure, what'll it be?'

'Sauerbraten, with Rotkohl and Spätzle, please.' She wrote

it down and went to put the order in. I pity people who have never had Sauerbraten. It is basically German pot roast except, like all great things German, it is far more complex than that. The roast is marinated in a vinegar-based marinade for three days to a week, and then – and only then – does the cooking start. It is roasted on a bed of vegetables and some of the marinade. Some recipes add raisins or gingersnaps to cut the sour taste. The meat is tender and flavorful, and out of this world when done right.

The Rotkohl is a sweet and sour version of red cabbage with onions and apples. It is cooked slowly in broth and is the perfect pairing for Sauerbraten. The Spätzle is the thing that balances it out. It is essentially German pasta, but the dough is worked more and cooks quickly. It is chewier, with more body, and there is nothing quite like it.

She came back to see if I needed anything. I put a twenty-dollar bill on the bar, and the picture of Dieter facing her. 'I'm a private investigator. This guy might be a witness to a car accident. A hit and run, and I need to find him. Have you seen him around here? He might be European or German.'

'I dunno, mister.'

'My client was hit by a big truck. His car is totaled, and his hospital bills are huge. If we can find this guy, we might be able to identify the company the truck was driving for. Please, he's got kids and he is out of work. Just take a look.' If I knew how, I would make puppy dog eyes at her.

'OK.' She picked up the picture and looked at it. 'He was in here a month ago, maybe six weeks.'

'And you are sure it was this guy, the guy in the picture?'

'Yeah, he was wearing those same clothes . . . he had that ring. You don't see a lot of guys wearing rings like that.'

'Yeah.' I finally had something approaching a lead. I wanted her to tell me more.

'Yeah. It was weird. He came in and went right to the bathroom. Two guys came in, fit looking, long hair, mustaches . . . like yours. They looked around and decided to sit down at a table. Your guy came out and watched them from the alcove. Then he came and sat down at the bar. He had a schnapps and went over to them. He said something to them like, "You guys need more practice." They all laughed and then he left. The two other guys looked embarrassed, maybe a little angry.'

'Did he have an accent?'

'Yeah, pretty thick one.'

'German?'

'No . . . Brooklyn.'

'He wasn't German?' I asked.

'Nope, not unless he moved to Brooklyn as a baby.' I slid the twenty to her and took the picture. She brought my food and another beer. I sat chewing my food mechanically, not tasting it. Trying to figure it out. Maybe she had the wrong guy. Or maybe the Stasi had taught Dieter to cover his accent well. Clearly someone was surveilling him and he made them. Either they needed some work or Dieter was that good.

After lunch I drove back to my apartment. The downside of two beers and a heavy German lunch was that I wanted to take a nap on the couch. My brain didn't want to think about anything other than closing my eyes. I stopped at my office long enough to put the picture of Dieter back with the others in the safe and futilely check with my answering service. Then I went back to the apartment.

In the end the idea of a nap won out and I stretched out on the couch. I closed my eyes and then I was flying in a Huey, feet out on the skids, CAR-15 resting on my thighs. We circled down to a bomb crater and I jumped off just in time to see the Karmann Ghia, with the girl in it, blow up. I was knocked on my ass and when I got up there was a crumpled Mustang, one side painted in gray primer, against a tree. I rushed up to it and I could smell the coolant and the melting plastic. Derrick Page's broken and bloody face looked at me from the smashed windshield. His mouth was moving but I could not hear the words. Then the car caught on fire with a *whoosh*!

I woke up with the afternoon sun in my face. I was hot and my mouth was dry. I went to the kitchen for some water. What had he been trying to tell me?

The phone rang, and I was expecting Sue. I made it to the phone before the machine picked up.

'Hello.'

'Hi, Roark.' It was Special Agent Brenda Watts, the woman with honey-colored hair. Cat abductor *extraordinaire.*

'Hi, Brenda. Calling to ransom my cat?' I said it jokingly.

'No, I will bring him by eventually. He is good company. A hell of a lot smarter and more charming than his owner.'

'So I remember. To what do I owe the call, then?'

'Oh, I had a busy weekend and only now have time to call.' I was sensing sarcasm.

'I'm sorry to hear you had a busy weekend. I hope it wasn't work related?'

'Funny you should mention it; it was.'

'Oh, that's too bad.'

'Yes, it is. It seems two guys got beaten up pretty good. One is a low level mob associate who works in the Combat Zone. Kind of a smallish drug dealer.' She could only be talking about Sailor.

'Oh, not too bad, I hope.' I too am well versed in sarcasm.

'Fractured skull and a concussion, could have been worse.'

'That's good, and the other guy?' I knew where she was going but, as my friends from Texas like to say, *You gotta dance with the one that brung ya.*

'He is busted up pretty bad. He has a broken arm, a broken ankle, a pretty bad concussion, and looks like someone black-jacked him a lot. Lots of blows to soft tissue, nothing too permanent, just painful. Funny thing was, he crashed his car and the local boys found guns and drugs in it.'

'Well, that is good. What does this have to do with me?'

'Well, it seems in both cases, before misfortune befell them, they were seen talking to a guy who, and I quote, "looked a little rough around the edges, had a mustache and needed a haircut," end quote. Someone described the person as "mangy looking."' Her voice tinkled; she was on the cusp of laughter.

'So naturally you thought of me?'

'Naturally. That, and also, while the FBI doesn't care much about the goings-on of local drug dealers and pimps – and half-assed PIs for that matter – we do care if it jeopardizes ongoing investigations into organized crime. My boss was looking to bring you in and have a talk with you about the status of your continued liberty and your ability to maintain your license.'

'Oh.' I had no desire to get arrested or lose my license.

'I reassured him that I could probably talk to you and that you could be convinced to put whatever your current crusade is aside in the interest of not making a bunch of already nervous mobsters jumpier and fucking up our investigation. Whaddya say, sport? Think you can help out?' Her sarcasm was artistic in its delivery . . . that was the only way to describe it.

'Sure, Brenda . . . anything for Mr Hoover's boys and girls.' She wasn't the only one who could be sarcastic. 'Watts, what about my cat?' I asked too late to the dial tone. As was her way when she was finished talking to me, she had just hung up on me. I was starting to think that I didn't bring out the best in her.

So the FBI was watching the Liberty Book Shop. And they had their eyes on K-nice too. I wondered what they were investigating. It wasn't drugs, because that would be the DEA's jurisdiction. They were looking into the mob angle, which would make sense. I'm sure that plenty of people in the Combat Zone paid protection money. Most of the businesses in the Combat Zone were cash businesses, which meant there were a lot of opportunities to launder money. There were plenty of activities in the Combat Zone that could be covered by the RICO statute. None of it was any of my business. I just wanted to find Dieter and Judy.

The next time the phone rang it was Sue. After we had said our hellos and asked each other about our days, Sue got down to business. 'Andy, I think you should take me out to dinner. Somewhere nice.' She was direct, to say the least. It was one of the things that I liked about her, and it was one of her most infuriating qualities.

'What are you in the mood for?' Boston has a lot of great restaurants, many of which are closed on Sunday nights.

'Fish. I'm in the mood for sea food.'

'Legal Sea Foods or the Union Oyster House?' The Union Oyster House was one of the oldest restaurants in America and Legal Sea Foods in the Park Plaza Hotel was considerably newer. 'The Union will be jammed, but it is worth the wait.

Legal's might be easier to get into, but it won't have the same ambience.' Frankly, nothing has the same ambience as the Union Oyster House.

'Hmmnn . . . Let's go to Legal's, it's closer.'

'OK, that works. Should I come pick you up?'

'No, I will come to your place. Say, six thirty?'

'Sure, I will make a reservation.'

'Cool, see you then.' Sometimes, without intending to, Sue reminds me that she is younger than me.

'See ya.'

I hung up and got out the yellow pages. I found Legal Sea Foods' number between a bail bondsman's and a criminal defense attorney's. I called, and eventually was able to get a reservation for two at seven. Thank god it was a Sunday night; otherwise we wouldn't have gotten a reservation, or wouldn't have been able to eat until almost ten thirty.

I had a couple of hours to kill before I had to get in the shower. There was nothing good on the TV, so I went to the bookshelf and pulled down a James Crumley novel that I had put there waiting for just such an occasion. It sucked me into the gritty world of Missoula, Montana: barflies, whiskey, drugs, and crime. Time passed quickly and before I knew it, it was time to get cleaned up.

I was dinner-ready with some boat shoes, faded blue jeans, and a white button-down shirt. I had a lightweight khaki sport coat to throw over it all. The sport coat was mostly to cover the fact that I was carrying the .38 holstered in my waistband. I had the usual – wallet, Zippo lighter, speedloader, and Buck knife – all in their appropriate places. I was wearing my Seiko dive watch on my left wrist. I looked reasonably presentable and had splashed on just a little bay rum aftershave.

Sue was a few minutes late, so we didn't waste any time heading to Legal's. I did have enough time to notice she was wearing a brown summer dress with flowers on it, buttons down the front, and wedge-heeled sandals. She had small diamond earrings in her ears and a gold chain that disappeared into her cleavage. She had put on perfume, and it was hard to take my eyes off her.

Legal Sea Foods is in the Park Plaza Hotel on the first floor.

It is the old Statler Hotel, which when it was built was the tallest building in Boston and a model for mixed business-use occupancy. It is a triangular building that takes up a whole block of Boston not far from the Common, the Greyhound station, and the Combat Zone.

The maître d' took us to a table by a window where we sat down. When the waitress came Sue ordered a martini and I followed her lead. There was a little candle on the table, but it was June and it wouldn't be dark for almost two more hours. It didn't matter, it was nice to be sitting across the table from a pretty lady in a nice restaurant. We looked at the menus and didn't say much until the martinis arrived.

'Andy, how do you feel about oysters?'

'As a rule, pretty good. They're tasty, but their reputation as an aphrodisiac is highly overrated. Would you like to order some?' Andy Roark, oyster critic.

'Yes, let's split a dozen. Then later we can put your theory to the test.' She smiled or, more accurately, leered at me.

'I like where you are going with this.' It is important to be supportive.

'I'm a girl of appetites.' The waiter came with the martinis. He put the martini glasses down, empty except for two skewered olives, and poured the clearer than clear liquid from the shakers, which he put down next to the glasses. I like martinis. It is impossible to drink one and not pretend for a second that you are James Bond. Purists like them stirred with gin, but I like mine to be made with vodka and shaken near to death.

Sue was holding hers up to toast. We carefully clinked glasses and she said, 'Here's how.'

'And how.' I took a sip and the vodka, with almost no vermouth in it as a dry martini should be, was cold enough to make my fillings hum.

'Emmn, that is good. Andy, this is nice.' She took her skewered olives out of the glass and nibbled on them.

'Yes, it is.' She smiled and I smiled back. The dozen oysters we had ordered came. They were nestled on a bed of cracked ice on a platter with parsley for garnish, lemon wedges, and two little dishes of cocktail sauce.

'Do you like lemon juice on your oysters?' Sue asked.

'Yes.' She squeezed lemon wedges over the oysters, drizzling the juice on them. She picked one up and spooned a little cocktail sauce on it. She lifted the shell to her lips – her bottom lip was a work of art – and tipped the whole thing into her mouth. I watched her throat as she swallowed it and began to wonder if there wasn't something to this whole aphrodisiac thing.

'Andy, you are staring.'

'Sorry, I was rethinking my stance on oysters as an aphrodisiac after watching you eat one.' I gave her what I hoped was a lascivious grin. Sue blushed, a pink-colored blush that started where her gold chain disappeared.

'Andy, you have a dirty mind.'

'It is one of my better features.'

'Yes, it is.' She smiled back at me. I took an oyster and put a bit of cocktail sauce on it, then tipped it into my mouth, slurping it down, enjoying the briny chewiness of it. You either love oysters or hate them . . . I love them.

'You know, Andy, after watching you, I might have a few ideas of my own.' I was about to reply with an ungentlemanly suggestion, but the waiter arrived to check on us. We ordered our entrees: lobster for Sue and a cod dish for me, and another martini each. We kept working our way through our martinis and oysters.

'Andy, how is the case going? You haven't found her yet?'

'No, every lead turns out to be a dead end.' Especially for Derrick Page.

'Ugh, that stinks.' She wrinkled her nose sympathetically.

'Yeah, it does. Though something odd happened.'

'What?' I watched another oyster disappear as she held it to her lips.

'Dave Billings said I should go back into the Army. That I could go back into Special Forces . . . maybe even be an officer.'

'Huh . . . that is weird. I can't see you in the Army, much less being an officer, having responsibilities. You are too much on your own . . . a lone wolf or a stray cat or something.'

'Yeah, Dave's selling point other than camaraderie is that it could provide me with a normal, steady life.'

'As a Green Beret. Jumping out of planes and stuff . . . well, if that is your idea of normal.'

'Jumping out of planes is fun.' Once the canopy opened, it was quite peaceful if everything worked and no one was shooting at you. Landing was a different story. 'I think he meant more having a place to belong again, having a steady paycheck and health insurance . . . stuff like that.' Possibly Dave was right in that maybe I needed some structure in my life. 'Plus, we aren't at war right now. The peacetime Army is very different from when we're at war.'

'But you would still be in the Army, still a Green Beret, right?'

'Well, that is the gist of Dave's offer.' The whole conversation was punctuated by the occasional oyster slurped or martini sipped. When the glasses got low, we topped them off from the sidecars that the waiter had left. There are few things as fine as an ice cold dry martini on a summer's night. Throw in a pretty lady and some oysters and it was about as good as it could get.

'Are you going to go back in?' She looked at me over the rim of a perilously depleted martini glass.

'It is worth thinking about. Dave made a lot of great points. Not the least of which was that when I was in the Army, in Vietnam, I felt like I had a sense of purpose. That has been missing lately. On the other hand, I have a lot of freedom now that I would be giving up if I went back in.'

The waiter arrived with our entrees. Sue had ordered a boiled lobster and steamed new potatoes with butter, garlic and dill. There was a ceramic ramekin of coleslaw to round it out. I ordered the special, which was a riff on a French bistro staple, baked cod with onions and potatoes, all with a trace of grated Gruyère on it. The original dish involved salted cod. Here it was fresh cod loin with butter, sliced onions that had caramelized in the oven, and new potatoes. It had been baked and seasoned to perfection. The art of it was in its simplicity. It was offered with a cup of New England clam chowder, not that clam minestrone that they try and pass off as chowder in Manhattan. The waiter had insisted that my meal be accompanied by a vegetable, and I chose spinach in cream sauce. Sue and I had wisely ordered another martini each. It was going to be one of those nights.

'Do you miss it? The Army, I mean, because when we were together you didn't seem like you did.' It was a fair question.

'I miss the guys . . . I miss having a sense of purpose . . . doing something important, but the Army itself? The big Green Machine? Not so much . . . but Dave's offer is still pretty tempting.'

'I think you would get pissed off. You like your freedom. I mean, even having me around regularly seemed to annoy you.' I had always thought that she was pissed off at me.

'You didn't annoy me. I just . . . I like to be able to do my own thing. Do things my way. It wasn't anything you did. It was never you.' She had been pissed off at me a lot when we were together. The long silences and the nights coming home late from watching cheating spouses hadn't thrilled her.

'Thank you. That is nice to hear. I had wondered.'

We ate our food and drank our cocktails. We probably should have been drinking a good white wine but sometimes you just want martinis. This was one of those times.

Later, back at my apartment, both of us a little drunk, I was slowly unbuttoning Sue's dress, and she was urgently trying to get me out of my clothes. She was her usual direct self, and we made love partially clothed on the couch. Later still she took me in hand and led me to the bedroom. We made love slowly and then fell asleep in each other's arms.

When I woke up after seeing Ger's face explode, after he told me again that the numbers were wrong, I managed not to wake her. I pressed myself against her trying to draw some of her warmth into me to abate the chill that was making me shiver.

SEVENTEEN

I woke up Monday morning to an empty bed. I could hear Sue moving around in the living room. I got out of bed and went to see what she was doing. She was buttoning up her sundress.

'Hey.' I said it softly, but it sounded loud in the apartment.

'Jesus, Andy . . . you startled me. I thought you were still asleep.' She sat down on the couch and pushed some hair away from her face.

'Yeah . . . I was. Where are you going? It's still early.'

'I have to go.'

'OK, call me later.'

'No, Andy. I don't think so.' She looked at me then. 'Andy, I'm engaged.'

'Huh.' Somehow of all the things I thought she might say, that hadn't been one of them.

'Engaged to a guy – you know, to get married.'

'Yeah, I know what it means. I didn't see a ring.' It is funny, in Army speak, to engage means to attack. Engagement refers to being in a fire fight. Maybe that is why I was still unmarried.

'I don't wear it at work . . . I don't wear it when . . . when I'm seeing you.' A tear started to slide over her cheekbone and then another followed.

'Oh . . . OK . . . um . . .' I was truly at a loss for words.

'He is a nice guy. A good guy.' The tears were coming more frequently now.

'Sure, yeah.' I had no idea what to say.

'But you walked into Anthony's . . . and I hadn't seen you, and you . . . and there you were, tall and handsome and dangerous. I had this vision of being married to a nice . . . safe guy. Then I wondered what it would be like, one more time. You know . . . just one more fling with you before I settled down.' She started crying in earnest.

'Sue, it's OK.'

'No, it isn't. He is a good guy. He doesn't deserve this. I thought that I could, you know . . . have the best of both worlds.'

'Sue, he is lucky to be with you.' She started crying even more at that. I sat next to her and awkwardly put my arm around her. She cried on me, tears running down my side.

'Let me get you some tissues.' I wanted to put something on. I pulled my jeans on and went to find some tissues. I was making my way back to the living room when I heard the door slam. I was standing barefoot wearing my jeans and holding a wad of tissues in my hand, staring at the door.

Maybe it was just as well. I had been starting to entertain thoughts of asking her to come by more often. Maybe even move back in. I had entertained thoughts of being back in the Army and of her in my life full time. They were the type of thoughts that made me want to have a more regular life, a BMW in the driveway, and a house with her in it to come home to. The type of life where on Saturday afternoons in the summer everyone washed and waxed their cars in the driveway. That type of thinking could get a guy like me killed.

Instead of going after her, I went back to bed. But the sheets and pillows were a mess. The whole thing smelled like sex, and I was starting to get annoyed with myself for thinking foolish thoughts. I got up, stripped the bed, and then got into the shower.

Later I was sitting barefoot in jeans and a t-shirt at my kitchen table. I had a cup of strong coffee, the remains of some toast, and a Lucky Strike burning softly in the ashtray. I had out my yellow legal pad and the felt-tip pens. I was adding to my notes. Everything involving Dieter ended in question marks. Was he such a skilled spy that he could pass for a New Yorker? Maybe a thick accent hid more mistakes? Was the guy the bartender identified at the Wursthaus really Dieter? Had I blown it?

I walked over to the phone and called Dave. He picked up on the third ring.

'Andy, do you have something?'

'No, Dave, nothing yet. I might have something, but I want to talk about it in person.'

'Sure, why don't you come up here tonight? I'm tied up all day, but why don't we meet at the Fort?' The Fort was a bar just off post where the guys from 10th Group hung out. It wasn't that other types of soldiers couldn't go there for a beer, but it was a Special Forces hangout. Legs and others were like children if they went in, best seen and not heard. It certainly wasn't a place to go to start a fight unless you felt you had too many teeth or not enough broken bones.

'Sure, what time?'

'I have a busy afternoon today. We're getting some trigger time in on the range. Let's say eighteen hundred?' He couldn't even arrange to meet for beers without it sounding like an Operations Order.

'OK, eighteen hundred hours at the Fort.'

I got out the yellow pages and went to the section that had universities. I found Harvard and started calling different departments to see if I could find Dieter. For a bunch of really bright Ivy League types it was surprising that no one seemed bright enough to find him. I mean I told them his first name, and that he was German and had a Brooklyn accent. What more did they need? I called all the other colleges and universities as well. But there was no joy. There was no Dieter.

I spent the rest of the day cleaning the apartment as if to exorcise my thoughts of having a normal life. A normal life with a nice, normal girl. I dragged the dirty laundry, bedding, and everything down the flights of the back stairs to the cellar where the coin-operated laundry was. While they washed and spun, I cleaned the bathroom. Had I really thought she was coming back to me? When the laundry was done and I had cleaned as much as I was going to, I sat back down with the legal pad and went over my notes. I read and reread them, and they brought me no closer to finding Judy Billings or the elusive Dieter.

I pulled into the parking lot of the Fort a little past six. The lot was mostly full, but I managed to find a spot. Dave's little BMW was not far from where I parked the Maverick. Most of the cars in the lot had small stickers on the driver's side

that indicated they were registered on post. The Army wasn't
content to rely solely on the Commonwealth's vast bureaucracy
and had to add its own layer.

I made my way into the bar. It was dark and smoke-filled.
It was crowded though it was only a Monday night. Everywhere
there were fit Special Forces types with hair and mustaches
that were a little bit too long, and women who were with or
looking to be with such men. What woman could resist the
charms of a real live Snake Eater? Apparently the ones who
always end up leaving me.

Somewhere a jukebox was playing Waylon Jennings, who
was singing about sitting in a spot and drinking instead of
romancing a lady friend. On the walls were pictures of men
in uniform, all Green Berets. The pictures spanned the period
from 1952 when the 10th Special Forces Group was stood up,
through Vietnam, to the new pictures of men in the standard
camouflage Battle Dress uniform. BDU's were splotchy
camouflage, unlike the olive drab green jungle uniforms we
had or the exotic, Hollywood style tiger-striped camouflage.
Here and there things like snowshoes, skis, ice axes, and
plaques with Fairbairn-Sykes commando daggers decorated
the walls. There were lots of plaques that had Jump Wings on
them too. There were tables with polished wood tops and
chairs with black vinyl upholstery. There was carpet on the
floor that was a dingy shade of green, the victim of too many
spilled beers over the years.

Dave was decorating a barstool, one foot on the brass rail,
one hand on a beer. He had pulled himself together since I
last saw him. His clothes were neat, he had shaved, and he
saw me coming in the mirror behind the polished mahogany
bar. He turned and smiled at me. We shook hands and I sat
on the stool next to him.

'Hey, Andy. Good to see you.'

'You too, Dave.'

'Beer?' He was already motioning to the bartender.

'Löwenbräu.'

'Sure,' then to the bartender, 'Löwenbräu for my friend.'

'So, I went to Harvard Square and showed a masked copy
of Dieter's picture around.' I didn't want Dave to freak out

about my showing his Top Secret pictures around. The Army takes the handling of classified material very seriously. Also, just having those pictures in my safe could get me in big, federal prison type of trouble. Over the years the Army had developed a thousand ways of controlling classified materials to ensure they didn't fall into the wrong hands. I wasn't sure how Dave managed to get the pictures of Dieter out of the office and back to his house.

'How'd it go?' We paused while the bartender put my beer down in front of me and Dave slid him a bill from a small stack of bills in front of him. Change from his last beer.

'The photos you gave me were taken in Cambridge, Harvard Square, so I went there looking for him. I showed his picture around to everyone: stores, bars, restaurants, newsagents, bookstores that deal in foreign books, pretty much every place I could walk into. Only the bartender in the Wursthaus recognized him. She said he sounded American. He must be good. From what she described, it sounds like he was under surveillance and he caught them at it. That was it. It is likely they drove him underground.' It wasn't much to offer a man whose daughter was being held ransom by a Stasi agent. 'I wish I had more to offer you.'

'I hope you were careful. We don't want to scare him off or make him come looking for you.'

'I think the surveillance probably made him cautious. If he does come after me that might not be a bad thing. Then at least we might get a bead on him.' I'm known on at least two continents for my cockiness.

'Andy, he plays rough. This is not a hood from Boston we are talking about but a real live Stasi agent. I don't think you appreciate how dangerous these people really are.' He leaned forward to half whisper, half yell over the country western music pouring out of the jukebox.

'I will keep it in mind, but I'm not losing sleep over it. He wouldn't be the first commie to try and kill me.' The North Vietnamese had tried awfully hard to send me home in an Army issue coffin. They had almost succeeded a few times.

'What's next?' Dave's voice betrayed a little desperation.

'We don't have a lot of cards left to play. I have a friend

in the FBI. If Dieter is under surveillance, they're the ones doing it. I will ask her discreetly.'

'Is that a good idea? I mean, how can you trust this FBI friend to be discreet? If something goes wrong, I could end up in serious trouble, and Judy could be killed. I could lose my security clearance, which means goodbye career.'

'My friend can be discreet, and she is the best chance of finding Dieter and saving Judy. We can worry about saving your career after we get her. After all, if you hand the FBI a genuine Stasi man, especially one they could pin a kidnapping on, that probably plays in your favor.'

'Andy, are you a hundred percent sure this is the way we should go?' He was leaning forward staring at me intently. Suddenly I felt like we were back in Vietnam doing mission planning for another one of his crazy plans.

'I think this is the only shot we have left.' Desperate men do desperate things. This was about as desperate as it gets.

'OK, well, that settles it then. We have a plan. We should drink on it.' He seemed relieved, and there wasn't much point trying to get Brenda Watts to help me tonight. After all, she had only just started speaking to me again. Progress was being made on all fronts. I touched my bottle of Löwenbräu to his glass mug. There didn't seem much point in being too sober either.

'Cheers.'

'Cheers.'

'I really appreciate everything you are doing for me and for Judy. I know I don't say it enough, but I do. When this is all over, I hope that you will take me up on the offer to come back into the Army, back to SF. I can really use a man I can trust with me.'

'It is a sensible idea, Dave. Everything you said the other day made a lot of sense.' I was never going to have a normal life, a house in suburbia, wife, kids, and a dog, but maybe I could have something with some stability. Maybe stability was almost as good as normalcy. Back to a brotherhood and being a part of something.

'It is a good idea. You were a good Recon man. You loved it too, admit it.' He was smiling his smile, the one that used to get us in trouble in the jungles of Vietnam and in the bars of Saigon.

'I did love it.' I had. It was the only time in my life that I felt exceptional. Like an Olympic athlete or a rock star. I had loved testing my plan, my wits against the best that the NVA and the communist world could throw at me. It had been exciting and terrifying. It had been addictive. Then I lost friends and brothers and it stopped being fun. Then it seemed like I was just doing it waiting for my chance to join my other dead brothers.

'You never should have left, man. Never. You were a sight to see on missions when I went on them with you. When they went to shit, that was when you were at your best!' Dave's sincerity and compliments made me feel uncomfortable.

'I was lucky, very lucky.'

'Better to be lucky than good.' He had ordered us another round. The beers came accompanied by two shot glasses of bourbon. Dave raised his shot, and it seemed obligatory that I did too. 'To Roark's luck!' We clinked glasses and the Wild Turkey burned its way down my throat. It hit my belly and warmth started to spread through me.

'Funny, I didn't feel so lucky. I lost almost everyone.' Not just guys on my team, killed or badly wounded, but friends like Tony who had been killed in a sapper attack in Da Nang.

'You always kept calm. No matter how bad it got, you worked the radio, shot straight, and always seemed to know where everyone was. More than that, it seemed like you knew what the NVA were going to do before they did it. You read the terrain and always seemed to know the right direction to move in. You seemed untouchable, like you were made to be there. It was more than just luck or skill. The only name that anyone could come up with for it was "Roark's luck." That didn't do it justice.'

'It wasn't anything special to do with me. I had a great team; the other Americans were good and the indig were great. We worked and trained and that was what did it. Sure, we got lucky, but it was mostly the skill and hard work that the team put in that made it work.'

'I don't care what you say. I believed in Roark's luck then and I believe in it now.'

'Dave, it wasn't anything special I did. I just worked hard and kept my head when it all went to shit. Like you said, I sounded calm on the radio, and that was half the battle.' The last thing I wanted was for Dave to think that I had some sort of mystical talent or quality. Or worse, for him to think that it would help me find Judy.

'That probably helped you a lot when you were a Covey Rider.'

'Yeah, that was like juggling, but there was nothing better than helping get a team out when they were in a Prairie Fire.' If Billy Justice hadn't suggested that I fly Covey, then I would have burned out . . . gone on one mission too many or taken one crazy risk too many. Then, like a lot of guys I knew, the jungle would have claimed me. Billy Justice wasn't wrong. I was thinking of crazy missions involving jumping in with one other guy so far north the NVA would never suspect we were there. Or using high end scuba gear to work our way down a river to infiltrate the Ho Chi Minh Trail.

Sergeant Major Billy Justice looked through me one day and said, 'Red . . . I need a guy to ride Covey. I think you would be good at it. Whaddya say?' The last sentence was him mocking my South Boston accent. I was flattered that he asked me. It took me years to figure out that Billy Justice knew that if he asked me to stop running missions I wouldn't know how to say yes. But offer me a spot riding Covey . . . he saved my life when I didn't even realize I needed saving.

'It wasn't just that. When you had to fight, man, Andy, you were just all cool and calm, all fire and maneuver.' He had a romantic way of describing what I remember as adrenaline-fueled terror transformed into action. During one Prairie Fire emergency, I don't remember ever having the time to acknowledge how scared I was. It was all just about action, shooting, moving, and trying to keep my team alive. If I had thought about how scary it was, then I never would have gotten on the bird to fly to a mission. Hell, I would never have gotten out of bed in the morning.

'I don't know any other way to fight. Especially in Vietnam, when the fight was on, it was literally all or nothing.' My attempts at trying to mellow didn't seem to be working as well as I would have liked. We had finished our beers, and Dave had ordered more, and more Wild Turkey. We drank a few more. We told the obligatory war stories and reminisced about dead friends. Eventually we were at the obligatory hugging, crying, and 'I love you' stage. We weren't drunk, but we weren't actually sober either. It was a little after eight, but Dave had another early morning.

We walked out into the parking lot and the fading sunlight of a June evening. Darkness was almost an hour off yet. We shook hands.

'Dave, I will find Dieter and Judy. I will do whatever it takes.' I had the sincerity that comes from having had a few drinks.

'I know, man. I know you won't stop looking until you find her.' He seemed so certain when he said it. So much more than me. He turned and headed to his BMW. I watched him for a second, wondering what he must be going through. I turned and walked over to the Maverick. I heard a car start up. Somewhere I heard a woman laugh. It was a fine summer evening. I was fishing for my keys in the pocket of my jeans. There was the soft scrape of a foot behind me. Stars exploded in my head and I pitched into an infinite pool of the darkest India ink.

EIGHTEEN

S lowly, my dive into the infinite pool of India ink receded. As if I was diving in reverse. My body told me it was receding by letting little bits of pain and discomfort make themselves known. I was damp, and there was the incessant high-pitched buzzing of mosquitoes in my ear. I felt them on my skin, drinking their itchy fill. The ground was cool underneath me. I was outside. That was something.

My head hurt. No, my head felt like it had been rudely cleaved open and crudely stuck back together. I didn't want to move, but the mosquitoes wouldn't let me sleep. Something was digging painfully into my shoulders. I could smell pancakes. Pancakes and mosquitoes . . . that didn't make sense. Slowly the smell of bourbon . . . cheap bourbon . . . filled my nostrils. The smell was as insistent as the mosquitoes were annoying.

My clothes were damp. I moved my hands to my face. It was damp too. My fingers probed my face, then worked their way around my head. The back of my head was sticky with what could only have been drying blood, and there was a lump. I opened my eyes, and the stars were out. I carefully turned my head from side to side. I was in a sparsely populated graveyard. There were candles in front of the headstones . . . and they were evenly spaced, yards apart to my left. I felt the ground around me. Grass, some sand or dirt. My hand touched something cold and hard. Glass. A bottle. I lifted it to my nose and answered the question I hadn't thought to ask about where all the bourbon had come from.

That was the pain in my back. I was lying against the hard concrete plinth of my own headstone. That couldn't be right, there would be no headstone on a plinth for me. I would get a rectangle of white stone in the local veterans' cemetery. Nothing fancier than little flags placed there by strangers and Boy Scouts for Memorial Day.

Mosquitoes were buzzing in my ears and Ger was whispering; '*Trung sĩ*, wrong numbers! Numbers wrong, *trung sĩ*.' I felt like I was going to be sick. 'I know, Ger . . . I know.' I smelled like cheap bourbon. Why was I drunk in a sparsely populated graveyard? The gravestones all looked the same. They were all silhouettes of men; they all looked the same. Uniformly spaced with their candles in front of them. Had I passed out at some weird séance? The candles weren't flickering. They were lights with dim bulbs . . . this all felt familiar.

'IS THERE ANYONE DOWN RANGE? IS THERE ANYONE DOWN RANGE? IF SO, INDICATE BY SIGHT OR SOUND.' The voice came from the bottom of a ship's hold. I had been in one once. I knew what they sounded like. I knew those words . . . those commands. Range commands. I blinked a few times, and when the pain cleared a little, I knew where I was. I had been to places like this graveyard a thousand times. I knew why the gravestones all had little lights on them.

The voice sounded like something out of a 1950s science fiction movie coming out of the PA system, Robby the Robot telling anyone down range to let him know by sight or sound. It was less annoying than repeating 'DANGER, DANGER' a bunch of times.

I was on a rifle range. An Army rifle range. It was the night fire range. No one could see me, and in a few seconds hundreds of 5.56mm rifle rounds would be loosed down range. Shit! They weren't gravestones but thick cardboard silhouette targets. The lights would flash to simulate muzzle flashes. It was supposed to be realistic training. Then the fusillade of 5.56mm bullets would punch through them, and through me too.

'IS THERE ANYONE DOWN RANGE? IS THERE ANYONE DOWN RANGE? IF SO, INDICATE BY SIGHT OR SOUND.' The command was repeated for the third and last time. I tried to say something, but my throat was dry, and I squawked something inaudible to the firing line. I rolled on to my stomach and started to crawl. I was close to the high berm that separated this range from the next.

'FIRERS, AT THIS TIME, TAKE UP A GOOD SUPPORTED FIRING POSITION.'

There was one more command. I knew that one more command was coming. What was it? I tried to gulp in air. Moving slowly, and thinking even more sluggishly than I was moving.

'ROTATE YOUR SELECTOR LEVER . . .'

A voice near me – no, not near me but from inside of me, bellowed out, 'GAS, GAS, GAS!'

There is only one command in the entire United States Army which requires everyone to stop what they're doing instantly. Even the command of 'HALT' when marching requires an element marching to take an additional step and then stop. The command of 'GAS, GAS, GAS' requires everyone within hearing to stop whatever they're doing right then and there and put on their gas mask. It is a testament to the level of fear and respect that the Army has for the Soviet chemical weapons program. The Army drills and drills its soldiers in responding to chemical attacks. They practice masking up, shooting wearing masks, putting on the chemical suits, and all sorts of other foolishness.

Behind me on the firing line, there were metallic sounds coupled with frantic motion as soldiers put weapons down and struggled to rip gas masks out of canvas carriers and get them on their faces. The Army said that you had nine seconds to get the mask out and secured on your face. Another six seconds to pull the rubber hood down over your shoulders and secure the straps. The soldiers on the firing line defaulted to years of training. They barked louder than Pavlov's dog. The range cadre were caught completely off guard by the unexpected flurry of flailing soldiers and did the only thing they knew how to do. 'CEASE FIRE, CEASE FIRE, CEASE FIRE!'

Fifteen seconds is not a long time except when your life is in immediate danger; then it is a lifetime. I probably had more time than that, judging by the shouting and general pandemonium. I managed to get upright and stagger to the berm, crawl up its sloped side and haul myself over the top of it. The next range over was dark and closed for the night. I crawled across it to the next berm and crawled up and over it. The next range over was deserted and I sat down heavily, with my head hurting but very much alive. I crawled over this one and slid down, landing with a soft thump on my butt. My head ached.

I sat there catching my breath and having a debate with myself about the pros and cons of being sick. A disembodied voice from the other range gave the 'ALL CLEAR' through the PA system. I sat and listened to the tower give the commands to get the night fire back on track. I sat there trying to clear my head. I was having trouble focusing and was reminded of the last time that I had been stoned on some really strong weed.

The sounds of rifle fire from the night fire range startled me. Even though there were at least two solid ten-foot-high dirt berms between me and the gunfire, I still didn't like being there. I was able to get up and stagger to the far side of the range I was on. I wanted to throw up but started to breathe deeply through my nose. The stench of bourbon hit me, and my stomach heaved, but I held it together.

I had only had a few beers and a couple of shots with Dave while we talked about Dieter. My aching head. Dieter must have followed me up from Boston and then waited for me in the parking lot. He was good. He had been quiet and knew how to sap a guy. He must have gotten on to the training side of Fort Devens and left me out on the night fire range. When they found my bullet-riddled corpse with an empty bourbon bottle and reeking of the stuff, they would have assumed that I was some drunk who'd wandered on to the range and passed out. It was, as the engineers say, elegant.

Was Dieter still out there? Was he the type to watch and see if his plan worked? Or would he take his chances and get away before my body was discovered, which would raise all sorts of hell. Should I stay here and try to wait him out? I couldn't chance it. Also, I didn't want to get picked up by the MPs. I had no idea where my car was and didn't have Dave's magic pass on me. At a minimum I would end up cooling my heels in a cell 'til mid-morning.

With some effort I managed to get to my feet and not fall over. I shuffled away from the targets and toward the empty firing points, the bleachers, and the Range Control tower. I got to the bleachers and sat down on the damp, cold wood. What if Dieter had hurt Judy because I was clumsy and Dieter had figured out I was on his trail? I shivered; the night had cooled off. I looked at the luminous dial of my Seiko dive watch. It took me a few minutes to make sense of its glowing face, but eventually I worked out that it was a little after ten p.m. I hadn't been out here that long. I didn't think I had.

Headlights flashed on the road, and I got down on the ground. A truck rumbled by, belching smoke and diesel fumes. It passed by, and in the distance I heard voices. Voices in the night were never good. I got up and started to walk again on unsteady feet. Soon they would start packing up the night fire range, then the soldiers would head back to main post or to a bivouac site. Either way, they would be on the road. Then there would be the occasional roving patrol of MPs trying to stay awake through their shift. If I was to get going, now was the time to do it.

On the other side of the road there was a thin strip of grass, some scrub pines, a barbwire fence, and the railroad grading. If I could cross the road and get on the other side of the train tracks, I could follow them all the way back to main post, or near enough. At least I could move and not be seen from the road. I waited, checked both ways, and shuffled across the road. I made it to the barbwire fence and managed to get through with all the gracelessness of a drunk at the end of a three-day bender. Somehow, I managed not to get caught up in the wire. I tripped going over the train tracks and landed in a heap on the other side. After a while I looked at the glowing dots on the face of the Seiko. It looked like it was going on eleven p.m. now.

I got up and walked along the tracks. I followed them until I noticed that the mosquitoes were getting thicker and the swamp was encroaching on my right. I crossed over the tracks without tripping and falling this time. I could have walked on them; they would have led me through the swamp, but trains come down these tracks frequently enough that I didn't want to risk getting squashed by a passing freight train bringing ammunition or something to Fort Devens.

At least it wasn't raining. The moon had come out and

provided a decent amount of light. The tracks were curving
off to my left. The moonlight was casting a funny shadow. I
looked up and there was a box in the sky in front of me. It
was Dave's mockup jump tower. I found the barbwire fence
by walking, painfully, into it. I made my way between the
wire strands with the type of grace that Billy Justice would
have described as 'a horny monkey trying to get it on with a
very reluctant duck.' I cleared the fence just in time to see
headlights come down the road and turn into the training area
for the jump tower.

I dropped down behind the nearest dirt mound left over
from the construction of the tower. The dirt was loose, and I
was a few feet behind the back corner of the tower. I heard a
Jeep pull up and stop. The engine kept running, and the lights
were shining at the ladder a few feet in front of me to the left.

'Why the fuck are we out here in the middle of the night?'

'Lieutenant Colonel Billings is worried that kids or enlisted
men are going to get up to mischief in his new jump tower.'

'So, we have to come out here, climb up, and check.'

'Yes, we do.'

'That sucks.'

'That is why they're called orders.'

I lay my face flat in the soft dirt hoping they wouldn't see
me while they made the thirty-four-foot climb. I listened to
their boots on the metal stairs and then clomping around in
the metal box above me. I was looking to my right and my
neck was getting stiff. I carefully and quietly turned my head
to the left. I heard them on the stairs, coming down, making
a racket, and my breath caught as I clenched my jaw shut. I
listened to the bored MPs talk as they came down. I heard
them as they bitched all the way back to the Jeep and spun
out of the field. I didn't bother watching them go. I was too
busy looking at a hand. A small right hand with nail polish
on the fingers.

I started to clear the loose dirt away with my hands. The
hand led to a wrist, and the wrist to a whole arm. I was digging
like a kid at the beach with no pail and shovel. When my
fingers grazed across the skin, it was cool to the touch, rubbery.
Soon there was hair, and then a face. I rolled over and dry

heaved in the grass for a few minutes. I was, for once in my career as private detective, uncharacteristically successful. I had found Judy Billings.

Dieter had killed her. Killed her and planted her here to implicate Dave. How much more symbolic could it be than burying her in a pile of loose dirt under the jump tower that he was so proud of. That was the type of ironic kick in the balls that I expected a Stasi man to find amusing.

I rolled over and slowly got to my feet. The world began to spin, and I was lucky enough to catch myself on the dirt mound before I fell over. I staggered on toward the road on rubbery baby deer legs. I got to the blacktop and started heading down it. The moon was shining, providing me with plenty of light.

I'd made it almost a mile down the road when two things made me stop. One was the fact that I was almost back at the rifle ranges, including the night fire range where Dieter had left me to be killed by my own Army. This guy had a thing for irony. He would have laughed at me heading in the wrong direction. It was his fault. He didn't have to sap me that hard.

The other thing that made me stop was a set of tire tracks leading off into the bushes. That and a bit of moonlight glinting off some red reflective plastic. I pushed the bushes out of the way and saw the distinctive taillights of a 1975 Ford Maverick, the sloped red rectangle with the clear squares that flanked the license plate on either side. My car seemed undamaged. That was a nice change. My last car had been beaten up and then blown up.

I pushed more bushes aside and was able to get the driver's side door open. The dome light came on, and I saw my keys were on the floor in front of the driver's seat. I had to get down on my knees to get them. If I tried to bend over, I was going to fall in and probably pass out. I slowly stood back up; then I got in and sat for a few minutes.

'*Trung sĩ*, numbers wrong . . . wrong numbers, *trung sĩ.*' My head hurt. My dead point man wanted me to know that I had fucked up and gotten him killed. He wouldn't leave me alone.

'Well, Ger, if you think I fucked up that badly, let's check the map.' He didn't say anything.

'I've got a flashlight in the glovebox; we can check the map and you can show me where I went wrong.' I had a penlight in the glovebox in case I needed a small, discreet light. Ger held up the paper he was looking at. 'Numbers wrong, *trung SĨ*.'

'I don't want to argue with you. I just need some rest.' I closed my eyes. Ger smiled at me and then his head exploded. The paper in his hand fluttered away. It had changed from the map to Dieter's picture. Dreams are weird that way.

I woke up with a mosquito buzzing in my left ear. I went to slap at it, but as I moved, my head reminded me of how much it was hurting. I leaned over and opened the glovebox. My .38 was there in its holster, and my speedloader with five rounds of .38 hollow points. My Buck knife was next to it, and under the whole pile was the penlight. Underneath that was all of the paperwork for the car.

The Maverick started with its usual throaty grumble, and I carefully backed it out on to the road and turned back toward the jump tower. I drove over to it and, as the MPs had before, bounced the Maverick over the open field. I turned off the lights and the engine and got out. I took the light, the gun, the spare rounds, and the knife out of the glovebox. I checked to make sure the .38 was loaded and clipped it inside my waistband. The knife went into my right pocket and the speedloader in my left.

I took the penlight and went over to Judy's body. I got down on my hands and knees and looked at her face under the soft glow of the penlight. I brushed the hair and dirt from her face. The smell was starting to escape from the mound, and I didn't want to be here anymore.

I got up and went back to the Maverick. My head hurt, but my mind felt clearer. I had to go see Dave. To tell him about Judy. I didn't want to be the one to deliver the news, but there was no one else who could do it, or should. I got in and started the car up and headed back up Range Road. I drove through the open gate past the Range Control office. The MP at Jackson Gate barely looked at the pass I showed him. He looked at how dirty I was and probably smelled the bourbon. He was satisfied that I wasn't a Soviet Spetsnaz infiltrator and waved me through the gate. Most likely the couple of hours of sleep in the guard shack were more important to him then seeing whether I was sober enough to drive.

I made the slow, interminable drive to the house on Walnut Street. I pulled up and sat in the car thinking of what I wanted to say to Dave. The words were important, and I wanted to get them right. I got out and walked up the driveway past his little BMW and unlatched the gate in the stockade fence and went into the backyard. I closed the gate quietly behind me.

I took out my Buck knife and opened it. I slid the blade between the French doors and worked it carefully and slowly up. The blade made contact with the loose metal latch, and I popped it open. I pushed the door open quietly and stepped into Dave's office. There was so little crime on Army bases that no one took their security that seriously. Why would you fix a loose latch on a set of French doors? I quietly pulled the door shut behind me and stood still, listening to the house. There were gentle creaks and noises but nothing alarming. There was no creaking of floorboards above me. I stood still, just waiting, for ten minutes.

According to my watch, it was almost four in the morning. Since I woke up on the night fire range, it had been a long night. None of it particularly good. If I had learned anything in the cops, it was that nothing good happens after midnight if it doesn't happen in a bar or a bedroom. Nothing good at all. I didn't see why tonight – this morning – should be any different.

NINETEEN

The office was much as I had last seen it. Dave's pictures, awards, and various mementos were still on the walls. The dollar bill was still under the ashtray, and the holstered Tokarev war trophy was still hanging on the chair. The bottlenecked Tokarev round was still on the desk where Dave had left it. The moonlight partially lighting the office made me feel like a ghost in someone's home.

After the time had passed, after I had waited, listening to the house, I decided to wash up. Dave wouldn't mind. I went quietly into the hallway. There was no need to disturb Dave. He would wake up soon enough. Behind the first door I tried were steps that led down into a darkened basement. Maybe there was a wash sink. No sense dirtying up one of Dave and Barbara's nice powder rooms. I moved slowly down the steps into the darkness below.

I should have turned on a light, but I didn't. I just took my time. My foot touched the bottom, and it felt different. I squatted down and touched my hand to the floor. It wasn't concrete but hard-packed dirt. The brick officers' housing had been built in the 1930s, and it wasn't uncommon for them to have dirt floors in the basement instead of the now required concrete slab. I looked around but gave up on the idea of a wash sink. I did find a basket of laundry by the dryer. I dug around until I found a t-shirt. It smelled clean and I took it with me. I went quietly back up the cellar stairs.

The next door I tried led to a small powder room. I shut the door and turned on the light. I looked at myself in the mirror. Dirt streaked my face and there was dried blood on the collar of my polo shirt. My shirt seemed to be as much dirt as cloth and was tattered. My hair was matted and clumped with dried blood and bourbon and dirt. At least all of that would wash out. There wasn't much I was going to be able to do with my blue jeans.

I stripped off my polo shirt and turned on the water. The sink was old and had separate taps for hot and cold water. I turned them on and took the bar of fancy French decorative soap that was never intended to be used. Barbara's choice, I was sure, as opposed to Dave's. Dave wasn't the type to care about French soaps and color-coordinated hand towels.

I washed, starting with my hands and arms. I splashed water on my face and lathered it and worked soap into my hair. The back of my head stung, but it was manageable. A few minutes later, I had dried my hands, chest, and hair as best as I could, but it was a damp, clean mess. Also, I smelled like lavender.

I put on the t-shirt I'd found in the basket. It was a little bigger than I wore usually, but Dave was bigger in the chest and taller than me. It was a t-shirt from a British para regiment with a little parachutist emblem above the heart. It seems like everyone has to have their own special shirt these days. They do make good fodder for trading. I threw my blood- and dirt-stained polo down the cellar steps. It could go into the laundry.

I was enjoying moving quietly through Dave's house. I imagined that I was a cat burglar. I moved quietly to the sideboard in the dining room. I took one of the nice crystal highball glasses. I dug around until I found a bottle of good scotch. This one came in a distinctive triangular bottle; Glenfiddich. I poured a finger and drank it neat in one long sip. It was so smooth it must have been old enough to vote. I guess that it is one of the benefits of having lieutenant colonel money. I took a second glass from the sideboard and took the bottle and two glasses into Dave's office. He would be up eventually, and the least I could do if I was going to drink his old, excellent scotch was to offer him one.

I turned on one of the floor lamps in his office. I put Dave's glass down on the desk next to the brass ashtray that was resting on the dollar bill. The Russian bullet was next to it, looking like a funhouse mirror version of a bullet. I poured a healthy belt of Glenfiddich into it. I poured my glass half full and put it and the bottle down on the round table between the chairs. I looked at the books on Dave's bookshelf. My head hurt, and I wasn't sure if I wanted to read anything. I settled on *Military Small Arms of the 20th Century*. It had a lot of pictures, and I could stand to brush up on what everyone seemed to be toting around these days.

I sat down in the chair that was furthest from Dave's desk but more directly facing it. I opened the book and took a sip of the excellent scotch. I wanted a cigarette. That smell of the lighter working on the paper and first bit of tobacco. That wonderful smell of a newly lit cigarette, and the first lungful of instant calm. But sadly, the pack of Luckies that I had with me hadn't survived the night's efforts.

I heard floorboards softly creak. Then a stair tread, and then a whisper of breath behind me. Dave moved quietly, I had to give him that. He was behind me in the doorway. It was rare for me to sit with my back to a door but there was nothing to fear in Dave's house. Plus, I could see his reflection in the French doors.

'Howdy, Dave.' My voice sounded like someone else's to me.

'Andy, Jesus! What are you doing here? Are you nuts?' I couldn't blame Dave for being shocked to see me sitting in his office in the wee hours.

'Had to come over. I have news.'

'Jesus, Andy, you could use the doorbell. I thought someone was breaking in. I could have shot you.' He had stepped into the office, and I noticed the pistol in his hand, hanging down at his side. It had been pointed at me until he saw who it was. It was a West German Walther P5. A nice gun, basically an updated version of the World War II era German P38 but with an alloy frame, enclosed slide, and shorter barrel. West German cops used them and, given Dave's taste in cars, I shouldn't have been surprised to see he favored a Euro-yuppie gun too.

'After the night I've had, you'd be doing me a favor.' I raised the glass. 'Cheers.' I held the glass up and Dave spied the glass on his desk. He put the pistol down and picked up the glass. The safety on the pistol was off but the hammer was down. The P5 was double action, which meant the first shot was fired like my revolver, then after that each pull of the trigger was single action. A shorter trigger pull, and much lighter too. Because the pull of the trigger was so heavy on the first pull, it meant that the safety was a bit redundant.

'Cheers.' He took a sip and then sat down behind his desk, the pistol in front of him momentarily forgotten. Dave had been raised with manners too good not to raise his glass.

'P5, nice gun. I have a P38 I picked up a few years ago. Mostly it lives in a safe deposit box in a bank in town.' The P38 had been a souvenir of sorts from an earlier case. It was of dubious legality, and I kept it just in case I needed to do dubious things with it. I have found in my short life that it doesn't hurt to be prepared.

'I picked it up in Germany. We did a lot of training with the Berlin cops and others. I liked this one, small and compact.'

'Good guns.' They were, and had a good track record going back to World War II.

'Better than that .38 Smith & Wesson you carry.'

'Hey, I like my Smith,' I said with faux indignation.

'It only holds five rounds, is slow to reload, and the .38 Special round is nothing to write home about.' He was right. Like a lot of guys, he believed that his choice in a gun was the best choice. I always thought of them as tools; the user was the real weapon. The best gun in the world is useless if the person holding it doesn't know how to use it. Dave knew what he was doing, I was sure of that.

'True, but it is small and doesn't jam. I can tell you from experience that I can put the rounds where they count. Also, I can't carry an M60 around with me, so the .38 will have to do.'

'Ha, that doesn't surprise me.' He smiled a tired smile at me. 'Andy, why are you sitting in my study in the middle of the night, wearing my t-shirt, drinking my expensive scotch?' That was a fair question that I was reluctant to answer.

'I was thirsty, Dave. I have had a long, shitty night. My head hurts, and I'm literally and figuratively a mess. I borrowed your shirt because mine is a bigger mess.' That was all true.

'What happened to you? Did you get into a fight at the bar after I left?' He was looking at me over the rim of his highball, of which he had taken a birdlike sip. Not even a very thirsty bird at that.

'We said goodbye and I went to my car and someone sapped me.' I took a good-sized sip of the excellent scotch. What the hell, I only drank stuff this good when someone else was buying or when I was at an Irish wake.

'Sapped you?'

'Yeah, hit me in the back of the head with a weighted, soft-wrapped weapon, inducing unconsciousness.'

'Jesus, you do live the private eye life to the fullest. Who was it? Dieter?'

'That would make a lot of sense, wouldn't it?' I took another sip.

'Sure, those Stasi guys are good, well trained. Maybe even better than you, Andy.'

'Could be. After all, I'm not the man I was in Vietnam.'

'Well, you do seem to drink a lot these days, Andy.' He said it reluctantly, almost apologetically.

'Yeah, well, my life lacks stability and that makes me thirsty.'

'That is why I keep trying to convince you to re-up . . . to come back in.'

'You are right, it would be good for me. Some stability, some friends, maybe a chance to grow up a little?' I have been told that I need to grow up, usually by Special Agent Brenda Watts.

'Yeah, man. Like I said, you would probably come in as an E-5, buck sergeant, but you would make rank fast. Or if you have college, you could get commissioned and come back in as an officer. You would come work for me. I would take care of you, and I could use someone around here I can trust.' It would be strange to have someone looking out for me.

'That sounds pretty good, Dave.' It did too. The thought of belonging to something again, the idea of having a sense of purpose again, those were things that had been missing from my life. I didn't know if I could have that back, but Dave was at least offering me a shot at it. I just worried about how high the cost of it would be.

'Jeez, Andy, I think it would be good for you and good for the Army.'

'Thanks. But what about Judy?' We had gotten off topic worrying about my future and my problems.

'I don't know. Dieter is good. He got the drop on you; I don't think a lot of guys do. I don't know what to do.'

'You know, Dave, I don't think Dieter is all that good.' I was, after all, still alive.

'Ha! You are sitting there with your skull split half open. The Andy Roark I knew in Vietnam would never let anyone sneak up on him, get the drop on him.' He was shaking his head ruefully.

'Yeah, you are right about that . . . I'm getting older. Losing my touch.' My sore head was proof of that. 'What was it you called it? Roark's magic?'

'Roark's luck. No, you just drink too much. I bet in a head-to-head you could take Dieter.' It was nice of him to say.

'No, Dave, I couldn't.' I was certain of that.

'Sure you could. You are still one of the toughest guys I know.' Now he was just being charitable. Being good in the woods didn't necessarily equate to being a tough guy. I certainly didn't think of myself as one.

'Well, thanks. But I can't take Dieter. I'm one hundred percent certain of that.' I took another healthy sip of Dave's scotch. I was only reaffirming his point about my drinking. I was a good friend like that.

'How can you be so sure?' Dave, sounding like an Army officer at a mission debriefing.

I took the bottle of scotch and dumped a few fingers into my glass. I held the bottle up to him with my right arm, offering to top him off. He shook his head no. I put the cap back on the good – no, great – scotch and put the bottle on the table. The book started to slide off my lap, and I caught it before it fell.

'Shit, I'm a mess.' I was, but that was nothing new for me. I put the book on the table. It rested mostly on the table in the shadow of the centurion's helmet.

'You could slow down with the scotch.' He sounded like a nagging father now.

'I could. I could,' I said without much conviction.

'Oh, listen to me like I'm a nagging mother. Have as much as you like.' Dave was all good manners and hospitality.

'I never answered your question. I got distracted.' That was true . . . I had strayed off topic. I blame the scotch, or maybe the split head.

'My question?' Dave raised an amused eyebrow.

'Yes, I said that I couldn't take Dieter. You said, how can you be so sure?'

'Oh, that question.'

'Yep, that question. Do you really want to know?'

'Sure.'

'Because Dieter doesn't exist.'

'Bullshit! Then who sapped you in the parking lot at the Fort?' Incredulous Dave now.

'You did, Dave.' He stared at me with a shocked expression.

'Andy, what are you talking about? I can't believe you would even think such a thing,' he blustered.

'There is no Dieter.'

'But you have the pictures of him. Classified pictures.' Dave would not be good on cross-examination.

'I have pictures of a man that are stamped "TOP SECRET," but they aren't, are they?' I shifted in the chair because the butt of the .38 was digging uncomfortably into my side.

'Andy, I took a huge risk showing you those, letting you take those home with you.'

'Do you dream about Vietnam, Dave?' He shook his head no. 'I do. I dream all the time about it. In many ways my dreams are like a time machine. Close my eyes and it is 1969 again, 1970, you know. Sometimes they're very literal memories of stuff . . . other times they're more free form. Usually, almost always actually, they're bad. You know what I mean. Dead friends bad. Seeing things happen and knowing I'm powerless to change the outcome. Or my CAR-15 shoots confetti instead of bullets. Stuff like that.'

'Andy, what does this have to do with anything?'

'Since the first time I sat in this study, I've been dreaming about our last mission together. The one that went to shit and decimated my team. You know, that one?' The one that was the reason why I stopped running Recon. Dave nodded.

'I keep seeing Ger, my point man, ahead of me on the trail. I see him turn his head and it explodes when the machine gun round hits it. He never had time to say anything. The NVA had laid a good trap for us. One second he was turning back to look at me, then the next . . . BAM! His head exploded and we were all running and gunning.'

'OK, so you dream about dead team members?'

'Yesterday, in the dreams, last night, Ger started to speak to me. He was holding what I thought was the map saying, "*Trung sĩ*, wrong numbers, numbers wrong, *trung sĩ*."' Dave shrugged, not interrupting, waiting for me to get on with the story. 'But it wasn't a map he was holding. In the last dream when he held up the piece of paper it was the picture of Dieter. He said his signature line again. Then it hit me.'

'What hit you?' Dave's face seemed tighter, like he was bracing himself for something unpleasant.

'Classified documents, high level ones, have serial numbers on them. You know, that way if any of them turn up in Ivan's hands they know who had them. Those pictures don't have any serial numbers. Ger wasn't trying to tell me something. He's been dead for over ten years and he's still trying to save my life. It was one of those little nagging details that my subconscious couldn't let go of.' I settled back in the comfortable chair and looked at Dave. There is a moment in every interrogation when you have pushed and probed and then you sit back and wait for the cracks in their defenses.

'Shit.' Dave said it quietly and sat back in the captain's chair.

'Yep. Who is the guy in the pictures, Dave?'

'Oh, him . . . that's SFC Charlie Holliday.' He said it like I might have heard of him.

'Let me guess, everyone calls him Doc,' I said.

'They do. Yes.' Certain last names came with unavoidable nickname options.

'Let me guess. It was some sort of training exercise, tailing and surveilling. That type of thing?'

'Yes, something like that. Guys going to Berlin must have those types of skills. We like to see who might be good at it before we send anyone over. It also gives guys a chance to practice their counter-surveillance skills.'

'Why the TOP SECRET stamp?' For a training exercise it should have been marked differently.

'The guys who took those pictures thought that it would be a nice touch. A joke.'

'So, Dieter isn't real? You invented him.'

'Yes.'

'Why?'

'Andy, I wanted you to keep looking for Judy. You were quitting and I wanted you to keep going with it.' His face was pale, and his voice was low.

'You wanted me to find her? Are you sure about that?'

'Yes.' Barely above a whisper.

'I think that is the last thing you wanted.'

'What do you mean?'

'Judy's dead, Dave.' No sense belaboring it. It wasn't going to make it any easier for him.

'Dead? Judy?' He was saying it slowly, like he was trying to wrap his head around the idea.

'Maybe part of you wanted me to find her. Like Ger telling me about the numbers, maybe your subconscious was working too. Let's face it, you didn't want me to find her because you killed her.' It is a strange thing to sit across from an old friend, a man who saved your life, and accuse him of killing his only child. It felt like vinegar in my throat watching him, waiting for him to say or do something. I sat listening to a clock ticking loudly only to realize that it was my Seiko, keeping time with the accuracy of the executioner counting cadence as his victim marches to the gallows.

TWENTY

'Andy, that's insane! I could never hurt my daughter.' His indignation was genuine enough.

'Dave, I found Judy.' I hated this part.

'What?'

'Yeah, in my mildly concussed travels tonight I ended up by your new jump tower. You know, the one you care so much about you have the MPs patrolling it at night?' I paused to drink some good scotch, my throat suddenly dry. He was looking at me, and his hands were resting on the arms of the captain's chair. He was squeezing the armrests hard enough that his knuckles were white, and I wondered if it was possible that the skin across his knuckles would split.

'I saw a Jeep pull in. I was near the mounds of dirt. You know, the ones you still have to clean up? I dropped to the ground, and while I was hiding, waiting for the MPs to check and make sure your tower was unmolested, I found her.' Dave's mouth was working but no sounds were coming from it. 'I found her hand. Maybe the rain yesterday washed the soil away. After the MPs left, I cleared away enough dirt to see her face.' I spared him all the bullshit about how peaceful she looked. Dave had seen enough of death to know it was all lies.

'You could have been mistaken . . . it might not be her. It was dark.'

'We both know I'm not mistaken. I know because I saw her. You know because you buried her there.' Dave made an anguished noise in his throat and began to sob. Real, large tears fell from his face, proving that gravity is always exercising its will on us. Even in grief.

'It makes a lot of sense to me. You buried your daughter in a place that you love, where you could see her whenever you wanted to. I imagine that you were going to go back and dig a proper grave and then cover her over when you got rid of those mounds of dirt. Hell, you loved her enough that you ordered the MPs to watch over her every night.' He was sobbing. There was no pretense of trying to regain his composure. I had no more pulled my punches with him than I had with K-nice in the parking garage. Only this time, instead of raining blows with a blackjack, I was expertly bludgeoning him with my words. 'Why don't you tell me about it? Tell me what happened, man. I might be the only chance you have.' Always offer a glimmer of hope, let them begin to see you as the source of their salvation.

At first, I didn't know if he heard me. Then he slowly collected himself with some effort. He blew his nose, drank some scotch, and then drank some more. He opened his mouth to start a few times and then closed it. I sat patiently, watching him and waiting. Then finally . . .

'She is . . . was a difficult kid. That part was all true. She takes after her mother in a lot of ways. Barbara is a lush. Even worse for an officer's wife, she gets around. You know how it is in Special Forces, you are either off on missions or you are off training and rarely home for long. I can't exactly blame her. When we PC-essed here, I told her she had to go to take the cure. I needed her to be sober and moderately discreet. I knew there was no way she would stop fucking around . . . all I asked for was a modicum of discretion.' I nodded. It was a story that was common enough on Army bases. Though I was fairly sure that Dave had gotten a lot of tail on the side too, there didn't seem to be any point in pointing out his hypocrisy.

'Well, Judy was a handful at the best of times, but Barbara was better at handling her. But when Barbara left for Palm Springs to take the cure, things got worse with Judy. Her grades got worse, she stopped going to school. She was doing drugs, seeing the boy in the motor pool.' That boy who had gone through the windshield of his Mustang. That boy whom I had been chasing. The boy from the motor pool who was dead for no good reason. Just another bit of human wreckage in Dave's little family drama. 'She was going to Boston all the time, going to bars and doing god knows what.'

'You told me all that. How did she die? Was she even alive when you hired me?'

'Oh, yes, yes, she was. I was really hoping that you would find her.'

'What happened?'

'She came home the night after I hired you. She was getting her stuff to run away with her boyfriend in Boston. I heard her moving around in her bedroom. I went in to confront her and we had an argument. She called me a limp dick asshole. Me, her father. She said if I had been any sort of man . . . if I had been any sort of man, then Barbara wouldn't have fucked all of those other men. That it was my fault. Then she tried to storm out. To push past me. I could smell the cigarette smoke on her. I could smell the sex on her. It was too much. I had it. Between her and her mother's screwing around, I just couldn't take anymore.

'I grabbed her by her shoulders. I was angry, Andy. I wanted to shake some sense into her. It is all a blur, but when I stopped and let her go, she took a step back, except her back was to the stairs. She stepped back, she was on the edge of the step, and she stepped back into the air and fell, tumbling down the steps, and landed with a crunch.' He paused, catching his breath. 'There she was, Andy, at the bottom of the steps, in a crumpled heap. My baby girl was dead.'

'What did you do next?' My voice was calm and even toned, like we were talking about the Red Sox instead of him killing his daughter.

'I went to check on her . . . but she was dead. The fall killed her. I know I should have called the MPs, but I thought they would pin it on me. I panicked. Look at how badly they fucked up the Jeffrey MacDonald case.' MacDonald was a doctor with Special Forces at Fort Bragg who had killed his wife and children. I didn't point out to Dave that the Army's own flawed investigation initially cleared MacDonald.

'So, what did you do?'

'I buried her in the basement. But I knew that was a temporary fix. The post maintenance people are in and out of the house every time something needs work. I couldn't risk it. Then you scared the hell out of me. You showed up as I was cleaning up, washing my hands.' It was hard to recall now, but I remembered him wiping his hands saying he had been doing the dishes. I had even been amused at the thought of a future general washing dishes.

'Later you moved her out to the jump tower?'

'I got her in the trunk of my car, wrapped up in a bed sheet. I drove out to the training area a little before dark and waited. Then I buried her where you found her. I knew that I would have to move her again, but it was a good temporary measure. I sat there by the pile of dirt and I cried. I thought about what I was going to say to Barbara . . . I thought about blowing my brains out.'

'Instead, you hatched one of your wild ass schemes and called me?'

'Instead, I called you,' he confirmed. He started crying again. Then he said, 'Andy, you have to believe me. I would give anything to have her back. If I could just undo those last few moments on the stairs with her, I would. You have to believe me. It was an accident. I could never intentionally hurt my own child.' I sat and listened to him and nodded sympathetically. 'Andy, you know me. You know I could never . . . would never . . . it was just a freak accident.'

'I know, Dave, it was an accident, and you compounded it with a mistake, a stupid panicky moment.' I used my most soothing voice.

'Exactly, Andy. Exactly. Now what do I do? Andy, you have to help me.'

'How can I help, Dave?' He took it as an offer of help, ignoring what I'd said about the futility of the situation.

'Andy, she's dead. It was an accident. You could keep quiet. I saved your life in Vietnam. You said yourself that you can never pay me back for that. No one has to know. You don't have to tell anyone.' Desperation breeds desperate plans.

'We just cover it up and pretend it never happened?' I asked him as casually as I could.

'Exactly. She ran away, that's all.' He said it like I was the kid in class who struggled but finally answered the question correctly.

'What about her mother, Dave?'

'Andy, it was an accident. Just bad luck.'

'You mean she fell down the steps and hit her head or broke her neck.'

'Yes . . . that's what happened.'

'No, it isn't, Dave. I have seen a lot of bodies in my time, in the Army, then more in the cops, even a fair amount as a private detective. I saw Judy, Dave, saw her face. Her neck wasn't broken. Judging by the bruises on her throat and the hemorrhages in her eyes, she was strangled. Even a rookie cop could tell that.'

'Andy, it was an accident,' he pleaded.

'No, it wasn't. You put your hands around your own daughter's throat, squeezing, pressing your thumbs into her windpipe. It isn't a quick way to kill anyone . . . you must have been angry.' It was an intimate way of killing someone, standing close and squeezing the life out of them. He must have felt the heat coming off her as she thrashed against him. Felt her go limp in his hands.

Then several things happened at once. Dave shifted his weight on the balls of his feet, started to stand up, and quick as lightning his hand snatched at the P5 pistol. In one fluid motion I grabbed the corner of the book I had been reading and side-armed it, skimming it across the desktop into the pistol. It knocked it out of Dave's reach and on to the floor. The highball glass of whiskey spun off into a wall and shattered into a thousand pieces. Dave was moving, trying to get up and over or around the desk. I sprang from the chair, snatching his Roman centurion's helmet, and winged it into his jaw. It didn't knock him out, but it sat him down long enough for me to pull my .38 and point it at him.

'Dave, this is the point where you should sit down and put your hands flat on the desk. Otherwise, we can see how academic your criticism of my choice of pistol is.' I had the gun pointed at his midsection, and we both knew it wouldn't take much to make it go off. He sat down slowly and put his hands flat on the desk. 'You killed your daughter in a fit of rage, but why did you try and kill me?'

He sat back and looked at me and then he smiled. He looked normal and ghoulish all at once.

'Andy, I think we both should have another drink. I think you can sport me to some of my own scotch.'

'No, I don't think so. I don't feel like getting close enough to you for you to try and finish the job you started on me tonight.'

He smiled again. 'It wasn't personal, Andy.'

'I know, Dave. It never is. Maybe one of these days someone will try and kill me for personal reasons. Might make a nice change for me.' It would at least be a change. 'What really happened, Dave? . . . All of it.' He smiled, and while it was the same becoming smile, all teeth and charm, it had changed too. Now it was the smile of a shark, an empty-eyed killer.

'Oh, Barbara was away drying out her liver for the umpteenth time. Judy was getting into more and more trouble. I tried everything to rein her in but nothing was working. I just couldn't stand the thought of her ruining my career with her antics. You know how it is with officers . . . careers are destroyed by whispers. I had run into one of the old CCN gang, Bill Winston. We got to talking and he said that he had recently run into you. That you were a private eye.' I had bumped into Bill 'Coffin Nail' Winston in April. I was still trying to make sense of the events that had led to my earlobe getting shot off. I was drunk and pretty gnarly looking.

'Bill said you looked bad. Drunk and a little disheveled. You hadn't shaved in a few days, and you had the sour smell of old booze coming off you like someone who had been drinking heavily for days on end.'

'Yeah, I'm sure the cigarettes didn't help any either,' I added. After all, it was my dime.

'He said you were down and out. That you looked bad. Then Judy went missing and I thought of you. The way you were in the jungle. You were just so fucking magnificent, and then to think of you here in the world . . . down and out. I reached out, figuring I could send some business your way. To help you out.'

'Well, that is mighty charitable of you.' Dave wasn't actually used to hearing me be sarcastic.

'Then you showed up and you looked nothing like what Bill had described.' Yeah, fuck you, Bill.

'I had been through some bad shit, and my way of coping was to fall into a bottle for a while. Bill caught me toward the end of that ride.' March had beaten me up badly.

'When I hired you, she was alive, and I really hoped you would find her. She came home and we had a horrible argument. After it was done, she was dead, and I had to come up with a plan. You were already in play and it hit me . . . she ran away . . . lots of teens run away to Boston, and like the teams that got swallowed by the jungle . . . they get swallowed by the city. No one would seriously expect you to find her.' He smiled and I wanted to throw up. He was proud of himself.

'So, you sent me on a fool's errand?' I tried to keep my voice even and not get angry.

'No, no, you were helping me build my cover. You didn't have to know why you were doing what you were doing. Just like in Vietnam. You had a part to play but you didn't have to know the significance of it.' It was weird watching him peel back the layers of his own onion . . . his own personality. As each layer was removed, I liked him less and less.

'You were great . . . the flyers, the calls, the reports. Then you wanted to give up. I had to figure out quickly what was the appropriate reaction. I have always been bad at knowing what the right way to feel is. What the right expression is to paste on my face when emotions are concerned. I always feel like I'm acting. Barbara says I'm a cold fish, unemotional, and that is why she drinks. She can't admit that she is weak, so she blames it on me.' He smiled at me. 'I thought of you, Andy, on those missions in the jungle. When you had declared a Prairie Fire and we were being chased . . . I thought of how you would improvise. I knew a real father who loved his daughter wouldn't quit . . . I had those pictures in my desk . . .'

'So, you invented Dieter, the East German Stasi agent.' There wasn't enough good scotch in the house to wash the taste of this out of my mouth.

'Sure.' He smiled his becoming smile at me with his empty eyes. 'Why not? He was a bad guy you could never find because he didn't exist. Also, I knew that you would believe that he was out of your league. You always did that . . . you never gave yourself enough credit. If a mission went south on you, it was your fault. It wasn't that the NVA were literally throwing their best soldiers at you, that the odds were so heavily stacked against you . . . nope, it was a personal failing of yours.' He was right. I had always seen it that way. 'That was why it was so easy to get you to go on those insane missions. You wanted everyone's approval – your CO, the Korean War hero, the sergeant major, Billy what's-his-name?'

'Justice, Billy Justice.' I was starting to feel hollow inside.

'Sure, you were just a kid looking for a family to replace the one you never really had. Always looking for approval from surrogate parents in green berets. Christ, you were perfect. Hard working. Smart, lucky, and disposable.' I wasn't sure if he was talking about Vietnam or now. It didn't matter.

'Then why did you come back for me on that last mission? It wasn't for the medal. There must have been easier ways of getting one. Why save my life if I was disposable?'

'I wasn't going to. We were taking fire, and I was running for the chopper. One of your team who was already in the bird broke open his M79 and popped the high explosive shell out. He held up a canister round, you know, one of those giant shotgun shell rounds. He made sure I could see him loading it into the grenade launcher. I was almost at the bird when he pointed it at me. He yelled, "No *trung sĩ* Roark . . . no *trung úy*." It wasn't subtle, but it wasn't supposed to be. If I didn't have you with me, he would kill me. I just ran back to grab you, and the rest . . .'

'. . . is history. What happened last night? Why try to kill me after saving my life in Vietnam?'

'You were determined to go to that FBI agent. It wouldn't take her long to figure out there was no Dieter . . . people would start asking questions. I had improvised, but it wouldn't hold up against determined scrutiny. I bought you drinks. I didn't want you to suffer – we're friends, after all.'

'So, you sapped me in the parking lot.'

'Yeah, I had a ten-inch piece of garden hose with some lead fishing weights in it. It was taped at both ends. It made an awful sound hitting your head. I thought I'd killed you right there in the parking lot. I got you to your car. If anyone had cared, I would have said you were drunk and passed out. No one noticed.' Story of my life. 'I got you in the trunk and quickly stripped you of your weapons. I drove out to the night fire range. No one was there yet, and I carried you out to the hundred-meter target. I put you down behind it and poured bourbon on you. I left the bottle.'

'Why not just kill me? Why the elaborate plan?'

'Oh, Andy, it was elegant. You had been drinking a lot lately. I was fairly certain you didn't have a girlfriend or much of a life, no one who would miss you. We were seen in public, and you were emotional. Talking about Vietnam and the guys you had lost. You drank too much, drove out down Range Road, and passed out behind a target. Another sad veteran killed by the aftereffects of a secret war within a war that no one cared about anymore. I wouldn't be killing you. I wouldn't be the one pulling the trigger. You're my friend, Andy. You must admit, it was an elegant plan.' He was annoyingly proud of his failed scheme to try and kill me. He might have set in motion the series of events that led to my death, but if he didn't actually pull the trigger . . . then in his mind he wouldn't have killed me. It must be nice to live on Planet Dave.

'How did you get back, and why didn't you wait around to make sure the job was done?'

'Alibi . . . we had been seen at the bar. No, I started walking back, I walked down the road and cut through post. It isn't hard to avoid people who aren't looking for you. If I saw a car, I would just step into the bushes and hide. It took a few hours, but I made it to the parking lot of the Fort and got in my car and drove home.' He was proud of himself.

'And you went to bed?'

'Yes, there was nothing else to do. I slept until I heard you moving around. That was awfully clumsy of you.' He admonished me as though I were a little kid.

'It didn't bother you?'

'Bother me?'

'Killing a friend? The thought of killing an old Army buddy?'

'Well, no. Andy, you don't have much of a life . . . it is sort of sad. But also . . . I saved your life once . . . I had given you more life than you would have had. You wanted to die a lonely hero in a futile rearguard action as part of a mission where you had no concept of what was really going on. Bother me? I had given you more years of your life than you would have had. You hadn't done much with them . . . no, it didn't bother me. I felt like . . . like it was mine to do with as I pleased.' And there it was.

'You made two mistakes, Dave.' I was angry at him, angry that he'd involved me, angry that he'd given me hope of a future, angry that he'd killed his daughter, angry about the dead kid from the motor pool. It was starting to show in the pitch and timbre of my voice.

'Which were?' He said it with a raised eyebrow and a trace of academic curiosity.

'You should have just killed me. No elaborate plan. No subterfuge, just killed me.' My voice was cold.

'And the other?'

'Hiring me to begin with. You never should have underestimated me, Dave. Then or now.'

'No, I shouldn't have.' He was looking at me and at the P5 on the floor. You could almost see him planning, like Wile E. Coyote with the blueprints.

'You wouldn't reach it before I put a few bullets into you. Even you would be slowed down by thirty-eight hollow points. I will put enough in you to ensure that you don't have to worry about the MPs or a trial.'

'I don't see myself spending life in a federal prison, Andy . . . but you . . . you don't have a life, not much of one . . . and you owe me.' Asshole; it might not be much of a life, but it was mine.

'Dave, in case you haven't noticed, dawn is breaking. In a little while, when the Range Control guys show up to open the range, they will find my note telling them where to find Judy and directing them to call the MPs. I tracked dirt from her burial site all over your house. The driveway, this study, the dining room, the cellar, and the bathroom where I washed up. There is a damp towel with dirt from the site hanging in there. I left my bloody sweat-soaked shirt with more dirt in it in your laundry. Even the MPs would be able to connect the dots. After all your careful work cleaning up your house, I left evidence linking you to the crime you covered up. You are, in a word, fucked.' As he should be.

'So, now what? I can't go to prison, Andy . . . I can't.' Pleading with me.

'Well, Dave, you can kick the P5 over to me.' He did, and I squatted down and picked it up with my left hand, covering him with the .38 snubnose. I put Dave's P5 in my waistband. 'I'm going to go home and go to bed. If you think you can stop me and want to try, then we can see how well you like getting gutshot. Otherwise, you have your war trophy . . . you can shoot it out with the MPs or you can blow your own brains out. You might get a couple MPs, but you won't get away . . . and your precious reputation . . . well, that won't exist anymore. Take your own life and all they will have is questions without answers. No trial, no conviction. Just a couple of corpses and a whole lot of conjecture.'

'Andy . . .'

'I'm leaving now Dave.' I stood up. The .38 was pointed at him. I reached down and pulled the dollar bill from under the brass ashtray. 'My fee . . . pretty sure I earned it.' Dave didn't move or say anything. I walked through the French doors into his backyard. I stuffed the dollar bill in my pocket and half expected him to shoot me in the back. Maybe even hoped he would. I walked down the driveway and stopped at his BMW. It was unlocked, and I wiped my prints off the P5 with my shirt and put it in the glovebox.

I had parked the Maverick a block away. I hadn't wanted to startle Dave. There were no MPs waiting outside. I had lied to Dave. I had never left any note. I was using what he called Roark's luck. Tap dancing and improvising, I would call it. I would call the MPs from a payphone in Ayer if I made it there in one piece.

It was morning now, and the post was coming to life. Somewhere in the distance I could hear a unit calling cadence as they were moving to PT.

'Hey, hey, Captain Jack
Meet me down by the railroad track
With that bottle in my hand

I'm gonna be a drinking man.'

As the unit moved away, their voices grew quieter with the Doppler effect. I had loved the Army. Maybe it had been my first love. Maybe my only love, but after Vietnam . . . I had just felt used up. Dave had been right about everything he had said about my being good at it, about my finding a family, and about my missing it. But I could never have what I had running Recon. Those days were over, and there was no way to have them back.

'Hey, hey, Captain Jack

Meet me down by the railroad track

With that weapon in my hand

I'm gonna be a fighting man

A drinking man.'

Their voices receded into the distance, taking my dreams of rejoining the Army with them. They moved further away until the voices were indistinct. I wasn't a soldier anymore, and no amount of dreaming would make me one. I was a private detective, and had been one longer than I had been a soldier or even a cop. That was just who I was now. Behind me I heard a single muffled gunshot.

'A killing man

A fighting man

A drinking man.'

I got in the Maverick and started it up. I drove south toward the main gate, cruising by at slow speed. There was no need to rush. Boston and my life there weren't going away anytime soon. I thought I heard the distant wailing of sirens as I pulled out of the gate and pointed my car toward home. Maybe Brenda Watts would answer when I called her. Maybe she would want to have dinner. Or at least I might get my cat back. Now that would be a case of Roark's luck.

ACKNOWLEDGMENTS

The author wishes to acknowledge the following people: CME for giving the first read and attempting to clean up my numerous mistakes, TFA who tirelessly answers questions and offers ideas. The late Sergeant Major Chris Callan who was an old and dear friend who answered question after question about gunshots, explosives, parachuting and provided invaluable insight into the history of US Army Special Forces.

Ed Stackler who gave the manuscript a close look and offered key advice.

Kate Lyall Grant who saved Andy from an early retirement.

Rachel Slatter, my editor at Severn House, and Natasha Bell and Nicky Connor at Severn House who work hard to make sure that you never see my numerous grammatical and spelling errors. The whole team at Severn House, I write the story but there are a lot of people who work very hard to bring the reader the book. I am very grateful to them for all of their hard work.

Cynthia Manson, whom I literally could not do this without.

Lastly Cathy, Henry and Alder, who very patiently put up with a husband and father who disappears into his office for hours at a time to hang out in the 1980s with Andy Roark.